Michelle Kenney is a firm believer in magic, and that doorways to other worlds can always be found if we look hard enough. She is also a hopeless scribbleholic and when left to her own devices, likes nothing better than to daydream about these worlds in the back of a dog-eared notebook. When not scribbling, Michelle can usually be found beachcombing with her family or rescuing Ted, their loopy Labrador, from himself. Michelle is the author of the bestselling Book of Fire trilogy, and a graduate of the Curtis Brown Writing for Children Novel Course 2015. She also has a LLB (Hons) Degree in Law, an APD in Public Relations, and an unhealthy obsession with all things Regency - Doctors say they're unlikely to find a cure any time soon.

- facebook.com/BookofFireMK
- x.com/MKenneyPR
- instagram.com/mich_kenneybooks
- tiktok.com/@michkenneyauthor

Also by Michelle Kenney

The Fairfax Sisters
The Mismatch of the Season
The Scandal of the Season
The Proposition of the Season

The Book of Fire
Storm of Ash
City of Dust
Book of Fire

THE PROPOSITION OF THE SEASON

MICHELLE KENNEY

One More Chapter
a division of HarperCollins*Publishers* Ltd
1 London Bridge Street
London SE1 9GF
www.harpercollins.co.uk
HarperCollins*Publishers*
Macken House, 39/40 Mayor Street Upper,
Dublin 1, D01 C9W8, Ireland

This paperback edition 2026

1

First published in Great Britain in ebook format
by HarperCollins*Publishers* 2026
Copyright © Michelle Kenney 2026
Michelle Kenney asserts the moral right to
be identified as the author of this work

A catalogue record of this book is available from the British Library
ISBN: 978-0-00-879286-2

This novel is a work of fiction. Any references to real people, places and events are used fictitiously. All other names, characters and incidents portrayed are a work of the author's imagination and any resemblance to actual persons, living or dead, events or localities is entirely coincidental.

Printed and bound in the UK using 100% Renewable Electricity
by CPI Group (UK) Ltd

All rights reserved. No part of this publication may be reproduced, stored in a retrieval system, or transmitted, in any form or by any means, electronic, mechanical, photocopying, recording or otherwise, without the prior permission of the publishers.
Without limiting the exclusive rights of any author, contributor or the publisher of this publication, any unauthorised use of this publication to train generative artificial intelligence (AI) technologies is expressly prohibited. HarperCollins also exercise their rights under Article 4(3) of the Digital Single Market Directive 2019/790 and expressly reserve this publication from the text and data mining exception.

For my brothers

Chapter One

Knightswood Manor, Devon
10th May 1826

Dear *Fitzwilliam Darcy*, Josephine penned in her distinctive loopy handwriting, having already denied Captain Wentworth and Mr Edward Ferrars the heady honour of becoming her new fictional diary husband. She smiled, picturing her favourite brooding hero, before continuing.

Today it rained all day... Josephine glanced up at her soaked window for inspiration. In truth, it was hard to find when most days consisted of the same three meals, a long walk and hiding from her eldest brother, but she liked to chart the time anyway. Then there was the fact that her fictional diary husband was her only confidant for her *tortured* thoughts about the perfectly heroic Sir Francis Percival Dashton. And she was certain that *tortured* was not an exaggeration if her pensive thoughts and veritable ache whenever she conjured his image, were taken fully into account.

Sighing, she stared down at her expressive handwriting, all hoops and swirls with several large blots of ink where she'd paused to ponder the use of a particular word over another. Her sisters would often laugh at her indecision when she told them, claiming one word couldn't be in any way superior to another, yet she was certain the opposite was true. Words were everything – they could change the world in a heartbeat – and she was certain no one understood this more than Sir Francis.

Sir Francis had first come to Knightswood during a New Year Hunt organised by Thomas. Each of her brothers had invited a companion for the sporting event but while twins, Edward and Henry, had been happy to enjoy the shooting party with their Oxford friends, dear Fred had hidden away with her. And it was while they were tucked up in front of the library fire, with the wintry rain cascading down the windows, that they were introduced.

In truth, after a dismal Christmas with Aunt Higglestone telling everyone that she *'really had tried her very best for her dearest, sickly bluestocking'*, Sophie announcing her third child, and Phoebe her first – at last – a New Year meeting with a perfect fictional hero was the very last thing she'd expected. Indeed, if her three long and tedious seasons with her persistent aunt had taught her anything at all, it was that perfect fictional heroes didn't actually exist, either within the confines of Almack's or any of the other ball or receiving rooms deemed appropriate for debutantes.

Which made Sir Francis Percival Dashton quite the exception.

Mistily, Josephine recalled the way he described the Acropolis in the moonlight, before espousing seamlessly on his favourite Shakespearean soliloquies and sonnets. There was little doubt his knowledge of art and literature far outweighed her own, which was hardly a surprise since he'd studied Classics at Oxford before enjoying a protracted Grand Tour with Fred. But it was his ready passion for books, as though he truly understood that words could burrow straight into the heart of a reader, that really captured her attention. He could just as readily recite passages from Sir Walter Scott's *Ivanhoe* as describe Michelangelo's works in the greatest of detail, and she really was quite cross with Fred for not telling her about the ceiling of the Sistine Chapel. The only wondrous sights he'd related at great length related to Turkish baths and smoking tents! She rolled her eyes.

Yet, the passion of Sir Francis's words had only confirmed her quiet belief that they really were the most unique magic that only a few knew how to wield well. There was a moment too when she thought he might have glimpsed an aspiring wordsmith in herself, for it was she who pointed out where Sir Walter Scott's novels were shelved when he claimed the bitter weather made him wistful for something poetic. And even if Fred had begun to snore behind his newspaper halfway through the first page, she'd felt so enraptured by the richness of Sir Francis's tone, she could not have enjoyed it more. He was the living, breathing hero she'd always dreamed about, from the high polish of his Hessian boots to the thick curl of his lustrous locks. In fact, Fred had been known to claim Dashton's romantic profile and natty dress sense could rival the great Beau Brummel himself – a suggestion which led her to wonder if her brother might not also be a little enamoured – before she dismissed the notion as nonsensical.

Rosily, Josephine conjured his flaxen hair, and eyes the colour of sea-spray. She'd spent her childhood on Devon beaches, chasing waves and building forts with her brothers and sisters, but there was a particular cove that she recalled for different reasons. She was twelve at the time, and suffering from a particularly bad spasm of the lungs, so Phoebe carried her down to the water's edge. Yet while her sister had urged her to take deep breaths of the remedial air, she'd been mesmerised by the ebb and flow of the glistening waves over the long silvery sand. And now that same colour had found its way into Sir Francis's eyes, as though he was one of Sir Walter Scott's heroes himself.

'Jo…?'

Matilda's voice pulled her back to the present with a jolt. She rose swiftly and stepped towards her bed, where she pushed her diary between the bed frame and mattress, her most reliable hiding place for as long as she could remember. She might not have suspicious Sophie to worry about anymore, but her youngest sister was no less ready to sacrifice her morals if there was a morsel of gossip to be had.

'Jo…!'

'I'm just…' Josephine began, as a slight tornado in blue muslin whirled through her bedchamber.

'There you are!' Matilda exclaimed impatiently. 'I might have guessed you were in here scribbling to your imaginary diary husband.' She chuckled as she crossed the floor towards Josephine's window seat. 'Though why you don't simply pick one and stick I'll never understand. It's bad enough imagining oneself with one husband, let alone a whole herd!' She pulled a comical face as she hoisted herself up and tucked her feet inside her skirts.

'Matilda Fairfax!' Josephine admonished. 'How many times do I have to remind you that my diary is my private property? It was bad enough with Sophie poking her nose in every five seconds. I most certainly don't think it is very polite of you to invade my personal—'

'Oh pooh!' Matilda interrupted, wrinkling her nose. 'It's not as though there's much else to do around here with Thomas worrying about the roof *and* the fences *and* the sheep, but not before replenishing the wine cellar, of course.'

'Matty!' Jo hushed through a chuckle.

'What? You know it's true! Thomas puts Burgundy before everything! Anyway, I've been trying to persuade him to revive the Knightswood Ball this summer. Not for the dresses and dancing, of course – I can't actually imagine anything worse than another dress fitting with Aunt Higglestone – but for the dawn steeplechase the morning after.' She drew a breath, her large inky eyes dancing. 'Did you know there used to be one every year in Mama and Papa's time? It was quite the event! All the gentlemen would turn out in their riding finery, while the ladies would stay up in their ball attire to watch them depart. *I* wouldn't settle for watching, of course,' she added with a grin. "I'd simply wear my riding habit to the Ball, because the race would be the only reason I'd go in the first place.'

Josephine eyed the obstinate tilt of her youngest sister's chin, wondering how the universe ever saw fit to leave the most fiery and independent Fairfax until last, and in her sole charge.

'Matilda, dearest,' she began patiently, 'the chances of Thomas reinstating the Grand Knightswood Ball while you are yet to enjoy a season and I have failed three of the things, are pretty much non-existent. Beside the actual cost of such an event, he'll be loath to spend money on a social occasion which has little chance of advancing either of our marital chances.' She sighed and walked towards her pretty sister basking in the spring sunlight. 'You're not out until the end of the year, whereas I've been such a resounding failure Thomas instructed Aunt to "*cut her losses*" and send me home last month. Like one of his non-runners! In truth, I think lavish balls and dawn steeplechases will be the very last things on our brother's mind.' She paused as she drew close enough to observe her sister's stockings and dress hem; both were streaked with brown mud. 'And what *have* you been doing?' She frowned. 'Please don't tell me you went to the May village show after everything Harriet said? You're eighteen now, on the cusp of your debut season, not some young schoolgirl climbing trees and grazing her knees!'

There was a moment's silence as they both stared down at Matilda's knees bearing earthy stains from her afternoon adventures.

Her younger sister yanked down her hem with an angelic smile. 'It was only a *tiny* chicken race,' she appealed. 'And I only went on account of Bertie Briggs saying Knightswood chickens were *half* as fast as *their* farm chickens, and he would lay sixpence on it. So, really, it was a matter of honour when all is said and done,' she concluded lightly.

Josephine closed her eyes in pained denial. 'Dearest, have you forgotten the Briggs brothers were responsible for

Phoebe's fall through the stable roof onto poor Higgins? And let's not even mention the pig race debacle...' She paused to shudder. 'Just tell me, *please*, that you didn't gamble sixpence with him – otherwise it will be the gossip of Knightswood village by now.'

'It will not!' Matilda retorted with an obstinate purse of her lips. 'For I won fair and square, and then I made Bertie promise he wouldn't tell anyone which he readily agreed to on account of being beaten by a girl.'

Josephine stared at the defiant gleam in her sister's eyes. 'He didn't agree, though, did he?' she quizzed suspiciously. 'Matilda Fairfax, did you wrestle Bertie Briggs? Is that how you got muddy?'

'I may have arm-wrestled Bertie Briggs *a little*,' Matilda replied mulishly, 'but he called Knightswood chickens lazy layabouts! Our chickens! What else was I supposed to do?'

'Did he now!' Josephine scowled, her demeanour changing momentarily. 'Now I'm almost glad you... But really, dearest, a chicken race and an arm-wrestle... if Thomas hears about this—'

'But he won't, for I shall change my dress, and neither of us will tell him. And anyway, I only came to share something that may help you write that gothic novel of yours...'

Josephine took a seat, unable to help smiling at her younger sister's dishevelled ringlets and moorland flush as she withdrew a piece of folded newspaper from her pocket.

'This is old, Matty,' she observed as she took the sheet and pushed her spectacles up her small snub nose. 'Nearly six years old, to be exact.'

'I know,' Matilda replied with a mischievous smile. 'Just

read ... *that* part.' She pointed out a small column in black type towards the bottom of the page.

'"A dark and bloody duel in the county of Somerset has left Huntingly Manor in the hands of trusted estate managers for the foreseeable future",' Josephine read aloud. '"The scandalous affair between Lord Alistair Huntingly, heir to the Huntingly estate, and George Pellham, son of the late steward, took place not long after dawn on the morning of the 3rd of March 1820, and, while neither party was to be located subsequent to the duel, their seconds and the local physician agreed it was a very serious matter indeed."'

'You wish me to write a gothic novel about a scandalous duel with no dead bodies to show for it?' Josephine quizzed.

'Well, why not?' Matilda grinned. 'You loved Shelley's *Frankenstein*, and who's to say the physician didn't stitch the duellists back together again? They must have had need of his services for him to say such a thing! But still, that isn't the reason I brought it. I looked it up in the library because I overheard Fred saying to Thomas that one of his old Oxford friends, who left for the continent six years ago amid a cloud of rumours concerning a murderous duel, had returned and that his name was Huntingly!'

Josephine smiled as a gleam stole into Matilda's eyes. 'How very dark and mysterious!' she replied, beginning to understand her sister's intrigue.

Fred wasn't the type of brother to keep bad company, let alone have a friend who'd been accused of murder.

'Precisely so!' Matilda agreed. 'And I say there's a story here which sounds far more interesting than any tiresome debut season.'

The Proposition of the Season

'I couldn't agree more.' Josephine laughed, reaching forward to squeeze Matilda's hand. 'But you really shouldn't think so, dearest, when you are the wild rose among us all. You have Phoebe's fire and Sophie's eyes, even if you must put up with my gorsy, moorland hair!' She smiled affectionately. 'So, there is no reason why you should not make the most ambitious match of all when it comes to the marriage mart. Yours is not the fate of the Fairfax bluestocking left on the shelf with her books.'

'Oh, don't say so, Jo,' Matilda replied wistfully. 'Our value should never be linked to success in a market which is prejudiced before we even begin...'

'You sound like Phoebe!' Josephine interjected.

'But it's true, isn't it?' Matilda sighed. 'And, if I had the choice, I would forsake the whole thing and do something meaningful like become a nurse instead...'

Josephine frowned faintly as her sister trailed off to stare at the old magnolia tree that had witnessed so many Fairfaxes making their first escape. 'Oh, Matty! Inspired by Dr Kapoor?' she asked, referring to the mild-mannered doctor who'd overseen her own care since Phoebe's marriage to the Viscount Damerel.

'Yes, definitely Dr Kapoor,' Matilda replied, nodding vigorously. 'Though also Captain Elliot's tales of his skirmishes in France, and of course both Alex and Thomas have seen some action too...'

'Viscount Damerel or Alexander, Matty,' Josephine corrected her sister gently. 'And do you really wish to apply soggy bandages in the middle of bloody battlefields? I would have thought a rural hospital far nicer,' she suggested, raising an eyebrow.

'I would make a difference, if I could!' Matilda declared passionately. 'For how else do we know what we're truly capable of, if we do not challenge ourselves?'

There was a brief pause while Josephine admired her obstinate, wilful sister who'd been born ready for life. 'You are an inspiration, dearest,' she replied genuinely, thinking of her own far less selfless pondering before she'd arrived. 'And anyone who meets you would be a fool not to know what a talented and caring soul you are, soggy bandages or not.'

'Pooh, much I care for all that! Unlike yourself when it comes to Sir Francis Percival Dashton,' Matilda added with a wicked gleam.

'Why? Whatever do you mean?' Josephine replied, feigning nonchalance and failing miserably.

'Don't act all innocent with me, Miss dreamiest Fairfax of them all, though she protests otherwise! I saw the two of you over the New Year, tucked up in the library, talking books for positively years.' She yawned. 'Besides, your diary told me the rest…'

'Matty!' Josephine glared, trying not to laugh. 'Sir Francis is very knowledgeable and pleasant to talk with, but that is all. I have no special interest.' She nodded emphatically.

'Oh really? So you won't be interested if I tell you I overheard Thomas say to Harriet that he and Fred are coming down tomorrow for the rest of the May Day Fayre?' Matilda asked airily. 'Something about Thomas not being free to judge the pigs, and Edward and Henry being in the middle of exams so unable to return – blah, blah – far too busy drinking Devil's brew more like!' She smirked. 'Anyway, I did offer to go in his stead but apparently *I* wasn't good enough.' She paused to look most indignant. 'As if Fred knows more than me about breeding sows!'

'Matilda!' Josephine groaned through a chuckle.

'What? I thought you might want to know so you can, you know, *make cow eyes* at him while pretending to talk more books?'

'Matilda Fairfax, you really are quite dreadful!' Josephine protested, descending into helpless laughter.

'And afterwards I thought we could challenge them to a game of tennis, if you're feeling up to it?' Matilda grinned, standing up and making her way towards the door. 'I'd prefer fencing, but didn't think either you or Fred would be keen on several rounds of competitive swordplay…'

'Tennis is fine,' Josephine agreed rapidly, '*if* Fred and Sir Francis are interested, but really, dearest, I don't think we should plague them to join us unless they really want to. One thing I've learned about gentlemen is that they so rarely like to be organised.'

'Well, this is where you and I differ! For one thing *I've* learned about gentlemen is that they so rarely know what they like at all, that the least we can do is tell them!'

'Matty,' Jo chuckled, throwing one of the window-seat cushions after her unapologetic sister. 'I do declare you are the very fiercest Fairfax of all, and the world should be very afraid.'

Matilda laughed as she dodged the cushion and pulled a face. 'You're not that different, Jo, you just put your fire on paper instead. But I do believe the day will come when someone will ignite that bluestocking flame of yours, and then we will all have to watch out! See you at dinner…'

Josephine stared at the space her younger sister had occupied seconds before, wondering for the umpteenth time how they could be related at all. Three long seasons standing at the sidelines of balls, assemblies and soirees had given her a very different impression of herself. And yet perhaps Matilda wasn't entirely wrong about some small Fairfax flame for while the vagaries of gentlemen were likely to tease her forever, she would protect her sisters come what may.

Wistfully, she recalled the many happy afternoons they'd spent in Phoebe's bedchamber, before Thomas started planning for the future. It felt like yesterday, yet now her sisters were building real families of their own, while Matilda waited in the wings and she… Josephine drew a steadying breath. It was far better Thomas had one of them to help him with the estate, and she would always choose the company of books over those who thought her a wallflower.

She glanced towards her novels and mustered a smile – for who could be lonely with a trove of heroes beside her bed, after all?

Chapter Two

The May Day Fayre; Tygers and Pigs
Two days later

'What say you, Miss Fairfax?' Sir Francis queried in his rich tone. 'Do you believe William Blake celebrates, or condemns, the fiercest of beasts?'

Josephine flushed, as Sir Francis fell into step beside her, on the country lane connecting Knightswood with the heart of the village. She glanced down at their shadows, one so much larger than the other, and briefly wondered how they would look with the additions of a top hat and wedding veil, before forcing her wayward thoughts forward. She'd always been the bookworm sister, the dreamiest sister, the lovelorn for a fictional hero sister – not the embarrassingly tongue-tied around a mortal gentleman sister.

'Are you talking about *The Tyger* again, Dashton?' Fred interjected, rolling his eyes. 'I'll never understand your incessant talk about poetic jungle cats, when we have *feral pigs* right here in Knightswood!'

Everyone chuckled.

'You were so scared at the fayre,' Matilda teased, hoisting up her muslin skirt as they reached the estate gate.

'That sow was going to bite me!' Fred defended himself hotly. 'And, if you ask me, motherhood makes any beast the fiercer.'

'And what makes you such a connoisseur?' she retorted.

'Well, *I* thought you did an admirable job, Fred,' Josephine placated, finally finding her voice. She pushed her spectacles back up her nose. 'The Oxford Sandy is attractive, but the Devon Black is hardier, and Thomas is certain they're easier to breed. And in answer to your question, Sir Francis,' she added, avoiding his gaze, 'I believe Blake may have been questioning why a creator who made the lamb, made the fearsome tiger too? Of course, he goes on to hint that both are necessary in our world – rather like love and fear, I suppose…'

There was a brief silence while everyone looked at Josephine, turning an even rosier pink in the dappled shade of the old apple tree.

Sir Francis cleared his throat. 'Most perceptive, Miss Fairfax.' He reached to open the small wrought-iron pedestrian gate. 'And I must own to being rather impressed that your personal studies have given you such insight. Best breeding pigs and Blake all in the same breath – there are not many young ladies who can claim such a ready and extensive knowledge.'

He paused to run his fingers through his flaxen hair, the spring sunlight reflecting in his eyes as a smile spread across his face. It was a picture worthy of a gallery and, briefly, Josphine couldn't help but gaze.

'You should know better than to try and catch Josephine out!' Matilda challenged. 'You and Fred might have degrees from Oxford, but Josephine is the most well-read and versed of us all. You would have to search far and wide to find any lady, or gentleman, as knowledgeable as she.'

'So I understand.' Sir Francis nodded. 'And I've always maintained there is something truly noble about knowledge gained through personal study, rather than in discussion with the professors and dons of Oxford.' He looked thoughtful as Matilda leapt down from the estate gate into the field of daisies. 'I say!' he added with a swift grin. 'I do believe that was a dismount worthy of an acrobat, Miss Matilda! Indeed, I recall Fred mentioning you once had ambitions for a career in the circus, is that true?'

He chuckled, as Fred reached down to grasp a handful of daisies and toss them at his tall, golden friend. Sir Francis retaliated instantly, grabbing handfuls of the meadow flowers in both hands, before giving chase.

'Matilda!' Josephine whispered earnestly as soon as the gentlemen were out of earshot. 'You must know that most gentlemen don't like it if we appear more well-read than they! I've had to bite my tongue countless times at soirees and social evenings, even though they talk as though they are quite the authority on everything. And don't ask me how many gentlemen have thought it acceptable to quote Byron *most imperfectly*, as a way of opening a conversation.'

She stole a sidelong look at her protective younger sister as the gentlemen gambolled ahead, throwing daisies like hapless schoolboys.

'Well, I think you should be proud of who you are!' Matilda retorted. 'And if a gentleman cannot cope with a lady having more knowledge than he, then he is not worthy of the lady! I'd take imperfect Byron over perfect Francis anyway,' she added cryptically.

'Pardon?' Josephine frowned.

'Oh nothing.' Matilda exhaled. 'They are very good friends, are they not?' she added curiously as they fell in a tangle of limbs and laughter. 'It's true I once had ambitions to join the circus, Sir Francis,' she called out in her next breath, 'but I've since decided more adventure lies with the army.'

'Matilda!' Josephine groaned.

At this latest intrigue, the two gentlemen ceased their play-fight at last and waited for the ladies to join them.

'And your eldest brother has approved this military life for you?' Sir Francis quizzed, as Fred snorted his faith in his sister's chances.

'Matilda has a great many ambitions,' Josephine defended swiftly. 'She also has her first season approaching at the end of the year, which I'm sure will bring many new opportunities.'

'And what of you, Miss Fairfax?' Sir Francis smiled. 'Have you left many admirers languishing in London? It is a little early to be returning to the country, is it not?'

Josephine willed herself not to flush, mortified Sir Francis should remark upon her unusual presence at home while the season was still in full swing. She hesitated, searching for a reasonable excuse not to be in town.

Thankfully, Fred came to her rescue. 'Oh, Lord, Jo needs

Knightswood air for her lungs!' he exclaimed. 'And my bookworm sister would far rather be tucked up with all her stories than dancing in Almack's, wouldn't you, Jo?'

Josephine nodded, torn between gratitude for his intervention and fresh annoyance that he'd mentioned her lung affliction. She wasn't ashamed, but Aunt Higglestone's frequent mention of it in town had attracted both suspicion and dismissal by several matriarchs, as though she was far too risky for any bridegroom to consider seriously.

'Indeed, it is true,' she covered brightly. 'Yet, what time is there to be thinking of languishing admirers when there is the mysterious tale of an infamous lord's return from the continent to consider?' she added, turning the conversation from herself.

'Ah, you must be referring to none other than Lord Alistair Huntingly of Huntingly Manor!' Sir Francis grinned, taking the bait. 'The scandalous lord who disappeared abroad after a murderous duel and hasn't been seen for six whole years...'

'Hogwash!' Fred called good-naturedly. 'And you know so too, Francis.'

Together, they turned onto the path that wound through Knightswood's avenue of oak trees, towards the grand house nestling at the top of the formal lawns. This morning, it was surrounded by a haze of bluebells and, briefly, Josephine wished she had her notebook with her to capture the springtime scene.

'*I?*' Sir Francis reposted, his sea-spray eyes widening so theatrically they all laughed.

'Was it hogwash?' Josephine asked shyly. 'I did so enjoy the newspaper reporting a bloody, murderous duel without a body to show for it.'

'Ah well, that was the sticking point,' Sir Francis chuckled. 'The gossip was rather more fun than the facts, wasn't it, Fred? Though he was a devilish cavy fellow, even at Oxford.'

'Cavy? Huntingly?' Fred frowned. 'Don't recall that? I mean, he was more *annoying* than anything else. The kind of bright, sporting fellow who was as popular with the gentlemen as with the ladies, but quite decent with it too... Anyway, you get the picture...' He broke off hastily.

Josephine glanced across at Sir Francis and was surprised to find him looking rather less mirthful all of a sudden.

'You knew Huntingly at Oxford, Fred?' Matilda demanded. 'Then you'll know whether or not he did it?'

'Or, at least, if he had the potential...' Josephine amended carefully. 'And perhaps the identity of his opponent? Do you know what they argued about, or what prompted the duel?'

'Yes, and *why* were there no bodies?' Matilda added impatiently.

'*So* many gruesome questions for well-bred young ladies.' Fred chuckled with a glance at his quiet friend. 'In truth, it was an age ago—' he shrugged '—and it happened some time after we graduated. I was probably halfway up some impossibly tall *chiesa* with Francis at the time.'

He glanced again at Sir Francis, who smiled faintly, prompting a tiny flutter in Josephine's core.

'Oh, Fred, you must remember something!' Matilda grumbled. 'At least what prompted the duel – everyone must have been gossiping about it.'

'Well...' He frowned thoughtfully. 'I can't recall precise details but, as far as I know, there was some dispute over old Lord Huntingly's will involving his steward's son.' He shrugged. 'Sounded a damned messy affair, to be honest, and suffice to say we were all a bit shocked when the news broke. I mean, it's one thing calling out friends over a game of faro, but the son of a steward who's shot naught else but rabbits his life long? It just didn't seem very ... Huntingly. Not that I knew him all that well. He was in with the fast set generally, all boxing and racing, laced with wild nights in between. Popular on the whole, but when a gentleman is in his cups and provoked...' He glanced again at Francis. 'Francis knew him better than me, but neither of us stayed in touch ... must have some flaw somewhere, I suppose.'

'But what of the duel? Don't you know why both gentlemen disappeared?' Matilda complained in a disappointed tone.

'Sorry, Matty, I don't,' Fred shrugged. 'All I ever heard was that the seconds were local and, while a physician was called, there were no bodies to show for the affair, either at the time or at any time afterwards.'

'What would make two grown men run to the continent, if there was no murder to cover up or hide?' Josephine mused.

'Unless there *was* a murder, but Huntingly hid the body and waited until the coast was clear?' Matilda smiled, a gleam in her eye.

'Or they chased each other onto the continent?' Josephine continued. 'Where one finished the other off?'

'Even better!' Matilda laughed. 'And one of them must have been injured, because the surgeon was called.'

'What a dark and terrible tale you Fairfaxes can weave!' Sir Francis quipped with a chuckle. 'Though it really wasn't as dramatic as all that. There was no murder charge, because there was no body. Perhaps the steward's son was pigeon-livered and Huntingly decided to cool off in Italy or France, or some such place, and stayed longer than he intended. Anyway, the estate was put into the hands of a manager, and Huntingly has been reliving his Oxford years abroad. End of tragic tale.' He turned to face the rest of the group as they reached the tall lead-framed French windows that looked directly into Knightswood's well-stocked library. 'And now we are back, what say we use this mood to divine our own gruesome gothic tales,' he grinned, sweeping his arms theatrically towards the top of the lawn. 'With the best one to be read aloud at supper?'

There was a brief silence.

'Write a story? We're not in the schoolroom!' Matilda objected indignantly. 'And you promised to play tennis. You won't stand a chance against Jo anyway. She's a terrible tennis player, but the best wordsmith I know.'

'Hush, dear, poor Sir Francis really mustn't feel cajoled into tennis,' Josephine protested, blushing at Matilda's compliment. 'And I'm sure he's a very skilled wordsmith, given his studies and travels.'

'Pooh! Fred has done both, and he's terrible with words, can barely string two of them together—'

'I say, that's a bit rich!' Fred intervened before his reputation was shredded. 'Though, dash it, Dashton, gothic tale writing does sound a little dark for such a bright morning! Unless *you* wish to, of course, Jo?'

'Unless Josephine wishes to do what precisely?' a dry voice interjected, stilling them all in the sunshine.

Dismayed, Josephine turned to see the library windows were slightly ajar and her eldest brother seated in his favourite high-back armchair. From this vantage, it was easy to spy Fairfax family heritage in his silhouette; he had the same high brow, stubborn chin and thick hair, though his was by far the darkest.

'Thomas!' Fred exclaimed. 'I didn't see you lurking beside old Duke Wellington's encyclopaedia! But don't take any notice of our nonsense, Francis was only trying to entertain the girls with a gothic tale – but I don't think—'

'A gothic tale about who exactly?' Thomas interrupted, a faint sardonic smile playing about his lips.

Josephine eyed the empty whisky tumbler on the French occasional table beside his chair warily.

'Oh, no one in particular…' she began.

'Boring Lord Alistair Huntingly!' Matilda scowled. 'When it would be *so* much more fun to play tennis.'

'Huntingly? Boring?' Thomas laughed as he rose from his armchair and placed his newspaper beside the tumbler. Then he sauntered forward with the all the nonchalance of a master of a large estate, with a wine cellar to match. 'Lord Huntingly, heir to Huntingly Manor and about two hundred acres of prime Somerset countryside, is anything but boring,' he drawled. 'In fact, our paths crossed only last week, and I was delighted to make his better acquaintance. His years abroad have given him wisdom and bearing, so the news he is looking for a wife to help restore Huntingly Manor's position was interesting indeed.'

A faint chill reached through Josephine as his gaze came to rest on her, the bright May sunshine accentuating the shadows beneath his eyes. 'Yes … perhaps tennis *is* the better idea,' he concluded abruptly, turning back into the quiet gloom.

'Finally, someone with a little sense!' Matilda exclaimed in an entirely unruffled tone, before setting off towards the estate office, where the lawn games were stored.

Yet as Josephine followed around Knightswood's stately front, she felt far from relieved. A wild and rakish lord who'd just returned from the continent amid a cloud of old murderous rumours might put some brothers off, but not Thomas. His Monstrous Marriage Masterplan had haunted them all. He was no less determined now than he had been when Phoebe had first come of age, and there was something in his tone that made her feel most unsettled.

'I wager Josephine and I will win three sets to love!' Matilda grinned as she pulled open the estate office door.

The gentlemen laughed, teasing her good-naturedly, while the note of unease in Josephine's heart intensified. She gazed at her sister's pretty, wilful face as she grasped the racquets and balls, and passed them out. Matilda was the most spirited and ambitious of them all, and yet she was also the most vulnerable. She truly believed that with enough determination, she could side-step the marriage mart altogether. Yet her wishes would matter for nothing if Thomas received a reasonable offer for her hand. She was a Fairfax female when all was said and done, a sister he would marry off, whether she willed it or not. It was going to be the biggest shock, and her fierce younger sister was going to need at least one of them by her side when the time came.

'Last one there has to pick up balls!' Matilda called, dancing on ahead towards the grass court, while she and the gentlemen followed at a more leisurely pace. Yet the jovial tones and joyful spring haze were at stark odds with the nature of her thoughts. With Phoebe and Sophie focused on their own families, she was the only one left who could support Matilda through her season. But not if Thomas resolved the problem of an older sister, who had yet to attract a single offer, first.

Josephine felt herself pale as she glanced at Sir Francis's tall profile, conscious of the oddest mix of feelings. With three seasons under her belt, she was looking more like a costly spinster every day. Yet to arrange her marriage to a wild and infamous lord, who might just be a murderer too…

Not even Thomas would do that, *would he?*

Chapter Three

Knightswood Manor; Soup and Sandalwood
7 o'clock

Josephine looked across her soup à la flamand, wishing she'd plumped for hashed venison instead. She was certain Thomas was eyeballing her more than usual, and as she lifted her spoon, she tried not to inhale Sir Francis's sandalwood cologne which, although pleasant, appeared to have pervaded every corner of Knightswood's grand dining room.

'I heard you managed to upset Jennings at the fayre earlier,' Thomas remarked drily, signalling for a second glass of Bordeaux.

He glanced at his younger brother Fred, the only Fairfax he ever addressed at dinner, who smiled nervously.

'He didn't like me overlooking Bertha, his prize Tamworth,' Fred replied, his voice faltering at his brother's demeanour, 'but I thought it best I chose a local breed…'

'Fred had a difficult task,' Josephine offered quietly. 'There were a number of our tenants competing.'

'More fool he then for choosing the smallest,' Thomas replied with a cold smile.

He tossed the wine back as though it was lemonade, before sawing into his venison joint with a violence that forewarned every Fairfax present.

'And the … er … winning tenant was happy?' Sir Francis enquired in a tone that made Josephine sink further into her seat.

'Undoubtedly!' Thomas snapped. 'A best in class means he has to show again next year, thus rendering the farm eviction notice I signed last week, *and* Jennings's application for a grazing extension, entirely null and void.'

There was a moment's silence while almost everyone stared at their plates.

'Well, it sounds as though he deserves another chance?' Matilda frowned. 'If he's our smallest tenant and *still* managed to produce a prize-winning—'

Thomas rounded on her bluntly. 'What it sounds like is that Alfred made a complete and utter farce of the one task I entrusted to him! Have you any idea how difficult it is to balance the accounts of an estate as large as this?' He growled. 'The decisions you have to make just to keep a roof over our heads and food on the table?'

'We would, if you allowed us,' Josephine interjected. 'And for what it's worth, I thought Fred made the right choice. The Tamworths were small for the time of year,' she added, her calm voice belying the shake in her hand.

Thomas eyeballed her intently while Josephine's eyes

flickered in Sir Francis's direction, urging Thomas to recall their guest. But his lips only twisted harder.

'And much you would know about right choices, with your three expensive seasons and no match to show for it,' he snarled. 'At least your sisters understood their duty to marry well and swiftly, but *you*? You seem to think you're living in one of your nonsensical novels! Do you think I spent hard-earned funds on new dresses and finery for you to look down your nose at every possible suitor who tried to solicit your hand?'

Josephine felt a dull flush of injustice creep up her neck as Thomas indicated for his glass to be refilled again.

'And don't even try to deny it.' He swirled his Bordeaux before tossing it down his throat. 'Aunt Higglestone wrote me how often she would look for you at soirees, only to discover you'd stolen away to some damnable library? She found it highly diverting, but she doesn't have to support you. It was the height of selfishness! What debutante indulges in such behaviour when they have all London's bachelors within reach? You're just lucky I wasn't there myself...'

'I'll call on Jennings first thing in the morning,' Fred intervened in a pitiful attempt at distraction, 'and explain to him personally about the land.'

'You'll do no such thing!' Thomas rounded back on him, eyes blazing. 'The only Fairfax with any business sense was Phoebe, and now it seems she's too indisposed to even *think* about travelling before July – even if I have need of her.'

Josephine frowned into her soup, wondering what possible need Thomas might have for her eldest sister in July.

'The library, you say?' Sir Francis quipped, his bright tone at direct odds with the mood in the room. 'I must admit I've often sought refuge in one, particularly if the speaker at a soiree has rather less of a grasp on poetry, or literature, than myself.' He chuckled before turning a golden smile on Josephine. 'I suspect that is what drives you to seek the company of books, is it not, Miss Josephine? To seek entertainment of a more *sophisticated* order? Indeed, I am quite certain it is the Achilles heel of the well-read... Alfred and I certainly indulged when we travelled around Athens, didn't we, Alfred?'

Josephine flushed, grateful for his attempted defence, while her brother gazed at his bronzed friend.

'Indeed,' Sir Francis continued, 'we quickly discovered the ruins of the ancient world were the perfect place to get to know one's fellow traveller. There are those who embrace a Grand Tour simply because it is considered *de rigueur*, and those – far fewer, I hasten to add – because they carry Homer's *Iliad* and the *Odyssey* in their hearts. Naturally, we inclined towards their company, or we would have been forced to hide in a library ourselves!'

He beamed his perfect smile then, leaving no one in any doubt about the sincerity of his relief, and Josephine pondering how one gentleman could win both the mind and features of an actual Greek god.

'Well, not sophisticated exactly...' she replied, her flush deepening under Thomas's intense glare.

She glanced at her siblings, eyeing her with sympathy, as Sir Francis continued to project his winning smile around the dining table.

'...And I did enjoy London, I just found some of the

company different to what I was expecting ... That is to say ... the libraries were hard to resist because...'

'Josephine prefers libraries because she has yet to meet a gentleman who knows half as much as she,' Matilda interrupted with a stubborn set to her lips. 'And I do not believe she should marry one who knows less! And while we're on the subject, I do not understand why gentlemen should be the only ones to pursue their travels or studies before marriage, when it seems a most sensible course for everyone!' She paused to draw breath in a way that made Josephine wither into her worn evening slippers. 'Just think how much more sense it would make for gentlemen to marry someone who can actually converse about real places and real sights, as well as sketch or play the pianoforte,' she continued passionately. 'Yet, we ladies are barely allowed to breathe before we're married, and required to provide an heir for some ancient line that sounds remarkably like one of Knightswood's prize-winning pigs!'

Fred sank between his collar points, as Matilda's valiant defence descended into a full-scale protest against the institution of marriage. 'And before you start casting aspersions on our character, or questioning our stamina for such opportunities, may I point out that we ladies didn't lose any of our serve points in the tennis!' she concluded on a note of triumph.

'It's true you did deliver a most bruising serve, to which my right arm will attest,' Sir Francis concurred fairly. 'Though I do believe Alfred also demonstrated significant skill when it came to the dreaded backhand: never my strong point.' He shot a swift smile at his friend. 'But in response to your interesting and forthright views, Miss Matilda, I must say I have no objection to the female mind being well-read. Indeed, I believe a match can be all the stronger if there is knowledge in common, for who knows what song the whimsical heart will sing a year or twenty years from now? A shared love of fine literature, however? Now that can be truly immortal!'

There was a moment's silence while everyone stared at the perfectly coiffured gentleman, who could not look more Herculean to Josephine. His hair was styled a la Brutus, with a flair that put poor Fred's efforts to shame, while his broad shoulders were perfectly accentuated by a coat of superfine blue, that reflected in the glint of his sea-spray eyes. His nose was proud in an academic way, and when his smiling lips parted to display a clutch of brilliant pearly teeth, they also suggested some heroic or mystical descent.

In short, Josephine had never seen a gentleman who so clearly belonged within the pages of the novels she loved, rather than around their fractious dining table – which only made his beaming presence all the more mortifying.

Josephine glared at Fred's wilting form, willing him to intervene before Thomas let him know exactly what he thought of his modern ideas.

'I do wonder at the idea of young ladies attending Oxford alongside gentlemen, though,' he continued thoughtfully. 'And perhaps any dedicated places of study should be carefully suited to the *sensitivities* of the female mind? Indeed, my tutor at Oxford quite often remarked that the nature of the female brain is such that it is naturally attracted to quieter studies such as poetry, classics and reading, not medicine, science or evolution—'

'Pooh, that is *not* the case at all!' Matilda objected heatedly. 'Why, my oldest sister Phoebe knows just as much as any doctor when it comes to Josephine's lung condition, and Josephine loves to read all the *extremely* gothic novels with all the *fiendishly* ghoulish murders, and don't even get me started about Sophie's obsession with—'

'So, Dashton,' Thomas drawled, cutting Matilda off midflow, 'from this admirable and progressive opinion that you so openly share, I'm supposed to believe you would take a wife who prefers the company of books to the drawing rooms of Mayfair?'

His tone was dangerous, and Josephine glanced at Fred, who only shrank further between his shirt points and intricately tied cravat.

'When I take a wife, and it is by no means certain that I will,' Sir Francis replied blithely, 'I will most certainly be interested in her conversation, as well as her lineage.' He paused to take a deep draught of his wine. 'Naturally, she should also be a consummate hostess, but again I would expect this as a natural development of truly understanding one another. This Bordeaux is excellent, by the way. You really must let me know who fills your cellar.'

'With pleasure,' Thomas replied, never taking his eyes from Sir Francis's face, 'though I am quite fascinated by your views on the female mind. Why don't we discuss it over another glass, and I shall endeavour to recall from whence it came.'

Josephine willed Thomas to look at her as she and Matilda responded to their cue to leave, but he only nodded at a footman in the manner of a gentleman ready to do business. Another wave of anxiety rose within her. She knew Thomas as well as any of her other siblings and there were only two things he ever spared the time to talk about – horses and wedding matches. Yet dinner was at an end, and she had no excuse to linger.

'Thank you, we shall wait for you in the drawing room.' She nodded, before turning and leaving the gentlemen to talk. It was usual practice, but all Josephine could think was that Thomas had seen an opportunity, and if he had the chance to enact another stage of his Monstrous Marriage Masterplan, he would.

She glanced at Matilda, her burnished ringlets aglow in the lowlight, as they made their way down the flagstone corridor. She might be next in line to be wed, but her clear ability to endure three whole seasons, without so much as a single suitor to show for them, had given her the faintest of hopes that Thomas might just leave her in peace with her books. Yet now it seemed he had his eyes on a match with Sir Francis Dashton too!

A rise of fear and chagrin stole through her. Sir Francis might be the most perfect gentleman she'd ever known, but the idea of him ever liking her enough to make an offer was preposterous. He could have his choice of any of the eligible young ladies this season, and undoubtedly the next too. Additionally, he'd given no indication of liking her in any special way, so the thought of her unfeeling brother trying to persuade him of the virtues of her spinster self was torturous. Not only would everyone know that she was an abject failure on the marriage mart, she would also have to suffer a flat refusal from the Adonis of her dreams.

'Are you feeling quite well, Jo?' Matilda asked in concern, reaching out to squeeze her hand.

'Yes, of course,' Josephine replied, reminding herself that, by his own tongue, Sir Francis was not looking for a wife, and her brother might not be able to progress the conversation at all. 'It's only I cannot bear the thought of Thomas discussing the female mind. It unnerves me.'

'It unnerves us all,' Matilda replied, raising her eyebrows. 'Best not think on it too long, dearest, lest it give you the headache.'

Josephine smiled, though she knew she'd have little rest until she knew exactly what had been said.

It was the early hours of the morning when Josephine finally heard the gentlemen stumble up the staircase and make their way towards the opposite wing. She'd spent the evening in the drawing room but, while the gentlemen had been amiable enough, there had been no mention of their dinnertime discussions at all. This lack of information had only agitated Josephine's feelings further, and by the time she and Matilda withdrew for the night, she could think of only one course of action.

Pensively, she lay down her quill and stared at the clumsily written passages on the paper before her. Usually, the act of writing provided her with inner peace and calm, but not tonight. Tonight, the words seemed barely her own at all but belonged instead to the wind and rain outside. With a heavy heart, she pulled her shawl tight, picked up her candle and trod to her door, where she paused to listen carefully. The house was silent, and when she stepped out into the hallway, the only movement was the flicker of candlelight on the sideboard.

Stealthily, she descended the staircase and crossed the hall floor towards the library, her chest thumping. She knew her brother's routine as well as her own, and there was little risk he'd retired yet, especially since he rarely slept in his bedchamber anyway. She inhaled deeply as she drew to a halt, and then knocked before she could change her mind.

'Shouldn't you be asleep?' came his dry response.

Josephine pushed open the door and Thomas was exactly where she expected him to be: in his favourite armchair beside the fire, a brandy in his hand and his gundog at his feet. Anxiously, she acknowledged his sullen expression and wondered if she should have waited until morning. Then his eyes lowered in the same way as at the dinner table, and she felt a surge of fresh determination.

'Thomas, you cannot pressure Sir Francis into marrying me!' she blurted, forcing her feet forward, and wishing she had Phoebe's authoritative tone. 'I have no desire to leave Matilda, and I am quite certain Sir Francis does not wish to wed at all.'

His answer was a curt bark of laughter. 'And what makes you think I would match you with that great fop?' he replied, his lip curling.

Josephine felt a curious mix of relief and indignation flood her limbs. Sir Francis Dashton was the least fop-like gentleman she'd ever met. In fact, she was pretty sure he was the living embodiment of every fictional hero she'd ever read and imagined for her own. She felt her cheeks flush. 'He wouldn't have me?' she asked, trying not to let him glimpse her inner turmoil. 'He is young and has ambitions before getting wed, I'm sure.'

'No, it's not that he wouldn't have you,' he replied, his smirk deepening, 'for I didn't ask him. Dashton is a coxcomb and a dandy, but he'll be a decent enough catch when he's looking for a wife. He just needs a little more time to realise it.'

Josephine exhaled quietly as Thomas tossed back a swift drink.

'Not that it matters,' he added, swirling his glass, 'for I have different plans brewing, anyway.'

Josephine felt a dart of cold fear as she conjured the only other gentleman Thomas had mentioned of late.

'Lord Huntingly, heir to Huntingly Manor and about two hundred acres of rolling Somerset countryside is anything but boring… The news he is looking for a wife to help restore Huntingly Manor's position was interesting indeed.'

She stepped closer until she could better read his face, noting the half empty bottle beside his chair. He was drunk, but not without reason.

'Tell me,' she asked, trying to keep a tremble from her voice and failing, 'have you made a match with the disgraced Lord Huntingly?'

He tossed back the remainder of his brandy, before reaching forward with the fire poker to nudge the smouldering logs. 'And what if I have?' he muttered. 'Why should it matter to you, when all you care for is books?'

'Thomas, you can't!' she replied, aghast. 'I know I've failed, but I haven't met anyone I liked well enough to marry. And I can be of use here … to Matilda … and to you. We don't know anything about Lord Huntingly, except that his reputation is clouded by rumour and he is most likely *a murderer*!' she whispered emphatically. 'Why would you make such a match? Even if you have no care for me, what of the Fairfax name?'

He turned back to her slowly, his lips twisting into a smile of disdain. 'What a goose you are, Josephine,' he replied mockingly. 'Of course I haven't arranged for you to marry Huntingly! Why would I waste my time trying to make a match that three expensive seasons amid a hundred potential suitors have failed to achieve?' He drained his glass. 'Have no fear, sister, I'm entirely in agreement with you. Your best course now is to live a quiet life here at Knightswood and, if I should exit this mortal coil before you, I'm sure one of your sisters will welcome the assistance of a spinster aunt with their growing broods.'

His cold words resonated through the room as Josephine lowered her gaze, wavering between relief and humiliation that her brother should dismiss her quite so readily.

'However, your younger sister is a very different matter,' he added, making Josephine still in her place. 'Huntingly is rich and in need of a respectable name to align with his own, while Matilda needs a strong hand. He is prepared to keep a wife in the most comfortable style, and I won't have another Fairfax costing money Knightswood doesn't have. The matter is quite settled – she will be presented and wed at the beginning of the season.'

For a second, all Josephine could hear was the sound of her own laboured breath. Then a multitude of feelings crowded her thoughts, making it impossible to articulate just one. She closed her eyes as her sister's face spun to the foreground, followed by a slow wave of horror.

'You can't,' she whispered. 'Matilda isn't ready... She's too young ... ambitious ... different from the rest of us... She needs time...'

'Yes, well, perhaps you should have thought of that before you wasted three perfectly good seasons doing exactly as you pleased.' Thomas shrugged, pulling his gaze back to the fire. 'You had your turn, Josephine, and I'm not leaving anything else to chance. Matilda will marry Huntingly this year, and there is nothing more to be said!'

Chapter Four

Huntingly Manor; Cherubs and Ghouls
One week later

Josephine frowned down at Viscount Damerel's copy of *Gray's New Book of Roads: The tourist and traveller's guide to the roads*, trying to calculate the time it would take to reach Huntingly Manor.

Thomas mentioned Huntingly owned two hundred acres in Somerset, and it hadn't taken very long for her to work out his estate lay five miles east of Ebcott Place; the country estate Viscount Damerel had dedicated to educating young ladies, with a doctor in residence. He and Phoebe still withdrew to it through the summer months and, fortunately for Josephine, her older sister had been only too happy to welcome her for a brief stay.

She'd arrived yesterday and enjoyed the happiest evening with her eldest sister, who looked as radiant as any female could in the eighth month of her confinement. Briefly, she recalled Phoebe's humble delight in her fuller figure and adjusted skirts, while the viscount looked on with clear pride. They still disagreed over everything yet were no less perfect for one another than they always had been. And now, after five long years of hoping and longing, their prayers had been answered.

She glanced out of the Damerel coach window at the dawn hedgerows speeding by, glistening with dew. The viscount certainly didn't spare any expense when it came to travel and, if his coach driver thought it a little unusual that his sister-in-law wished to take the family coach on such an early outing, he was much too polite to query it. Indeed, she was grateful, for she was certain Sophie's scowling tiger would have been far less agreeable to the idea. Momentarily, she conjured Horace's permanently disgruntled expression since Rotherby and Sophie married – an expression that had only worsened since the Rotherby tribe began appearing – and now, with their third child on the way, he really was looking quite thunderous. Her lips twitched as she recalled Thomas's terse reference to *'the gloomiest groom he'd ever set eyes upon'* before the coach jolted, forcing her back to the present.

Carefully, she rearranged her skirts and recalled the letter she'd left for Phoebe should she rise before her return. It was as brief as possible, detailing her desire to visit a local acquaintance, and assuring her swift return before the morning was much advanced. She suppressed a frown. It wasn't exactly a lie for she fully intended to acquaint herself with Lord Alistair Huntingly; it was just that she hadn't detailed her intention for the visit.

The moment Thomas told her about Matilda echoed through her thoughts.

'You had your turn, Josephine, and I'm not leaving anything else to chance. Matilda will marry Huntingly this year, and there is nothing more to be said!'

They were just a few words, and yet they'd changed her entire world. She'd tried to dissuade him, but he'd refused to speak further, and she knew her brother far too well to believe anything would alter his mind now. She clenched her fingers in the folds of her sensible jade muslin, the dawn chorus at odds with her churning feelings as she contemplated the real reason for her assignation. It was the most courageous, if not outrageous, thing she'd ever attempted – but if she didn't act, Matilda's life would be ruined.

As for her own life?

For a moment, she contemplated her future at Knightswood Manor if she didn't pursue her current course. She'd have the comfort of her books and family home for as long as Thomas wished it, but how could that count for anything if she could have saved a beloved sister from a fate that would suffocate her? Her thoughts lingered on her younger sister, from parasol-wielding pirate, through fire-breathing acrobat, to the breath of fresh moorland air she'd become now. Matilda was an opinionated whirlwind of a Fairfax, with a heart of pure gold, who deserved everything the world could offer, not a lifetime clouded by her husband's shame.

She swallowed to steady her thumping chest. Her plan had seemed so rational when she left Knightswood, her consideration only for Matilda, but now the hour was drawing near, every rumour she'd heard about Lord Alistair Huntingly of Huntingly Manor began surfacing with startling clarity.

What would make a gentleman run to the continent for six long years? Why had he duelled in the first place? And what had prompted him to return and take a wife now?

A wife. Josephine swallowed again. There was the no small consideration that she was not a beauty like her sisters, and Thomas had undoubtedly promised a striking bride with spirit to match. Yet she had it on good authority that her figure was neat, and her eyes more than pleasing, once one got past the spectacles – and she was certainly the most well-read and accomplished musician of her sisters.

Josephine blinked and pushed her spectacles back up her snub nose. She had to believe that Lord Alistair Huntingly's reputed desire for a wife would outweigh such superficial considerations, and to that end one Fairfax would be just as acceptable as another. They might not be rich, but they were an old and respected family, and she was well aware of the worth of her name.

It was with all these thoughts running amok that the driver finally turned through a pair of imposing stone pillars, giving Josephine her first view of Huntingly Manor. And for a moment she could only stare, for it was everything she'd imagined the home of a disgraced, self-exiled Lord of the Manor to be.

The driveway and hedgerows were hideously overgrown, throwing much of the weed-ridden carriageway into shade, while an old oak had split and fallen, forcing the coach driver to draw to a premature halt. Josephine opened her door with a mixture of foreboding and relief. She was more nervous than she'd ever felt in her life, but the thought of Damerel's coach driver driving her up to the entrance of Lord Huntingly's derelict residence, was somehow worse.

'Thank you, Johns, this will do perfectly well. I can take it from here!' she called with a briskness she was far from feeling.

'Are you sure, miss?' Johns replied, climbing down with a concerned look upon his kindly face. 'This doesn't look the type of place a young lady should be left alone. Perhaps I should accompany you, miss. Wait in the servant's hall or the kitchen?'

He glanced around the quiet estate, clearly aware there was very little likelihood of a servant's hall or kitchen, and even less chance of anyone to populate it.

'No ... thank you, Johns. I know the owner and it's better I visit alone. They're a little ... shy of company, you see.'

He nodded, his thick grey eyebrows saying everything he wasn't.

'Right you are, miss. I'll wait right here, then... Ready to go the minute you are, miss.'

Josephine smiled brightly, and gathering her skirts, picked her way across the old stone carriageway, towards the gloomy entrance of Huntingly Manor.

She paused just as she reached the wide, crumbling steps and gazed up at an imposing colonnade entrance, presided over by an old copper lantern on a rusted chain. Briefly, she stared at its tarnished casing before glancing back at the once formal rose garden, now running wild around a silent water fountain while open-mouthed cherubs glared through the choking thorns. It was a strange and ominous sight amid the echoes of a grand past life, and she turned back to the house with growing unease.

Thomas said Lord Huntingly had taken up residence at his ancestral seat in Somerset since his return. Yet, despite the determination of a towering cherry tree to shower everything with its pale blossom, there was a distinct absence of care or life wherever she looked.

Josephine tried to shrug off the chill creeping through her limbs. She was used to being thought *the ailing one, the bookish one, the failure when it came to ordinary, practical things one*, but on this she refused to capitulate. She was determined to protect Matilda and, even if it did feel as though she was walking into one of the haunted houses of her gothic novels, it would take more than a glaring cherub to make her run now.

Ignoring the thump of her heart, she grasped the bell pull, only to stare in dismay as it came away in her hand. Swiftly, she let it drop amid the leaves and debris at her feet, before reaching for the knocker instead, which was precisely the moment the heavy oak door began to inch open.

Josephine watched the widening crack of musty darkness, feeling as though she would never underestimate the heroine of a sinister tale again. A wave of dread rose from the pit of her stomach, chased by the certainty that if a stitched, muscular arm reached through the gloom towards her, she would absolutely not be the courageous leading lady she'd always imagined herself to be. Indeed, such was her expectation, that when a thin, balding face with pale blue eyes emerged instead, she was almost disappointed.

'Yes?' came his querulous enquiry.

'Oh … good morning… Please excuse the hour and

unannounced visit,' Josephine stumbled, 'I was wondering if I might have an audience with Lord Huntingly?'

For a moment, the elderly retainer stared as though she was speaking in a forgotten tongue, before appearing to collect himself and slowly open the door.

'Of course, miss,' he replied in a bemused tone. 'His Lordship is just finishing his breakfast, but … if you care to wait in the library, I'll let him know you're here.'

'Thank you, that is most kind,' Josephine murmured, stepping over the threshold into a flagstone hallway that smelled distinctly of rotten potatoes and dust. She glanced around at the dirty windows, unswept floor and dimly lit passages, and forced a smile.

'Actually, I'd be grateful if you could take me straight to the breakfast room, if that's not too much trouble?' she asked, aware that no wilful heroine in her books ever waited in the library. 'I have risen early myself and would be glad of some coffee.'

At this, the elderly retainer stared as though she'd asked for oyster soup and a fork, before shuffling towards a long murky corridor.

'As you wish, miss, of course, though His Lordship did not sleep well, and was not expecting visitors, so perhaps you could excuse his … informal attire…?'

Josephine murmured something resembling a polite reply, but her mind was already awhirl with the villain she was likely to confront in the breakfast room. She'd expected a gentleman actively shunning society, one reluctant to meet with an unaccompanied young lady perhaps, not a recluse who didn't even bother to dress.

And yet, she'd come this far.

Resolutely, she followed the manservant along the dimly lit hallway, and through a formal hall with a minstrel's gallery, until he reached a closed door. Then he lifted his hand and knocked awkwardly, as though unused to the formality.

'That you, Henry?' a gruff voice answered. 'What foolery are you playing at at this hour? You'd better have brought that Chateau Margaux I sent for or you can walk Brutus too, and we both know how much you'll enjoy that!'

Josephine glanced up at the elderly retainer, who appeared somewhat frozen, and swallowed to quell a spiral of her own fear.

'Thank you, Henry,' she whispered, wondering if she too ought to be concerned about Brutus. 'I can take it from here.'

Then she turned the door handle and stepped inside, to be greeted by utter disarray. A long breakfast table dominated the centre, with little space for any guest to sit for it was littered with used crockery and glasses, as though several meals had been eaten at once. Silently, Josephine glanced at an astonished gentleman seated at the top of the table, before stepping around the clutter to a small fireplace, where a large hound eyed her with suspicion. She regarded the creature carefully before drawing to a halt, when it lowered its head and resumed snoring.

'Thunder and turf! Didn't I tell you not to bring the applicants directly, Henry?' the astonished gentleman bellowed. 'Take the girl to the library where I can interview her properly!'

'No ... thank you, Henry,' Josephine countered in a tone that quite belied her terror, 'it's all right.'

Then she settled her gaze on the scowling gentlemen to whom she was to propose the most daring agreement of her life.

Lord Alistair Huntingly of Huntingly Manor looked most unlike any gentleman she'd ever seen before. He was sprawled, rather than seated, across a chair at the head of the table, and wearing buckskin breeches, muddied boots and a creased day shirt, unbuttoned at the neck. He was also surprisingly tall, even when seated, with long athletic limbs and a glinting scar that ran down his left cheek to his throat. The rest of his face was heavily bearded, while his hair – which was much the same moorland colour as her own – reached as far as his wayward collar, giving the impression of the survivor of a shipwreck, rather than the lord of a manor. Yet, despite the swarthiness of his appearance, all Josephine's regard was for his eyes. They were the colour of horse chestnuts, accentuated by bruises of tiredness, and heavily lidded.

For a moment, her racing thoughts conjured the faded newspaper report of six years ago, when two gentlemen with bloodlust faced one another in the early morning mist. Then she recalled that this was the gentleman to whom Matilda was betrothed, and a wave of urgency reached through her.

'Pray excuse the intrusion,' she began stiffly. 'It was not Henry's decision that I should come to the breakfast room, so please spare him any retribution. Neither am I in search of a position,' she added before he could respond, 'for my name is Fairfax.'

She paused to push her chin into the air so that he might better observe the profile for which the Fairfaxes were famous, and yet his blank stare only served to confirm her suspicion that she really was the exception to the rule.

'Miss Fairfax,' she repeated with a brief glare. 'I think you may be acquainted with my brother Sir Thomas Fairfax?'

At this, the bemused lord's thick eyebrows forked skywards.

'Fairfax?' he repeated in a brusque tone. 'So, you're not a prospective housekeeper? Should I be expecting you?'

Josephine's glare intensified. 'No, I am not a prospective housekeeper, though the Lord knows you're in need of one!' she flashed, with a purse of her lips. 'And you, sir, are drunk, which is not at all what *I* was expecting at such an early hour of the morning.'

She caught her breath, aware she'd committed the sort of verbal affront for which Phoebe and Matilda were famous, but unable to bring herself to regret it. His Lordship was clearly a terrible host and, it seemed, intent on insulting her too.

At this he tipped his head back and let out a bark of laughter, stirring his hound. Josephine took a wary step sideways. She was not in any way afraid of dogs – indeed, she had grown up around many, but this one was unusually large and looking at her as though she might be a new species of rabbit.

'Oh, take no notice of Brutus, he's the biggest coward I've ever known. But you … you're beginning to interest me.'

He rose suddenly, throwing his chair backwards, and affording Josephine her first real glimpse of his towering frame. She shrank back, aware that her well-intentioned plan mightn't be as straightforward as she first thought.

'Thomas said I'd find you spirited but, egad, no female I've ever known has had the effrontery to waltz into my house and tell me it needs a good clean, before accusing me of being drunk!'

He paced towards the door, making Josephine sidle back towards Brutus, who suddenly seemed the least terrifying prospect of the two.

'And the purpose of your trip, Miss Fairfax?' he mocked. 'Was it to inspect the manor over which you might preside? That's somewhat understandable, yet I might remind you that, while Thomas appears to have done his homework, I have yet to make an offer.' He paused to run his fingers through his mop of unkempt hair, his eyes gleaming. 'Though why I shouldn't drink wine in my own home, and in my own time, eludes me. I'm sure many would agree it's far less unsociable than waltzing into a stranger's house before they are even dressed, without so much as a by-your-leave. Furthermore, while I am usually the last to observe any kind of social protocol, there are still certain formalities to be attended to, are there not? As well as a little familiarisation?'

He ran his gaze over her slim, neat person while Josephine reddened, aware Thomas had likely described a very different sister.

'No... Yes... Of course!' she replied in confusion, trying not to think about whatever Thomas may have said. 'I am not who you think I am,' she continued, clenching her fingers tightly. 'My name is Fairfax, but I am *Josephine*, Matilda's older sister.'

At this Lord Huntingly frowned, while reaching for the back of a chair as though to steady himself.

'If you're in need of assistance, sir...' Josephine began,

suddenly noticing a cluster of thick, ugly scars encircling his left wrist and reaching up his forearm.

'No! I am not in need of assistance, any more than I'm in need of inspection, if that's what this is about?' he growled. 'And Thomas made no mention of surprise visits from…' he looked her up and down again, 'bluestocking sisters! Tell me, what is your impression? Are you to tell your sister to run while she still can? I would I could run from me too.' He scowled as he picked up a nearby bottle and drained the contents directly.

Josephine gritted her teeth. An arrogant, shamed lord she could manage, but a self-pitying one?

'Really, sir!' she remonstrated. 'I have younger brothers with more pluck than you!' Her tone was severe as she eyed his scars. 'And you can think again if you consider your injuries will frighten me, for my oldest brother fought at Waterloo and the rest are keen sportsmen. Through their combined efforts, I am no stranger to a wide array of injuries, which to my knowledge they have never used to plead sympathy!'

Her scolding words echoed around the high ceiling, while Lord Huntingly eyed her in fresh astonishment. 'Haven't they, egad?' he repeated in wonder, running his fingers through his unkempt hair, his knot of scars glinting in the pale light. 'And you've come here today to read me a lecture on all my deplorable habits?'

Josephine flushed, realising it was going to be much harder to achieve her original aim if the lord in question was eyeing her with distinct abhorrence. 'No…' she stalled, wracking her head for inspiration and failing to find any. 'I've come here to ask you to marry me.'

Momentarily, he stared as though she were a madwoman who'd accidentally wandered into his home, while a defiant heat bloomed across her cheeks. Josephine forced herself to stand tall. She might not have Sophie's face or Phoebe's and Matilda's spirit, but she was still a Fairfax and, from what Thomas had said, that was his only requirement.

'I am a quiet person, sir, and will give you no trouble. I am also organised and well able to manage a household, for I have been helping my brother since my older sisters left Knightswood. I understand you are looking for a wife to assist with Huntingly Manor, and, to that end, I respectfully suggest one Fairfax is as good as another, is it not?'

His Lordship gave another bark of laughter, although it was marginally less certain, as he reached for a half-filled goblet. He eyed her intently, before tipping its contents back, affording Josephine a full view of his muscular neck and chest through his barely buttoned shirt. She swallowed and averted her eyes. She'd witnessed most of her brothers in a state of undress at some point or another, mostly through banned swimming outings to Knightswood's lake when she and her latest novel were chief sentry, but this was different. For some inexplicable reason, his half-dressed person made her feel oddly breathless, as though she was wearing one of Sophie's pelisses after a large breakfast.

'Take off your glasses?' he asked in a curious tone, replacing his goblet.

'I beg your pardon?' Josephine blinked, feeling her flush reach down her neck. 'I assure you, sir, I can see little without them, and you would not wish me at any disadvantage because I am not familiar with your home.'

She was already regretting so much, but to agree to be inspected, like some sort of bottled specimen, was a stretch even for her. Defiantly, she pushed them further up her nose, which was precisely the moment he began to move around the foot of the table, and across the flagstone floor towards her.

'I am not asking you to navigate my home without them,' he returned as she watched his progress in horror. 'I am simply asking permission to see your face without them.'

He paused directly in front of her and, for the first time, Josephine wondered if she'd been an utter fool. To come here alone, without bringing one of Phoebe's maids or even the kindly coach driver, was misguided to say the least. She'd been so intent on saving Matilda that she hadn't paused to consider herself at all, and now she'd never felt more vulnerable.

'You make an interesting proposition, Miss Fairfax,' he murmured, 'so let us understand one another completely. I am well used to people judging me by what they see, or hear, and rarely looking further. But if I am to consider your offer properly,' he paused with a glinting smile, 'I would like to see you without your armour.'

Josephine caught her breath as she stared up into Lord Huntingly's dark eyes, feeling her blood pound as though she was atop a tor in a moorland storm.

'Sir,' she replied, by now certain she had made a grave misjudgement. 'Your request is not … seemly, given our brief acquaintance.'

'Seemly?' he quizzed in an amused tone. 'But I thought we'd dispensed with all the usual formalities? Perhaps then, it would be more gentlemanly if I levelled the field a little?' In a heartbeat, Lord Huntingly pulled his open-necked shirt over his head and reclined back against the breakfast table, wearing only his breeches and boots.

Josephine flushed flame-red as she had little choice but to face his honey-toned chest and tangible warmth. She pressed back into the mantle behind her, wondering if the poker was within reach.

'So now, Miss Fairfax, you may observe at your leisure the gentleman to whom you are making an offer.' His eyes gleamed. 'It is a somewhat terrifying sight, is it not, a form that is less than perfect? Feel free to leave when you have looked your fill, for I will not stand in your way.'

Josephine inhaled as she glanced across his chest, tracked by long white scars, towards his left arm. She swallowed. The newspaper had described the duel as a bloody affair, but his arm, while usable, was corded in the thickest welt of angry scarring she'd ever seen. He looked truly battle-worn, and she tried not to conjure the moment the injuries had occurred, or the fate of his opponent.

'I beg to differ, sir,' she replied in a steady voice. 'I do not look for perfection, and I consider a person without scars is one who has barely lived. It is our blemishes and imperfections that define us, not the opposite.' Then, before she could change her mind, she reached up to remove her spectacles and look straight at the semi-clad lord. Instantly, the background of the room disappeared into a blur of shapes and colours, as was usual with her sight condition, but His Lordship's face remained clear. She lifted her chin, and waited for his inevitable disappointment or indifference, but his expression only seemed to soften. She took a deep breath. 'I may not be my sister's equal in appearance or temperament, my lord, but as neither of these things were specifically detailed, I assumed they were less important than my name... And, unless your opponent was murdered in cold blood, it will take more than a few battle scars to scare me,' she added, replacing her spectacles.

There was a moment's silence while Lord Huntingly regarded Josephine, his eyes never leaving her face, before he pulled his shirt back over his head. 'You are deceptive, Miss Fairfax,' he drawled. 'I had you pegged as a bluestocking do-gooder, but now...' He frowned as he shook out the sleeves of his shirt and buttoned the neck more respectably. 'Tell me,' he began, his tone gentler than before. 'What's prompted this course of action? Is my reputation so very ghastly among the Fairfaxes?'

'No, not at all,' Josephine replied carefully, 'and the idea was mine alone. But, in truth, there's little that can be said or done to induce Matilda to marry you willingly – and I am quite certain that even the knowledge that she is promised could make her run to the ends of the earth.'

At this, the bemused Huntingly gave a shout of laughter. 'Good Lord! And so you're the sacrificial lamb? I'm not sure I think much of the rest of your sisters for letting you face the fire alone, or did you draw lots?' he enquired, visibly shaking with mirth.

'Well, no.' Josephine frowned, concerned that any gentleman should find his own terrible reputation quite so amusing. 'No one else knows I'm here, and I would be in awful trouble if they did. I offer myself in Matilda's place

The Proposition of the Season

because…' Her voice trailed off as she stared at his gleaming eyes, noticing a fiery ring of amber around his irises for the first time. What did they indicate? A passionate nature that could kill a man and disappear for years, before confronting a lone female with the scars of his misadventures?

The faded newspaper report of a murderous lord, who disappeared abroad after a bloody duel, reached through her thoughts. It was followed swiftly by a vision of the thorn-choked fountain on his front lawn, and she closed her eyes to suppress a shiver.

'I offer myself because I am not like Matilda, or expected to make a match at all,' she forced calmly, 'so if it's just the name you're after, you might as well have me!'

She pushed her chin in the air defiantly but was conscious her chest felt tighter than it had in a long while, that this was the moment to which she'd been building, that he could still say no and it would all have been for nothing. There was a protracted pause when she thought he might laugh again, but instead he only regarded her quizzically.

'Well then, Miss…'

'Josephine,' she supplied quietly.

'Well then, Miss Josephine Fairfax, you intrigue me and, as *"nothing on this earth will induce Matilda to marry"* me, I say we throw our lots in together and make the most of it.' He held up a hand as Josephine tried to interject. 'I may not yet have had the pleasure of meeting your sister,' he added, amber sparking in his eyes, 'but you make a very strong point, and your selflessness in offering to take her place when faced with such a monstrous predicament … pleases me. In short, Miss Josephine Fairfax, I accept.'

Chapter Five

Ebcott Library; Old Paper and Scars
Later that day

The scent of old paper and sealing wax soothed Josephine as soon as she entered Ebcott library, Lord Huntingly's parting words still ringing in her ears. Every time she thought of her early morning mission, she reddened to the point that she barely knew what to think anymore. How she'd ever managed to convince herself she could waltz into his manor house and propose herself as an exchange for Matilda, seemed so foolhardy now as to be ludicrous.

There was a reason she was still unmarried: she was everyone's *dearest sickly bluestocking*, universally terrible at dancing and conversation, already wed to her books. Yet now, she was secretly betrothed to a … what? A shamed gentleman, for sure, but a self-confessed monster?

She caught her breath and flushed again, recalling the way he'd asked her to remove her spectacles. It had been the smallest thing, yet distinctly unnerving too. Was he trying to make her feel that way, to punish her for having the audacity to make such a proposal? Or was it something deeper, something that reflected his own sense of self? And then there was the fact he'd accepted her proposal, or at least claimed to, with a smile that made her wonder if it was the bravest, or most ridiculous, thing she'd ever done.

Was he, even now, writing a letter to Thomas and laughing at her?

Scowling, she reached out and ran her fingers along the worn spines of the novels closest. They were bound copies of *Sense and Sensibility*, *Pride and Prejudice*, *Mansfield Park* and *Emma* she'd insisted the viscount bought while she and several others were schooled under the watchful eye of Dr Kapoor. How innocent and carefree those days seemed now, and how certain she was that none of their heroines would have ever made the blunders she made without trying.

'I thought I might find you in here,' a familiar voice called, interrupting her brief escape.

She smiled instinctively as her sister appeared in the library doorway. Phoebe had been a mother figure to her for as long as she could remember, and no one could have been more supportive when her London seasons proved to be fruitless. She'd even reminded Thomas that neither she nor Sophie had secured a match in the usual way, and that their marriages were much more the product of coincidence than strategy.

And yet neither had returned home after three seasons without so much as a sniff of an offer either.

'I was just daydreaming about old school days,' Josephine replied, half truthfully. 'Are you feeling quite well, dearest?'

she added, observing Phoebe's pale countenance and stiff stature.

Phoebe laughed and placed a hand in the middle of her back to accentuate the considerable bump beneath her loosened corset and skirts.

'I'm not sure anyone can claim to be quite well with one of these ruling every thought and movement they make,' she replied ruefully. 'Truly, Jo, I'm not sure how Sophie has done it so many times already.'

Josephine laughed, though she was conscious of a stir of concern too. Damerel and Phoebe had smiled through their efforts to become with child, while Rotherby and Sophie had made it look easy. Then, when the news they'd all longed for had transpired at last, she'd suffered more than she'd bloomed. Even now, in her final month, Phoebe's usual colour and spirit hadn't quite returned and, while she beamed with gratitude, Josephine could sense her discomfort too.

'Sophie has always been the most practical of us,' Josephine soothed. 'She was destined to have a tribe of her own, while you, dearest, are one of the bravest – save for Matilda, of course!'

It was Phoebe's turn to laugh. 'Was there ever a Fairfax as daring as Matilda?' She groaned. 'And yet, her spirit and fire are so akin to my own heart, I cannot chastise her for it.'

'We know!' Josephine rolled her eyes.

It was an old joke among them all that Matilda and Phoebe were spirit twins, and that neither could criticise the other, even when their behaviour was clearly wanting.

Phoebe's eyes danced as she took her sister's arm. 'It's a pity they aren't here tonight,' she sighed, gently steering her sister out of the library and towards the dining room. 'I do so miss them both, but considering Sophie is heavy with child, Matilda is distracted by the May Fayre and I didn't even know you were coming, I shall just count my blessings instead. I also have a small surprise for you too, dearest, a special dinner guest!'

Josephine glanced up sharply, briefly considering the likelihood of Lord Huntingly following her back to Ebcott, to shame her in front of her sister and brother-in-law. A wave of fresh fear threatened, just as a footman opened the dining room door to reveal a jovial gentleman, smiling back instead.

'Captain Damerel!' she exclaimed in relief, abandoning Phoebe to greet the viscount's good-natured brother who'd stolen all their hearts in Bath six years before. 'And Dr Kapoor too,' she beamed, proffering her hand to them both in turn. 'It's been too long!'

'Miss Josephine, you are looking quite flushed and radiant,' her childhood physician observed in his studious manner.

'Of course she does, she's come directly from Knightswood!' Phoebe smiled.

'I would I received such a joyous reception,' the viscount observed, greeting his wife as though they hadn't attended the village fete together that same afternoon.

Phoebe chuckled and returned his embrace with a warmth to which they'd all grown accustomed. Yet there was a flicker of concern in his eyes as they rested on her, before he leaned close to murmur something that made her blush.

'And how is life treating you, Miss Josephine?' Captain Damerel enquired as they took their seats. 'Or should I ask how you have been treating life? For I am sure you have been taking the town by storm!'

His chestnut eyes danced as their first and second courses arrived together, including a tureen of white soup, turbot with a lobster sauce, and a dish of oyster patties served with a sparkling champagne.

'Josephine has decided the chaos of the London season cannot compete with the peace of her books,' Phoebe interjected, coming to her rescue, 'and I for one do not blame her. When I consider how stifled I felt in Bath, it's a wonder I ever found a husband at all!'

There was a ripple of smiles and chuckles around the table.

'What?' Phoebe defended. 'If you are all thinking of the handful of misadventures that befell me…'

'Handful?' Her husband remonstrated affectionately. 'You had more adventures that season than anyone I've ever met in my life! And I *still* don't think your poor aunt has recovered from the sight of my ruined evening suit after your canal swim.'

'I wasn't swimming!' Phoebe retorted. 'And it wasn't the *suit* that made a lasting impression!' She side-eyed Josephine, who snorted into her patties. 'Though it is true I've had finer moments,' she added with a sigh, 'and all while Josephine behaved like her usual angelic self, of course.'

At this, Josephine nearly choked on her wine, while all parties around the table eyed her with concern. 'You were the one who rescued Matilda,' she pointed out when she could, smiling reassuringly at Dr Kapoor. 'I'm sure she wishes you could do the same now, too.'

'Rescue her? From Knightswood or her impending season?'

Phoebe enquired. 'Don't tell me Thomas is talking matches already?' she added, her brows drawing together sharply.

Josephine hesitated, torn between wanting to tell her sister the truth, and conscious she hadn't yet broken the news of her morning's work to Thomas. 'Nothing official,' she reassured, 'though there has been mention of a few possibilities – including a Lord Huntingly, who has recently returned from the continent—'

'Lord Huntingly?' Viscount Damerel interrupted. 'Lord Alistair Huntingly who owns Huntingly Manor but five miles away from us, across the border in Somerset?'

The table suddenly went very quiet, making her wonder if she should have said anything at all.

'Yes, I believe so,' she replied, feeling her cheeks grow warm. 'Fred and Sir Francis knew him at Oxford, and Thomas mentioned he recently returned to his country seat in Somerset.'

The viscount glanced at his brother. 'You know about this, Elliot?'

Josephine frowned. She'd expected the viscount to have a view, but the captain had only recently returned from duty himself. 'Do you know Lord Huntingly?' she asked, aware he suddenly looked much more sombre.

The oddest prickle crept down her spine, as the captain glanced at his brother before turning back to her. 'I do indeed,' he replied, though it was clear he was picking his words with care. 'I had the pleasure of serving with him for a time, though he kept himself to himself, and we both sold out before the regiment was sent to the Gold Coast. Last I heard, he was in Italy, and then well ... there was that business with Pellham ...

and now it seems he's back in Somerset,' he concluded with a swift frown. 'I didn't know he was considering taking a wife, though.'

Josephine glanced from the captain to the viscount to Phoebe, before conversation was paused by two footmen who removed some of the dishes and replaced them with a glazed ham and fowl à la Montmorenci, garnished with a ragoût à l'allemande.

'Why does the name Pellham sound familiar?' Phoebe asked her husband as she accepted a slice of the ham. 'Should we be concerned Thomas is considering Lord Huntingly?'

Josephine tried not to look avidly interested as her oyster plate was cleared.

'You might remember the name from a somewhat infamous duel,' the viscount replied drily.

'Yes, that's it!' Phoebe nodded. 'Wasn't there a scandal? I thought they both disappeared?'

'They did,' Captain Damerel interjected. 'Which is hardly surprising, given the rumours.'

'We don't know what Pellham did for certain,' Dr Kapoor murmured, 'only the extent of the injuries.'

Josephine hardly dared breathe as the conversation around her started to turn to some of her own questions.

'Huntingly's weapon backfired, and they were Pellham's Flintlock pistols,' the captain frowned. 'That's evidence enough for me. If a man can't be honourable in a duel, no soldier will defend him in battle.'

'It may have been loaded incorrectly,' Dr Kapoor insisted, with a glance at Josephine. 'I have known terrible injuries from the like.'

'Unusual with seconds present. And it nearly took Huntingly's arm!' the captain argued.

'What happened to Pellham?' Josephine's voice rose above the rest, drawing the conversation to an abrupt halt.

Everyone turned towards her as a memory of the unusual scars that scored Huntingly's arm and chest reached through her thoughts. She swallowed: she had to know the truth.

'Yes, what did happen to Pellham?' her older sister echoed in a tired tone. 'And do I need to talk to Thomas?'

The viscount lay his hand over Phoebe's. 'There's nothing you need worry about just now,' he reassured, 'and there were never any charges, so Huntingly is free to look for a wife if he wishes. Though I'd be surprised if Matilda doesn't lead Thomas a merry moorland dance if he tries to shoehorn in a match before her season!'

At this, they all laughed as the viscount lifted his wife's pale hand and kissed it.

'And may I ask how you are feeling this evening, Viscountess?' Dr Kapoor added with a kindly smile. 'Did you try the roasted apples? Unlike many of my colleagues, I do not believe pregnancy to be a disease, but rather a physical state that deserves medical care and attention.'

Josephine half-listened as the viscount and Dr Kapoor steered the conversation away from bloody duels. She was relieved her sister was receiving such good care, but also highly distracted. Huntingly's mocking eyes flitted through her thoughts, and a blush stole across her cheeks. How she'd ever had the audacity to ask him to marry her was becoming a mystery of epic proportions. Thomas's judgement had never been in more doubt, and nothing was more important than knowing the truth.

'What *did* happen to Pellham in Italy?' she repeated, stilling the conversation a second time.

'I think enough has been said on this subject, Josephine,' the viscount replied. 'It's a discussion for another occasion.' He frowned in warning, and she understood, of course. He was trying to protect Phoebe, and a wave of guilt rose within her as she acknowledged her sister's pale and anxious face. Yet, she had no time to waste either. Unless Huntingly was intending to publicly humiliate her, she was committed to marrying him, which meant she had to find out the truth. She tried to stem the panic coursing through her limbs as she looked from the viscount, to Phoebe, to Dr Kapoor and lastly to the captain, before drawing a shaky breath. 'You see, I need to know,' she blurted in a rush, 'because I've asked Lord Huntingly to marry me!'

There was a moment's pregnant silence, and then everyone began speaking at once.

'Jo! What on earth do you mean?' Phoebe gasped.

'Did you say *marry*?' the viscount demanded sharply.

'I always said it's the quiet ones you have to watch!' the captain groaned.

'I hope you have not overly excited yourself.' Dr Kapoor frowned.

'It's only because Thomas already agreed to a match … for Matilda.' Josephine flushed. 'And I know, without a shadow of a doubt, that she'd rather join the foreign legion than marry any gentleman just now…'

Thomas berated her through her panicking thoughts:

'What a goose you are, Josephine. Of course I haven't arranged for you to marry Huntingly…! You had your turn and I'm not leaving anything else to chance. Matilda will marry Huntingly this year, and there is nothing more to be said.'

'…so I went to see him this morning.' She pushed her spectacles back up her nose, conscious her least shockable sister was looking more shocked by the second. 'It was quite clear from his reaction that he hasn't given the match much thought at all, that Thomas is right and he is simply looking for a respectable name to align with his own.' She drew a deep breath. 'As you all know I have three seasons behind me and no expectations, so it just felt … sensible to offer myself in Matilda's place, and he has accepted, which is why I ask about Pellham.'

She swallowed and pushed her chin a little higher, though she was conscious she was trembling too.

'Jo, no!' Phoebe exclaimed wretchedly. 'I knew you were distracted … but *this*? A thousand times, no! Why didn't you come to us? Alexander could have spoken with Thomas and—'

'Most likely achieved nothing,' the viscount drawled, his eyes glittering. 'Surely you know your eldest brother by now, my dear? Not that I approve of your reckless course of action, either, Josephine.' He frowned heavily, before nodding at his brother. 'Tell us everything you know, Elliot, and we'll see if a plan can be fathomed.'

'Well, that's just it,' Captain Damerel replied, shooting Josephine a worried glance. 'I know very little, only that Pellham died in Italy.'

There was another silence as Josephine felt a coldness whisper across her skin.

'Go on,' the viscount drawled, his eyelids sinking even lower.

'It was just after we both sold out last year. Huntingly went on a short tour while I came home. Next thing I heard was that Pellham had been killed in some skirmish in Rome ... swords, or so I understand.'

Josephine recalled the long, thin scars on Huntingly's chest and shivered. Weren't they just the sort of injuries that might befall someone in a swordfight?

'Not unusual for Rome, of course, except Huntingly was also travelling through the south of the country around the same time...' The captain glanced at Dr Kapoor. 'Anyway, there was never any evidence he was responsible, or even near the location of the fight,' he finished with a shrug. 'As I understand it, Huntingly went on to travel for a few more months before returning to England earlier this year. That's all I know.'

Josephine drew a breath as Phoebe closed her eyes. 'If there were no charges, there can't have been any evidence,' she offered logically, 'which means Lord Huntingly must be innocent.' She looked around the table. 'Thomas must have arranged the match knowing the same, and when I spoke with him, he was insistent Matilda would marry before her season even began. I know Matilda, and this knowledge would have forced her to run away or something equally as desperate, so really there *is* no plan to be fathomed... I will wed Lord Huntingly, Matilda will get more time, and there is nothing anyone can say or do to change it.'

Chapter Six

Ebcott Place; Shadows and Tales
Midnight

The silence was thick and foreboding, immobilising Josephine in her bed, as moonlight pooled on her bedchamber floor. She listened intently, yet it wasn't so much that she'd heard something, as she could just *feel* something was wrong.

Frowning, she pulled on her dressing gown, and padded softly towards the door before inching it open. The corridor was gloomy, and all seemed quiet until she caught a whisper of voices from the direction of Phoebe's bedchamber. And then she knew.

Without hesitating, she flew down the corridor, only slowing as she turned the corner and nearly collided with the viscount. He was pacing outside her sister's door, while his brother reclined on the hall settle in his nightgown, half-asleep. It was such a comical, unexpected sight that, at any other time, she would have laughed, but one glimpse of her brother-in-law's pale face was enough to silence her.

'Phoebe?' she croaked, ignoring the sudden pounding in her ears. She'd always been the ailing one with Phoebe her faithful nurse – she'd never known her robust older sister to experience a day's ill health in her life.

'Josephine,' the viscount exhaled, his whole appearance so uncharacteristically dishevelled that for a moment he reminded her of Rotherby, Sophie's husband.

She caught a breath as he took her hands, his dark eyes clouding with a fear he was clearly trying to hide.

'The child has begun early, Jo.' He smiled in a way that didn't reach his eyes. 'And I thank the heavens above she is in the care of Dr Kapoor. He is with her now, as is her monthly nurse, and while she is in some pain she is making good progress.'

He broke off to run his hand through his hair, as a soft moan reached through the bedchamber door.

'Though it is damnably hard to listen to,' he added, with a sidelong glance at his snoring brother, 'for some of us.'

Captain Damerel snorted then, as though to add insult to injury, yet Josephine's thoughts couldn't be further from sleeping.

She stared, guilt bleeding through her like a gathering tide. Had her confession at dinner started this? She was sure Phoebe had said there were another two weeks before her time, yet she'd looked so drawn at the table. She would never forgive herself if the child's delivery was affected by her confessions. Briefly, she closed her eyes, trying to ease the barrage of thoughts competing for attention, yet she knew exactly what she needed to do too. 'I'll go to her,' she reassured in a low voice, much like the one Phoebe had always reserved for herself. 'She will be easier if one of us is there.'

She didn't mean herself or Alexander, but herself or one of her sisters. Despite the passage of time, and Phoebe's undisputed love for her husband, there was no doubt in Josephine's mind that she would need one of her sisters more than anyone else at this time.

The viscount exhaled in clear relief. 'Will you? I'm not sure if you should, but she will want one of you there, I know ... I'd go in myself but I know it's not the damned done thing...' He ran his fingers through his unkempt hair again. 'Perhaps I should, anyway?'

Josephine pressed his hand reassuringly, just as the door opened to reveal Dr Kapoor still in his evening wear, though his jacket had been discarded and he'd rolled up his crisp white sleeves. Not for the first time, she noticed the natural air of authority he exuded in a crisis and felt comforted.

'The infant was breeched, but the cephalic version appears to have worked which is encouraging.' He nodded in his calm way. 'I'd still like to request permission to use a little ergot of rye to help the viscountess, if you will permit me? As it transpires, she's been experiencing some mild birthing pains for the better part of the last two days, but says she did not wish to trouble anyone...'

At this the viscount groaned. 'Isn't that just like my wife? Of course, please do everything in your power to help her! I believe Miss Josephine will also bring her comfort and ... if there is anything I can do ... anything at all?'

'Miss Fairfax's presence will be most comforting to her

sister,' Dr Kapoor agreed soothingly. 'As yours would too, sir, if you are so inclined? I am not typical of my profession, as you know, and consider the presence of a supportive husband to be beneficial to both mother and child – though I must warn you that birthing pains, while natural, can be difficult to watch.'

As if to accentuate his point, another guttural groan reached through the doorway at precisely that moment. It was all the invitation Josephine needed, and pressing the viscount's hands one last time, she slipped through the door and into the candlelit bedchamber.

The room was warm and dark, yet light enough to see her sister wasn't on the birthing bed she'd been gifted by Sophie, but in her own bed. She hesitated as she gazed across at her sister's agitated form, surrounded by a swathe of fresh linen, while her monthly nurse, an experienced woman from the village, bathed her brow. Then Phoebe groaned again and, without another thought, Josephine rushed to her side.

'Jo … thank goodness!' Phoebe panted in short breaths. 'I have … no … idea how Mama did it … more than … once! For I am … certain this will be our first and last … whether through choice or not,' she added before breaking off to groan in a way that reached through Josephine's bones.

Josephine smiled, though her sister's pained and drawn face was shocking. Mama used to say Phoebe had the constitution of an ox, yet all she could see now were her pale and thin arms amid the swirl of birthing sheets. How had she been so wrapped up in her own problems that she'd failed to notice she was in pain?

'Such talk,' she scolded lovingly, though her stomach was churning. 'I distinctly recall someone not so far from me claiming there was nothing a Fairfax could not do! In fact, I believe that anyone who can duel a highwayman with a theatrical épée is more than equal to bringing a new human into the world, isn't that right, Alexander?'

She looked in relief at her brother-in-law who'd taken Dr Kapoor at his word and followed Josephine into the bedchamber.

'It is!' The viscount smiled, the furrow between his eyes saying everything he wasn't, as he made his way to Phoebe's other side. 'Not forgetting the courageous young lady who jumped into a canal in full evening dress to rescue her sister,' he added, dropping a tender kiss on his wife's forehead.

She smiled wanly. 'You know I don't like to swim in anything else...' she panted before tailing off to groan again.

This time Phoebe gripped her hand so tightly that it made her eyes smart, yet Josephine forced herself to murmur words of encouragement. 'That's it, won't be long now,' Dr Kapoor consoled, stepping forward to count her sister's pulse when she lay back against the pillow.

Josephine waited, momentarily reassured by his unruffled air before he turned away to speak to the nurse, which was precisely the moment that everything changed. Without warning, Phoebe uttered a sudden, strangled yell that made Josephine's every nerve strain. Startled, she glanced back as her sister arched dramatically, her face contorting with pain, before she fell against her pillows – while a strange, dark stain grew amid her twisted sheets.

There was a moment's silence as Josephine's veins filled with horror. 'Dr Kapoor...' she whispered.

'Outside, now! Both of you!' Dr Kapoor ordered urgently.

The nurse didn't even wait for Dr Kapoor to finish before ushering them from the room and closing the door. For a moment Josephine stared at the viscount's stricken face, conscious his brother was still gently snoring, oblivious to it all.

'If anything should happen to her...' he whispered wanly.

'It won't,' she whispered, her own problems forgotten now she was facing the loss of a most beloved sister. 'This is Phoebe, the strongest, the bravest, the most ... alive person I know!' Her voice caught as she pressed her brother-in-law's hands. 'And as she would say herself,' she added hoarsely, 'she's a Fairfax.'

Three days later

The spring sunshine warmed Josephine's face as she made her way down the meadow, awash with bluebells, dandelions and wild garlic. It was like being immersed in a painted landscape and briefly, she closed her eyes, letting the pastel surroundings soothe her. It worked better than one of Dr Kapoor's tinctures and she smiled, recalling the happy months she'd spent at Ebcott in his care. Her siblings had spent summers here too when Phoebe and the viscount had removed from town for the warmer months, and now their young voices permeated every nook and cranny. They were halcyon days she'd thought would never end, not become shadowed by an event that stilled her heart every time she thought on it.

Carefully, she allowed her thoughts to reach back over the

past two nights, to the moment she thought she'd lost both her sister and the infant she carried. Pain flared instantly, tightening her chest against the fresh May air, despite her efforts to recall that both Phoebe and her new son lived.

'Baby Alexander,' she whispered, reaching down to brush her fingers through the long meadow grass, taking comfort from the dew that cooled her fingers. It reminded her of the circle of day and night, life and death, and she took a steadying breath.

She wasn't maudlin, but her near loss had shaken her, and she'd never felt so mortal in her life. It was clear Dr Kapoor's swift and skilled intervention had saved them both, yet while young Alexander was a perfect, cherubin infant with a set of lungs to match, Phoebe had yet to regain her strength.

Josephine frowned, recalling her sister's pallor and exhaustion ever since that night. Dr Kapoor insisted she was in the right place to recuperate, yet she'd never known her so weak.

'That you, Miss Josephine? Come to see the new chicks, I'll bet!'

She glanced up, relieved for her thoughts to be interrupted by the querulous voice of Ebcott's elderly gardener.

'Yes, of course I have, Williams. How are you?' Josephine called, hurrying towards his stooped figure at the bottom of the meadow. The last three days had been so beset with worry, some tiny carefree life sounded the perfect tonic. She smiled as she reached his familiar figure, his elderly face as wizened as the small orchard surrounding them.

'Oh, I'm fit as an old flea, thank y'miss … and how's the

mistress now?' he enquired as she turned to peer over the coop fence.

True to his promise, half a dozen tiny yellow balls of life peeped back at her, before darting towards their clucking mother. Contentedly, she watched the mother hen fuss around her demanding brood. Phoebe had been no less enamoured with infant Alexander, despite the trauma of his arrival, and hadn't yet let the nurse remove him from her bedchamber.

'She's making slow progress, thank you, Williams,' Josephine replied, reaching down to scoop up the nearest chick, which chirruped its protest to the world, 'while Alexander seems as determined to embrace life as one of these little souls.'

Williams nodded, his faded blue eyes full of care. 'I'm glad to hear it, miss. It's no easy business bringing young'uns into the world, an' no mistake. The master and mistress deserve many years of happiness together, not all this worry. I'm sure I wish them a whole brood of healthy chicks too, just like Betsy here.'

Josephine couldn't help but chuckle. 'Well, Betsy has done a fine job.' She released the tiny adventurer back inside the coop. 'And Phoebe was always the sturdiest of us all – I pray she will be back to full health soon.'

'Aye, as do I, miss.' Williams smiled kindly. 'They always say that those who work hardest to bring them into the world make the best mothers... Be you waltzing down that aisle next, miss, and I'll make sure you have a bouquet of May-bells in your hands, if I can. They were always your favourites, and the estate woods is full of them just now.'

He turned to shuffle away, just as a thought struck Josephine.

'Williams,' she frowned, 'do you know any of the domestic staff working at the bordering estate?'

'You mean Huntingly Manor, miss?' he replied. ''Bout five mile from here?'

'That's it,' she replied, pan-faced. 'The son has recently returned from the continent, I believe.'

'Aye miss, I know the one.' He nodded, reaching up to stroke his chin in a manner of someone thinking back over the years. 'The old lord kept a man – Henry was his name – we was in school together, and I still see him from time to time. He was the quiet type, did what he could to look after the place, but the manor still fell into ruin while the young lord was away, of course…'

'So, you know what happened … with the duel?' Josephine ventured.

The situation with Lord Huntingly had receded to the back of her mind over the past few days, but now it returned with glaring clarity. Silently, she berated herself for not thinking to ask Williams before: the Ebcott and Huntingly estates neighboured one another, and he was the longest-standing member of staff, after all.

'You mean all that went on with old man Huntingly and Pellham?'

Josephine glanced up. 'Yes, if you don't mind?' she replied, trying not to sound too hopeful.

'No, I don't mind.' He stooped to pick a blade of grass and begin chewing on it. 'Though it was summat of a shady business, truth be told. Pellham's father was as thick as coves with old man Huntingly, as he was his estate manager. He was a nice enough fellow – rough and ready but knew his business too – so when he died, old man Huntingly adopted his son … not officially, but took an interest and the like,' William continued, frowning in concentration. 'Young Pellham was quite the sportsman, as it turned out, much like Huntingly's own son, and so of course the pair quickly became inseparable … like brothers some might say…'

Josephine listened with bated breath as the elderly man recounted Huntingly's story, filling in gaps with his memories.

'So what happened?' she prompted as his voice trailed off.

He bent down to pick up a small pail of water and shuffle towards the chicken coop. 'Old man Huntingly died in a hunting accident with only Pellham there, and afterwards, when the will was read, the young lord discovered Pellham was to inherit part of the estate.'

'Oh,' Josephine commented cautiously, though her mind was cartwheeling at the revelation. 'So, the duel was prompted by jealousy?'

It was logical, and yet she could tell Williams wasn't quite done yet.

'Perhaps.' Williams frowned again. 'Though I wouldn't have thought that would bother young Huntingly – he wasn't exactly the rich landowner type – he was a bit of a hothead, happiest with his dogs and horses. His father had made no secret of the fact he was fond of Pellham too, and the young lord seemed to love Pellham like a brother…'

'So, why then?' Josephine prompted. Recalling the half-dressed young lord with his hound, she could readily believe he'd never been an easy gentleman about town.

The Proposition of the Season

'I'm not entirely sure, miss.' Williams scratched his head. 'But there are those who say the accident itself was unusual. Old Huntingly was, as his name suggests, a fine sportsman, and the coroner ruled he fell from a bolting horse... It's only hearsay, mind, and folks do like to gossip, but I believe his son may have issued the challenge because of his grief following his father's death.'

There was a silence as Josephine watched the elderly gardener fill up the wooden chicken troughs, the joyful springtime chorus at odds with the strange story he'd just related. She shivered. 'So young Lord Huntingly challenged his best friend to a dawn duel, because he was suspicious of the circumstances surrounding his father's death...' she pondered. 'That's really sad.'

'Aye, miss, it was sad for them both, and I think it would have pained old Huntingly to see it too. They both seemed nice young gentlemen in their own way, truth be told. Then, of course, the duel wasn't without its own cloud...'

Josephine frowned, trying to recall what Captain Damerel said the night Phoebe went into labour.

'Huntingly's weapon backfired, and they were Pellham's Flintlock pistols... That's evidence enough for me. If a man can't be honourable in a duel, no soldier will defend him in battle...'

'There was a problem with the pistols,' Josephine paraphrased carefully.

'Yes, that's it,' the elderly gardener nodded. 'I'm not fond of fighting in any form, mind, think there's plenty of better ways to settle a fall out without offering yourself up as target practice... Anyway, the pistol backfired, and young Huntingly suffered badly, an' no mistake.'

Josephine imagined the scene as the pistol backfired and shuddered: little wonder the newspaper report had called it a 'bloody affair'.

'They stopped the duel, of course, but far from reconciling their differences, it only made things worse. Last I heard, they both went off to France, and now the young lord is home again, not that he's recalled any staff to service other than Henry, or seen anyone much at all. The Lord knows what state the manor is in now, for it were completely closed when the young lord went abroad, and it were such a pretty house in its day too.' He sighed before seeming to recall Josephine's presence. 'Not that you need worry your head about all that, Miss Josephine, for I'm sure it's naught to do with you, eh?' He stooped to pick up his pail. 'And now the viscountess is over the worst I'm sure we can all rest a little easier too … especially you, miss. 'Tis a lot for a young'un like yourself to take on,' he added kindly, letting himself out of the coop. 'Hopefully, a little fresh air and sunshine will work its magic on us all now, as will a few of old Jemima's eggs, which I sent up this morning. I've also a posy of May-bells in the potting shed, if you're happy to take them to the viscountess? I thought they might cheer her bedchamber.'

Josephine wasn't sure if the elderly gardener knew of Pellham's subsequent death in Italy and was sparing her, or wasn't aware himself, but she'd heard enough either way. 'I'd be delighted, Williams.' She smiled warmly.

Chapter Seven

Knightswood Manor; Wrath and Honour
One week later

'You did what?' Thomas exploded.

Josephine flinched, wishing for the umpteenth time that she had the same ready courage for herself as she'd had for Matilda on the day she visited Huntingly. But it had entirely deserted her, and now Williams's fresh knowledge of the duel compounded the whole situation.

She glanced out of the coach window and tried to draw strength from the haze of wild flowers blooming into life despite the long, cold winter.

'I'm sorry,' she replied quietly, 'but it made little sense for Matilda to marry so soon when I have three seasons behind me—'

'So, you thought you'd arrange things to suit yourself?' Thomas interrupted scathingly. 'Tell me, how did you muster such confidence, when I have it on the best authority that you barely muttered a word to any gentleman throughout three whole seasons?'

Josephine reddened and clenched her fingers, as Harriet pursed her lips at her eldest charge.

'I wasn't motivated by confidence,' she replied. 'I wanted only to protect Matilda and give her some time. I know it was ... forward, foolhardy even, but you said he was only interested in a respectable name to align with his own. And if I marry Lord Huntingly there will be one less charge upon the future estate,' she finished with a faint note of hope.

'And what of my name?' Thomas thundered in the small space. 'I gave Huntingly my word! Am I to accept that now counts for nothing? Let alone bear the shame of a sister offering herself as an exchange. It is not only *forward*, Josephine, it's scandalous! And I would have thought you'd learned the outcome of such things from Phoebe's near disastrous escapade or Sophie's ridiculous jaunt across Paris!'

'They're both happily married now,' Josephine defended.

'Yes, but through luck rather than design!' he countered furiously. 'It could have ended so differently for them both, but *you*, Josephine... I expected so much more of you! You're just lucky Phoebe's delicate situation will serve as a half-decent excuse for your folly!'

Josephine glanced up. 'What do you mean?' she asked, suddenly fearful.

'Well, obviously I can't let things stand as they are,' he scorned. 'I made a gentleman's agreement with Huntingly, and he'll be waiting to hear if it still stands. I'll write to him as soon as we're back at Knightswood to assure him your actions were the result of your sister's recent birthing experience – that your nerves were strained. Though I'll be surprised if he doesn't rescind on the whole thing altogether; the gentleman needs a respectable alliance to quell gossip, not a ramshackle wife who thinks she can behave like one of her ill-advised heroines!'

'You can't!' Josephine whispered, aghast. 'You ... you don't know what Huntingly is like.'

Thomas' lip curled. 'If you mean I haven't listened to all the rumours, you're quite right!' he replied glibly. 'Papa hunted with old Lord Huntingly, and he would have approved of the match. His son is little different, and his nature will suit Matilda.' He paused to look Josephine up and down. 'Far more so than it will your reclusive nature.'

Josephine reddened, picturing the towering, chestnut-eyed lord reclining against his breakfast table, eyeing her with clear disbelief. She could readily believe he was a hothead just like Matilda, and already knew he possessed an unpredictability, a wildness, that was both terrifying and drawing at the same time. Yet, however could two such fiery souls produce an alliance to quell gossip? And the thought she might have meddled in a match that might actually suit Matilda? It hadn't crossed her mind. She'd acted to protect her sister and give her precious time, but if she'd thought Matilda might embrace the match, she never would have interfered. She closed her eyes, Thomas's bleak words piercing her like tiny darts. She'd never considered herself a match for Matilda's beauty or spirit, yet his description felt more scorching than any criticism she'd ever levelled at herself.

'But Matilda has other ambitions,' she defended quietly, staring down at her knotted fingers. 'She needs time.'

There was a heavy silence before Thomas spoke, and

when he did, it was with finality. 'Matilda may have as many ambitions as she pleases,' he said coldly, 'but her duty will always come first. I promised her to Huntingly, and by my troth, he will have her, if he still chooses. And, in the meantime, I suggest you take time to reflect upon your selfish and nonsensical behaviour which disappoints me more than I can say. I expected more sense from you, Josephine, but now I can see you're just as damned foolish as the rest!'

Dear Fitzwilliam,

So much has happened since I last wrote you that I hardly know where to begin, yet perhaps it should be with the most joyful news that Phoebe is on the road to recovery…

Josephine broke off at the sound of faint voices in the hall downstairs, and yet the past three days had been so quiet, there was a distinct chance she could be imagining them.

In truth, baby Alexander's entry into the world was so beset with challenges, Dr Kapoor calls it a miracle that he and Phoebe survived at all, which only makes my sister's improving health even more of a blessing. And miracle does seem to be an apt description, for a more heavenly bundle it would be difficult to find … such tiny fingers, such sweet infant eyes… I truly believe he has the look of the viscount, and yet there is something in his ferocious cry that is Phoebe through and through.

She exhaled as memories of Phoebe's pride and joy were slowly replaced with recollections of her own dismal predicament.

As for my own plan, I can safely say I have never felt more wretched! Not only has Thomas written to Lord Huntingly to assure him their gentleman's agreement still stands, he has claimed my actions were the result of overwrought nerves. I am sure Lord Huntingly will take little persuasion that this was indeed the case, he eyed me with enough suspicion, but more importantly my efforts to protect Matilda will count for nothing! Thomas is determined my nature will not suit Huntingly, but our old nurse Harriet spoke with more truth when she said Thomas will not be crossed. Truly, he must be the most heinous brother to force the hand of one sister when another will give hers most readily.

She swallowed, trying to quiet the barrage of hurt and confusion within her slight frame. Thomas had lectured her all the way from Ebcott until, finally, his grievance turned to silence. Harriet had extended looks of sympathy throughout, but even she knew better than to intervene when Thomas was in one of his darker moods.

In truth, she'd never known him so damning before, except perhaps when Phoebe was pinked by a highwayman, or Sophie decided to accompany a known rake of the ton to Paris... She smiled faintly, recalling her sisters' calamitous adventures long before she'd raised her own bookworm head above the parapet, yet wouldn't she do the same again, for any of her sisters? Her smile faded as she recalled their arrival back at Knightswood, when Matilda learned of her match with Lord Huntingly:

'I don't care what you've arranged, you can un-arrange it as fast as you like! I'm not your daughter, and I won't be told who I'll spend the rest of my life with – especially if it's some scandalous cad!'

'How dare you speak in such a way! You are my ward, and my responsibility. And by my troth, you will marry who I say you will marry, so help me God.'

She closed her eyes, remembering the way Matilda had stormed from the dining room, her moorland face stained with fury and tears. It was a scene she'd tried so hard to prevent, yet it seemed she'd achieved little but her own disgrace.

Josephine glanced up as a soft rap at the door jolted her from her thoughts.

'Excuse me, miss. Sir Fairfax wonders if you might join him in the library, miss?' Betsy asked timidly. 'And he requested you … tidy yourself before you come down too, miss.'

One glance at Betsy's wide-eyed expression was enough to ascertain that it wasn't an ordinary request as she turned to inspect herself in the mirror. She looked neat enough in her old plain muslin with her hair twisted into a low bun, yet Thomas's mood was far from easy.

'If I may say so, miss,' Betsy sniffed loyally, 'you look lovely just as you are.'

Josephine smiled and pinched her cheeks. 'Thank you, Betsy,' she replied ruefully. 'Let's hope my brother agrees.'

From the moment she entered the room, Josephine knew something was different. For a start, Thomas was smiling, prompting her to glance behind in case her arrival had coincided with a delivery of Burgundy.

'Ah, sister!' He called in a jarring, affectionate tone. 'There you are! Do come in so we may talk with you.'

Josephine edged into the room, glaringly aware that Thomas's new brotherly affection was due to the presence of a third person, seated in his favourite high-backed chair. She swallowed, wondering if this was the moment she was to discover that he was to have her committed to an asylum – just as the person stood up. Josephine drew in a shaky breath, momentarily bereft of speech, as she stared at his clean-shaven face and long locks swept à la Brutus, to his impeccably dressed person. And yet there was that same towering frame, fiery chestnut eyes, and familiar mocking smile too.

Was this Thomas's idea of retribution? Was he planning to chastise her in front of Lord Huntingly?

'Look who has graced us with a visit, Josephine! I'm sure we're both delighted to make Lord Huntingly's better acquaintance, especially given recent exciting news.'

Startled, Josephine glanced at Thomas, but there was no hint of irony in his face, only genuine satisfaction.

'Lord Huntingly has been kind enough to confirm his satisfaction with the new arrangements. He is a country man, with little interest in town and outside distractions, and feels your nature will be well suited to his lifestyle. I have to say, I am of the same opinion! Let me congratulate you, dear sister, for Huntingly has made a formal offer for your hand this morning, and I have accepted.'

Josephine blinked at her older brother as he wrung Huntingly's hand before turning to nod approvingly at her.

'It is a fine offer, sister, and I will ensure you have a wedding that befits your new status, for the Huntinglys are a very old family indeed.'

'Old, but not ostentatious,' Huntingly amended, his eyes never leaving Josephine's face. 'In truth, I would be quite happy with a modest affair, Fairfax, and I wager Miss Josephine feels the same way?'

Josephine managed to nod, blood drumming in her ears. She had no idea how things had turned about so swiftly, only that Lord Alistair Huntingly had apparently decided to take her marriage offer seriously – and persuaded Thomas to do the same. He appraised her now, his dark eyes taking her straight back to his breakfast room when he'd closed the distance between them. It was such an intense, vivid memory that she felt a flush steal up her neck, prompting a gleam of recognition in his eyes. She reddened further, aware she might still appear a figure of fun in his eyes. Yet, whatever his reasoning, she'd done it, she'd changed his mind, and now their match would protect Matilda for a while longer.

Josephine lowered her eyes, searching for words while he seemed content to gaze. In truth, his youthful, clean-shaven face unsettled her more than she cared to own. He looked barely older than Fred now, which was curious for someone who'd lived so much.

'I would be content with a very quiet affair, thank you, my lord,' she murmured, wondering how differently her sisters felt when they received their offers.

'Excellent!' He smiled disconcertingly. 'Didn't I say we

The Proposition of the Season

would deal famously together, Fairfax? Miss Josephine has as little desire for pomp and ceremony as I, and she has already expressed a very particular view about the condition of Huntingly Manor...' His lips curled as he forced Josephine to recall her comments about the dilapidated condition of his ancestral home. She swallowed and flashed a glance at Thomas, who was beginning to frown. '...which I found excessively fresh and useful,' he added smoothly. 'In short, Fairfax, I believe Miss Josephine will breathe new life into Huntingly Manor without exacerbating mine – which is precisely what is needed.'

'Excellent ... excellent!' Thomas boomed, clearly relieved he wasn't required to defend Josephine unnecessarily. 'What say we toast this new arrangement at dinner? I might even crack open a bottle of my favourite Blandy's Madeira to mark the occasion!'

'I should be delighted,' Lord Huntingly replied with a swift smile, 'as I shall be to make your sister's better acquaintance.'

'Excellent!' Thomas repeated, crossing the room. 'And now I shall give the two of you a few moments in private. Suffice to say, I'm very happy to conclude this business with you, Huntingly – very happy indeed! Until dinner!'

Then Thomas pulled the library door shut, leaving Josephine alone with her new, most unexpected, fiancé.

'You look perplexed, Miss Josephine,' Lord Huntingly commented with a faint frown. 'Yet I only came to make our agreement formal. If you have changed your mind, pray tell me now, for I am sure your brother will be understanding.'

Josephine's eyes flew to Lord Huntingly's, their amber flare just visible.

'You do not know my brother, sir!' she returned, a thousand thoughts racing. 'And I can assure you that any surprise on my part is due to the fact that I thought my behaviour might have … scared you off.'

Lord Huntingly's sombre expression changed suddenly, giving Josephine a glimpse of a sunnier face she barely recognised, before it faded again. 'You really are most refreshing, Miss Fairfax,' he observed, closing the gap between them with a few easy paces. 'You are aware of my reputation, are you not? I cannot recall the last time anyone accused me of being scared of anything, least of all an over-protective bluestocking!'

Josephine lifted her chin, aware of a rise of chagrin.

'But to be quite clear,' he continued in a softer tone, 'no, you didn't scare me off, quite the opposite, in fact. And, in truth, I owe you an apology: I should have never asked you to remove your spectacles. It was most … ignoble of me.'

He was barely an arm's length away now, towering over her with his chestnut eyes and derisive smile. She stole a shallow breath, aware of the oddest rush of feelings. This lord was so different from the one she'd encountered in the manor. His coat was expensive, his manner sophisticated, his shaven face far more handsome than she'd ever realised… Suddenly, Josephine realised the enormity of what she'd done. She'd proposed marriage to the sort of gentleman she'd made it her life's work to avoid, in the knowledge they would never find interest in her. She flushed furiously. Perhaps Thomas was right; perhaps he would have dealt better with Matilda.

'I've never before met a female prepared to make a lifelong sacrifice merely to protect another.' He raised an eyebrow, stilling her response. 'Please, I have it on the best authority that *nothing would induce Matilda to marry me!*' Josephine's flush deepened. 'And the fact you were prepared to risk your own reputation, in order to secure the arrangement, only makes your selflessness all the more admirable.' He smiled then, but in a way that made Josephine's toes tingle quite oddly. 'Indeed, I can quite honestly say that I have not felt this intrigued by someone for some time, Miss Josephine, and as your offer makes perfect logical sense, I am quite content to move forward with the new arrangement. Which leaves you, my dear?'

He reached out then to take her hand and lift it to his lips – a move that took Josephine entirely by surprise – before planting a chaste kiss on her back of her fingers. It was the briefest of touches, yet the warmth of his lips startled her.

His eyelids lowered as she caught her breath.

'There is no need for … any apology, sir,' Josephine stumbled, 'for I too am … quite content. I have not changed my mind, for the happiness of my sister is everything to me… And I shall endeavour to breathe new life into Huntingly Manor, sir, without interfering in your life at all. You have my word.'

Momentarily, he observed her, a faint quizzical light in his eyes. 'And what of your happiness, Miss Josephine?' he asked softly. 'Or does that count for nothing?'

Josephine returned his regard, wondering if he was testing her. 'My happiness shall derive from the satisfaction of knowing I helped a sister, sir, and that shall be enough to sustain me.'

'Good grief!' he exclaimed. 'What a truly selfless creature you are!'

'And what of my reputation?' he continued in a low tone that made her feel curiously vulnerable. 'Are you sure you shouldn't be a *little* wary, my dear?'

Josephine swallowed as he echoed her inner thoughts perfectly, everything Sir Francis, Fred, Captain Damerel and Williams had ever said surfacing in vivid detail. Viscount Damerel had referred to an Italian court ruling Pellham's death to be accidental, and that Huntingly was innocent as a result – *but on what evidence?*

She crossed her fingers in the folds of her skirt. 'I know little of your reputation that would make any real difference, sir,' she replied carefully. 'Indeed, if any of it *were* true, I would be even more eager to assist my sister, lest she befall a similar fate.'

At this, Lord Huntingly's lips twisted into a crooked smile and, alarmingly, Josephine found she rather liked it.

'By my troth, I believe you would,' he whispered so closely that she could watch the amber flares dancing in his eyes. 'Which makes you either very brave, or very foolish,' he added, before leaning in to brush her lips with his own.

It was such a bold and unexpected move that she barely realised what he was doing before her lips were tingling unfamiliarly. She stared up in shock, exhilaration chasing her veins, wishing for nothing more than to escape back to her bedchamber. Yet, he only straightened and walked back to the fireplace as though they'd exchanged the most civil of pleasantries.

'I shall be staying at the White Stag in town for a while and hope we can use the time to become better acquainted,' he suggested, as though he hadn't just stolen every logical thought from her whirling mind. 'Thomas and I are both keen to conclude the matter this year, so I think we'll find ourselves wed without too much delay. I trust that fits with your expectations? I am keen to rescue Huntingly Manor from its current state of decline and would like our union to be settled before undertaking any major work.'

Josephine stared as Lord Huntingly talked, conscious of words collecting like stones in her throat. She knew she should be trying to order her wayward thoughts, but felt only the human equivalent of her very plain brown muslin instead.

'I ... can see little reason to delay, sir,' she responded colourlessly, as Betsy arrived with a tea tray, 'and a private affair will enable us to move swifter than most.' She swallowed, searching for suitable pleasantries while her lips burned.

'Excellent! I had a feeling our thoughts would be aligned, Miss Fairfax,' he drawled, eyeing her in amusement until Betsy withdrew, 'just not *how* aligned.'

'Tea?' Josephine tried valiantly, approaching the tea table and focusing all her attention on the small teapot.

'Thank you.' He smiled disarmingly, taking the seat next to her.

Josephine nodded and began to pour, determined to behave as though nothing untoward had happened, yet his teacup shook traitorously in its saucer as she passed it to him. 'I trust the flavour is to your liking, sir?' she asked in an attempt at distraction, though the question sounded pointed, even to her own ears.

'Indeed,' he replied, taking a drink with dancing eyes, 'the flavour is very much to my liking. A small wedding, no objection to restoration work, and a skilled hostess – you are in danger of making me like the flavour a great deal, Miss Fairfax.'

Josephine nearly choked on a sip of her own hot tea. None of her literary heroes had ever lived on the page long beyond a kiss, and now she knew why: it was mortifying! She knew not where to look, what to say or how to think, but she could not let him know so.

She stood abruptly, unable to sit any longer. 'I thank you, sir, but I am not renowned for my hostess skills, any more than I am for the features for which my sisters are celebrated. I am a Fairfax, it's true, but other than a love of music and novels, I am the over-protective bluestocking you think me to be. Please do not confuse this with an accomplished debutante, for I will undoubtedly disappoint!'

Then she swept from the drawing room with as much dignity as she could muster, and when she finally reached her bedchamber, she closed the door in relief before turning to her looking glass. Momentarily, she stared at the trembling, wispy-haired girl before her – her cheeks flushed, spectacles askew, and chest still pounding.

'I do believe you enjoyed it!' she whispered accusingly as she reached to touch her lips. She'd read a number of passionate interludes in her novels, but nothing had prepared her for the violent sensations coursing through her veins now. She was ashamed and unsettled and ... aware of a very strange coiling at the pit of her stomach, all at the same time. She flushed, recalling the promise in his warmth, even though she was quite alone.

Yet why would he look on her as anything other than a contract of convenience? The thought was like pure gravity, drawing her back to earth as she spun to vent her feelings about the perils of marrying a likely murderer, to her much safer fictional fiancé.

Chapter Eight

A Moorland Breakfast; Plum Jam and Thistles
The following morning

'We could both join the army?' Matilda suggested, as they trotted along the old bridle path that bordered the Knightswood estate.

Josephine wasn't the keenest rider, but she'd felt a distinct need for moorland air this morning, and Matilda hadn't taken much persuading. She looked up from her quiet reverie, her eyebrows forking. 'You and I both know that, unless a soldier was in need of an emergency poem, I would be a positive disadvantage on the battlefield!'

'Actually, I think you'd be perfect!' Matilda defended. 'You've spent so long being nursed yourself, you'd know the inside of a medical bag without any training at all.'

Josephine chuckled. 'Unfortunately, being invalid oneself does not in any way qualify one for nursing anyone else. And, in truth, I've had my fill of the medical world at the grand old age of two-and-twenty. I'm not sure I'd be terribly patient.'

It was Matilda's turn to chuckle. 'It's not that you're not patient, it's just you're rarely in the present… You're a thinker, Jo.' She reined Misty, her elderly pony, back from the hedgerow dandelions. 'Perhaps that's what changed Thomas's mind?' she added, frowning. 'I mean, Lord Huntingly doesn't know either of us, so he wouldn't have any reason to prefer one above the other. Thomas must have suggested your nature would suit him better after all… In truth, I shudder to think what he said about me!'

She broke off to laugh as Josephine looked away towards a distant hill covered in a haze of flowering gorse. She'd managed to break the news about Lord Huntingly's change of mind before dinner, but she still hadn't told her of her visit to Huntingly Manor. The last thing Matilda needed to know was that her sister had chosen to marry a likely murderer to protect her from the same fate.

'I … don't know,' Josephine replied, a memory of the barely dressed lord in his cluttered breakfast room suddenly surfacing among her thoughts. 'I don't think he's typical of most gentlemen. The only thing Thomas said was that Lord Huntingly is in need of a respectable name to quell gossip since his return, and that he has little interest in outside distractions. Perhaps our brother decided that my nature was better suited to this,' she added carefully, guiding her pony around a ditch. She crossed her fingers in the folds of her riding habit, knowing she couldn't be more different to the headstrong lord. 'And I suppose I don't have too many options left after three seasons, I'm virtually on the shelf.' She laughed unconvincingly.

'Oh yes, such an old lady at two-and-twenty!' Matilda retorted, glancing at her sister. 'I think we marry too young, as a rule, anyway. We've barely begun to think for ourselves before we're tied to a gentleman who believes it's his job to think for us! Anyway, what of Sir Francis now?'

Josephine frowned at her ready turn in thought. 'Sir Francis could marry anyone he chooses, this season or the next, so I'd as lief *not* hang on until he notices me, for it is likely to be never!'

'Oh, Jo, you're much too good for him, anyway. I've always thought so. Sir Francis is much too in love with himself to ever love anyone else properly!'

'Matilda!' Josephine protested, unable to help laughing. 'I'm not sure such a thing is even possible. Sir Francis is an academic; he doesn't talk or even think in an everyday fashion, so it's not right to judge him by the same standards as everyone else.' She paused to collect her thoughts. 'He's well-travelled, well-read and unafraid to share his stories, and I for one admire that. If I'd been born a man, I would have leapt upon the chance for a Grand Tour and be full of such stories myself. Indeed, I may never have returned, so I'm most grateful he is generous with his knowledge for, if had been left to Fred, I would know nothing at all!'

'"Generous with his knowledge"?' Matilda laughed, wrinkling her nose. 'Well, if talking forever about the *marvellous* works of Michelangelo without allowing anyone else to get a word in edgeways makes one generous with knowledge, then yes, I suppose he is ... but I think he just likes the sound of his own voice! After all, Darcy never expounded on the merits of studying Greek mythology to Elizabeth, did he?' she challenged. 'And however Fred puts up with all his guffawing, I'm sure I don't know! Still, I know you respect his literary studies, and for that reason alone I'm prepared to put up with him, which is not the same as wishing him for my brother-in-law.'

'Well, I'm very happy to spare you the pain of that prospect,' Josephine replied, rolling her eyes. 'Not that it was ever a likelihood. And while I understand Sir Francis can expound on any subject *considerably*, I do admire him because he is unafraid of expressing an opinion, unlike most of the young gentlemen I met in London, who seemed only to talk about horses and boxing! Besides,' she added lightly, 'is it not possible to admire a gentleman without imagining oneself desperately in love with him?' She looked out again at the distant moorland hill. 'Either way, I am to wed Lord Huntingly now, and the matter is quite settled.'

Josephine tried not to acknowledge the sudden tightness in her chest as she uttered the last words. Her lung affliction had grown much milder under the watchful care of Dr Kapoor; the last thing she needed was a relapse because she'd allowed herself to become overwrought. And despite all the rumours, there was no clear evidence that Lord Huntingly *was* an actual murderer. Briefly, his scars sprung to mind, and Josephine forced her pony into a brisker walking pace. She'd been afflicted by illness all her life – even the ton had rejected her as too risky to make a good wife – yet she had never let it define her. By contrast, Huntingly's appearance and behaviour would suggest the very opposite. She frowned.

'So, what did Phoebe say about Huntingly's proposal, anyway?' Matilda pursued, catching up easily.

'I knew little of his intentions when I stayed at Ebcott,' Josephine replied, praying her inquisitive sister didn't notice the telltale blush stealing up her neck. 'But they have their hands full at the moment, and I suspect there is little she and the viscount could do to change Thomas's mind – even if I wanted them to.'

She broke off to muster a smile, pushing Phoebe's wan face to the back of her mind. Phoebe had been anything but silent on the subject, but her worried letter to Thomas had only brought him hot-foot to Ebcott, resulting in the shortest of conversations with the viscount and the swiftest of departures for herself. Josephine swallowed. In truth, she'd been happy to depart and relieve the viscount and Phoebe of one headache. She could tell the viscount was much too worried about Phoebe to lend her own situation much attention, and she wanted nothing more than her dearest sister to concentrate on recuperating just now. 'And Sophie is too busy populating Grosvenor Square with miniature Rotherbys to have time for anything, so it's just as well I am content, isn't it?'

A whistle sounded behind them.

'Both our sisters are much too distracted,' Matilda grumbled, having listened, with decidedly mixed feelings, to the account of her nephew's dramatic arrival. 'And I'm sure I'll never understand how such small humans can have such large needs! Anyway, it looks like we have company,' she added, her countenance brightening as she glanced behind. 'And I do believe it's the boys!'

At this, Josephine's spirits lifted too, knowing by Matilda's tone that she couldn't be referring to Thomas or Fred – Thomas never rode out this early and Fred never rode at all. Their twin brothers, Edward and Henry, on the other hand, were keen riders and rarely off the sporting or hunting field when not up at Oxford.

'Why have they returned mid-term?' Matilda asked, slowing Misty to an amble so they could catch up.

'Something to do with an exam exeat,' Josephine replied, her brow wrinkling. 'Not that either will open a book while they're home, of course.'

She'd raised her voice deliberately to goad Edward, who grinned as he cantered towards them. Edward was the more serious academic of the two and planned to become a zoologist when he finished Oxford, while Henry nursed hopes that Thomas would buy him an officer's commission in the cavalry.

To Josephine, however, neither would ever be out of their skeleton suits.

'I take it you're on the hunt for the Greater Crested Newt too?' Edward called jovially.

Josephine smiled as the youngest Fairfax brothers, wearing fashionable cutaway tailcoats, fitted trousers and gleaming riding boots, caught up. Neither could be termed a dandy, despite their fashionable attire, though Henry liked to consider himself a Corinthian, given his prowess in the sporting field.

'But, of course! Or Duke Wellington's grandsons!' Matilda grinned, referring to the family toad who'd graced their bedsides for many years before croaking off to the great pond in the sky.

'Great-great-grandchildren, you mean!' Edward corrected with a wink.

'Always so proper!' Matilda teased.

'Well, that's a relief anyway,' Henry said, 'for we plan to breakfast over at the old stepping stones, and I thought for a moment we might have to *share*!'

He pulled a face while patting his overfull saddlebag.

'Henry Fairfax!' Matilda laughed accusingly. 'I do believe Cook has made us *all* a packed breakfast and charged you to bring it us. *And* that she has sent my favourite plum jam, too!'

'I decline to comment on all three charges,' Henry replied solemnly. 'And if you wish to discover what Cook has made for breakfast, and whether it includes hot rolls, butter and the aforesaid jam together with the most divine *sugar cakes* ... you'll need to catch me!'

Then the most mischievous of the Fairfaxes urged his pony into a canter and raced away towards the moorland wading spot they'd all loved for as long as any of them could remember. Matilda wasted no time in giving chase, and soon enough the pair of them were disappearing into the middle distance, while Josephine and Edward followed at a more leisurely pace.

'I wonder if he recalls the way?' Edward pondered, following Matilda's speedy pursuit, her dark hair streaming out behind her.

'Well, if Henry doesn't, Matilda will enjoy reminding him,' Josephine smiled as a faint whooping floated through the air.

'It is good to see them together, even if they do sound like overgrown infants.'

'They really do,' Edward chuckled, raising his eyebrows.

'Oh, it's so lovely to have you both. back with us, Edward,' Josephine returned warmly, 'even if it's only for the weekend. I was beginning to think Fred and Sir Francis were going to be our only visitors this spring, and the Knightswood fayre can only entertain so much.'

Edward grinned. 'Fred and his companion not kicking up enough larks?'

'When has Fred ever kicked up a lark?' Josephine retorted. 'And Sir Francis is far too…'

'Boring?'

'Sensible,' Josephine corrected reprovingly, as Edward snorted with laughter.

'That's one word for it,' he murmured. 'Anyway, I believe Thomas has a special weekend plan for everyone.'

'What kind of plan?' Josephine frowned.

'Well, I *could* tell you, but if we don't hurry up, we'll be eating crusts for breakfast!' he exclaimed, urging his pony into a canter and leaving Josephine no choice but to chase him the rest of the way.

'So, what *is* Thomas's special weekend plan?' Josephine asked a half-hour later, tucking into a warm buttery roll and jam.

She gazed at the trickling river, and then the canopy of whispering oaks over their heads, as the tightness in her chest eased. The mossy stepping stones and gurgling brook were a favourite play spot when they were younger, and there was a serenity in the dappled light that always soothed her.

'Ah!' Henry grinned from his mid-stream perch, catching minnows with his cupped hands. 'You mean his plan to send everyone to the Davenport Derby for the evening, rather than go to the trouble of hosting his guests himself?'

Josephine chuckled. The Davenports were a local family with five unmarried daughters, who regularly held soirees to entice local gentlemen of a marriageable age into their circle. While she and her sisters tolerated the occasions, their brothers were far less enraptured and often referred to them as Davenport Derbys, given the competitive performances.

'Fred, Sir Francis and Lord Huntingly too?' Matilda queried through a mouthful of cake.

Edward frowned. 'Apparently so... Not that the latter said above two words to me this morning.'

'You've met Lord Huntingly?' Josephine asked quickly. 'I thought he was staying at the White Stag?'

'I believe he is, but he was also riding past the lower gate early this morning as I was heading out. He'd enjoyed an early hunt, judging by the number of hares swinging from his saddle,' Edward mused, 'and is obviously a keen sportsman... Though, in truth, I'm not sure what *you* see in him, Jo.'

'You know?' Josephine asked, startled by her brother's candid comment.

Her brothers had arrived at Knightswood long after dinner, which made the sharing of her betrothal news fast work even for Thomas.

'Yes, I hailed a greeting in good humour, and he barely acknowledged me. Then a moment later he called: "You must be a Fairfax, you've the look of Fred without the nerves. I'm your new brother to be," before riding off as cool as you like!' Edward muttered indignantly. 'Anyway, he seemed cavy to me but, if he's the one for you, Jo, I'm sure I wish you well!'

Satisfied he'd more than fulfilled his brotherly duty, he rested back on a mossy cushion in the sunshine.

'He could have been referring to me!' Matilda protested through the last of her warm roll. 'I am eighteen now, remember.'

'Nah, no one will take you!' Henry interjected, sneaking up from behind. 'You're far too prickly, like a dewy moorland thistle.' Then he took great delight in shaking handfuls of icy river water over his younger sister, who shrieked and set off up the riverbank in pursuit.

'Could tell Huntingly wasn't referring to Matilda right away,' Edward grinned. 'He was far too calm. Anyway, it's your turn first, isn't it? He just seems a little different from what I expected, that's all.'

Josephine drew a breath and, not for the first time, marvelled at the world of young gentlemen, where everything happened fairly and in step.

'Lord Huntingly is Thomas's choice, not mine, but the matter is quite settled,' she replied firmly. 'And Lord Huntingly doesn't do small talk,' she added, having decided to spare her younger brother the full drama of his story. 'Though he does enjoy sport, like you.'

'Most gentlemen enjoy sport to one degree or another.' Edward shrugged, pushing a whole sugar cake into his mouth. 'Well, most except Fred that is. I don't know, I suppose I expected Thomas to pick more of an academic type for you, but perhaps he has hidden depths.'

Josephine pictured Lord Huntingly in his breakfast room, forcing her to gaze on his scars, before his unexpected visit to Thomas and the kiss that had seared itself into her thoughts. And now there was Edward's view of his skill as a huntsman, his glass-eyed trophies hanging from his horse's saddle. A dart of fear twisted somewhere deep inside. She wasn't sure she wished for any knowledge of her betrothed's hidden depths, even if he did possess them.

Chapter Nine

Davenport House; Gods and Angels
7 o'clock

It was less than a half-hour carriage ride to the Davenport's country residence, though Josephine's siblings managed to make it feel twice as long. She sighed. Things hadn't much changed in five years, and she had even less leg room than ever, but at least they were amphibian-free for the journey across the village.

'I still don't see why Fred gets to go in Thomas's stylish phaeton with *Sir Dashing* when we are cramped in like Cook's sardines!' Matilda grumbled, swatting away Henry's attempt to open the sash window.

'It's Sir Francis *Dashton*, Matty, as you well know,' Josephine reprimanded, ignoring Edward's smirk, 'and it's very understandable – they're friends.'

'Well, I've no desire to arrive looking crumpled *and* windblown,' Matilda remonstrated, glaring at Henry who'd managed to inch down the window and was now pretending to gasp like a goldfish. 'The Davenports have a new dress every time one of them so much as opens their mouth to sing.'

'Yes, and that's far too often,' he scowled. 'They all sound like drowning cats! And Sir Dashing is *far too sophisticated* to travel with the Fairfax milieu, don't you know ... he might catch some devilish Devon plague!'

Matilda and Edward started to laugh, while Harriet, who'd been sent as chaperone in Thomas's place, frowned at them all. 'If I didn't know any better, I'd imagine you were all still in the nursery,' she admonished from her quiet corner of the coach.

'And really, Sir Francis has been nothing but kind and sincere to us all,' Josephine added, 'so we might do well to afford him some respect.'

'Perhaps more than a few others anyway,' Edward murmured drily, eyeing his sister. 'And I do believe we have arrived!'

Josephine sighed as the coach trundled to a standstill outside the Davenport residence, comprising a rambling Georgian house and long glass orangery, Sir Davenport's pride and joy.

'Good luck, gentlemen!' Henry saluted dramatically as they climbed out. 'If we're not all hitched to a wailing Davenport before the evening is done, I'll eat my new crav—'

'Henry!' Fred warned, from the phaeton which had drawn up behind them.

His younger brother grinned and swept a mischievous bow before proffering his arm to Matilda, while Sir Francis jumped down beside Fred. Josephine blinked. In the dusk, he looked even more of a fallen-to-earth Olympian; his bronzed skin was aglow in the half-light, while his stature and presence put her in mind of a combatant in the ancient Greek games. Briefly, she pictured him with a crown of laurel set upon his golden head, as his sea-spray eyes searched for hers among the cheering crowd and... She blinked again – she really had to cease daydreaming now she was betrothed.

'Might I say how delightful you look this evening, Miss Josephine.' Sir Francis bowed with his straight-from-an-oyster-shell smile. 'Like a veritable Ophelia!'

'You are too kind, Sir Francis,' Josephine protested, pushing her spectacles back up her nose. 'Though, in truth, she did meet more of a watery end than I would care for.'

'Yes, an excellent point,' Sir Francis acknowledged. 'Perhaps Hermia would be more apt? I've often thought there's something of the forest nymph about you.' He proffered his arm. 'You don't mind, do you, Fairfax?'

Fred shrugged his indifference as Josephine mumbled something unintelligible, and then they all made their way inside.

Miss Venetia Davenport performed two arias in a row, and was clearly prepared for a third, before her fiercely smiling mother propelled her from the piano. 'For fear there will be no time for other young ladies, dearest!' One of the equally fierce sisters then proceeded to perform a minuet with more flats than Josephine knew existed, before sinking into a curtsey that Matilda termed 'entirely attention-seeking'.

'I must admit to looking forward to your performance, Miss

Fairfax,' Sir Francis murmured from her other side. 'For I hear you are quite the talent.'

Josephine murmured her second, unintelligible response of the evening, before shrinking back into her seat. While she could play the harp proficiently, she'd always suspected any compliment was given in relief by those who discovered there was one thing she could actually do tolerably well. Yet she was no willing performer and quite aware she had none of Phoebe's wit, Sophie's beauty or Matilda's charm to sustain her should things go awry.

'Oh, Lord, they don't expect me to croak something out, do they?' Matilda whispered in a mortified tone. 'I haven't practised in an age!'

Josephine tried to smile reassuringly, though she knew exactly how her sister felt. Not only were three of their unforgiving brothers present, it seemed Lady Davenport had seen fit to invite half of Knightswood's gentry to the gathering: perhaps the weight of five unmarried daughters was beginning to tell.

'You'll have to perform *for* me, Jo,' she added urgently. 'Unless you want me to stand up there and belt out three rounds of "Roy's Wife"?'

'Matilda!' Josephine hushed in a pained tone. 'This is not the place for Bertie Briggs's inappropriate ditties. How do you know such a thing, anyway?'

'It wasn't intentional,' she protested. 'He was humming it at the chicken race and it just kind of got … stuck.'

And whether it was the guilt in her voice, or the pressure of a looming performance, her whisper wobbled, and Josephine could no longer look at her. Her gaze watered as she stared at another wailing Davenport, trying not to give in to the rise of irrational laughter. It was just like Matilda to pick up an entirely inappropriate ditty without trying, and entirely probable she would stand up and sing it too. Then a flurry of movement on the opposite side of the Davenports' drawing room distracted them both. A footman was trying to be discreet. The edges of the room were in shadow, but there was no mistaking the newcomer's imposing silhouette.

'Huntingly,' she whispered to Matilda, who raised her eyebrows.

'Thought it was unusually decent of Thomas to entertain him at Knightswood,' she muttered.

Josephine swallowed. Despite Edward's sighting that morning, she'd not seen Huntingly all day, and assumed he and Thomas had decided to keep company this evening. Yet she might have known her eldest brother would foist his responsibility elsewhere.

Anxiously, she watched as the eldest Davenport bungled her way through her second performance, before an entirely unknown young lady, no older than Matilda, was called forward. She had a pretty smile and perfect ringlets and when she began to sing, she reminded Josephine of a canary songbird. She glanced at Matilda who shook her head, yet there was something about the girl's delicate features and wedgwood-blue eyes that felt distinctly familiar.

'Miss Amelia Carlisle,' Sir Francis murmured with impeccable timing.

Josephine nodded, silently wondering at the coincidence of a young lady sharing a surname with Phoebe and Sophie's oldest nemesis.

'Miss Amelia Carlisle of…?' she prompted, as soon as the music allowed it.

She was aware Aurelia had married a European baron a few years before but knew nothing of any younger relations.

'Youngest daughter of Lord and Lady Carlisle,' Sir Francis replied. 'An old London family. She's staying with the Davenports currently … as I understand it.'

Josephine felt her eyes grow rounder as Miss Amelia finished her song with the confidence of a seasoned performer, before sinking into a demure curtsey. Then a round of rapturous applause followed, led by her own brothers, as Miss Amelia smiled and made her way back to her seat.

Matilda glared and shook her head. 'And this is why I refuse to stand up there and bray like a donkey,' she whispered. 'I will not give my brothers reason to tease me mercilessly for months when one of us is *actually* talented – please, Jo, do this for all of us?'

'Now, which of the young ladies have yet to perform?' Lady Davenport called in her permanently delighted voice. 'I have three Davenport songbirds waiting, but I do believe every young lady should have an opportunity…'

Josephine closed her eyes, knowing Lady Davenport would not give up until at least one Fairfax had been publicly humiliated.

'Perhaps I might offer something a little different this evening, Lady Davenport?' Sir Francis suddenly interjected in his rich tone. 'After all, this is 1826, and the young ladies deserve to be entertained as much as the gentlemen, do they not?'

He smiled his golden smile at Josephine then, who felt her

jaw drop slightly as she returned his regard. She had no reason to believe he'd come to her aid, and yet his intervention was certainly timely. She tore her gaze away, conscious a number of the young ladies were staring.

'Why ... *thank you*, Sir Francis,' Lady Davenport gushed after a brief pause. 'I'm sure the young ladies would be delighted if you would grace us with an anecdote or a reading from your literary studies, perhaps?'

'The pleasure would be all mine, Lady Davenport,' Sir Francis replied, already rising and moving to the front. 'As you know, I've relished the opportunity to study classical literature and poetry over the past few years, and flatter myself I might know a few small pieces that will entertain the more *delicate* minds here.'

There was a ripple of sighs that Josephine was sure had nothing at all to do with Sir Francis's promised performance.

'I'm surprised he does not recite something in honour of himself, and be done with it,' a low voice murmured behind them.

Matilda stifled a snort, as Josephine felt a rise of indignation. Lord Huntingly had clearly decided to sit close enough to tease them, but that he should mock their friend too? Sir Francis was the most noble gentleman she knew, and certainly never a murder suspect!

'And what of my reputation? Are you sure you shouldn't be a little ... wary?'

She stiffened as fragments of their library conversation surfaced, while Matilda tried to contain her mirth. *'Which makes you either very brave or very foolish.'*

Without warning, her traitorous lips tingled with the

sudden memory of his kiss. She flushed as Sir Francis cleared his throat, conscious of Lord Huntingly's unexpected proximity. Silently, she willed her thoughts elsewhere, and yet she couldn't stop the heat of her furious thoughts reaching up her neck and across her cheeks. Was he trying to goad her? She glanced at her radiant younger sister and felt the oddest churn of unease – or perhaps he'd changed his mind?

'She walks in beauty,' Sir Francis began from the front of the room, *'like the night of cloudless climes and starry skies…'*

A further sigh of delight rippled through the watching ladies as Josephine clenched her fingers in her skirts. Ordinarily, she loved Lord Byron's poetry and kept a volume beneath her pillow. Yet, while Sir Francis's golden tone suited it beautifully, she could think only of Lord Huntingly's scorn.

'I do believe half the audience actually think him Lord Byron, come back to woo us!' Matilda gurgled as the ladies around them gazed, enraptured by his dulcet tones.

Refusing to look at her, Josephine glanced down their row and glimpsed Fred, entirely mesmerised by Sir Francis's performance. She frowned, perhaps he too was feeling out of sorts.

'They'd as lief believe it of a crowing peacock!' Lord Huntingly whispered again, making Matilda shake with the effort of containing her laughter.

Josephine clenched her teeth. She'd borne so much without complaint: a childhood battling a lung affliction, Thomas's constant criticism, three unsuccessful seasons, the knowledge that all her sisters would likely marry while she didn't – all to arrive at a moment she would truly treasure, were it not for the presence of a gentleman she wasn't even sure she wanted to know, let alone call husband.

'If you are so certain of his poor performance, why not show us all how it should be done?' she replied fiercely, angling her head so only he and Matilda could hear.

A pregnant silence followed while Sir Francis meandered through his last lines: '...*a mind at peace with all below, a heart whose love is innocent...*' before the room erupted with rapturous applause.

'Thank you so much, Sir Francis,' Lady Davenport gushed. 'I believe you might not only have entertained the more delicate minds here, but won a few *hearts* too! And now, perhaps another of our young ladies would like to...'

'If you might be generous enough to indulge another gentleman, Lady Davenport?' a low voice called suddenly, making Josephine freeze in her seat.

The audience hushed as the authoritative tone garnered the attention of everyone in the room, including Sir Francis.

'But of course ... Lord Huntingly,' she responded valiantly, though it was clear she was dumbfounded. 'What a treat that we should be entertained by *two* eloquent gentlemen this evening! I'm sure Lord Davenport can learn much from this...' She paused to allow for several guffaws of laughter. 'Please do come forward – the floor is yours.'

The room fell silent again, but this time there was a murmur of curiosity and briefly, Josephine wondered how many knew of the rumours surrounding Huntingly's past.

'Thank you, Lady Davenport,' Lord Huntingly began, his melodic tone somehow quieting the air. 'I perhaps ought to mention that I am no poet, but I did learn something of the world on my travels abroad.'

He smiled then, his amber flares catching the flickering candlelight, as Matilda suddenly fell quiet.

'And, if you will permit me, I will break with the current mood and recite a passage from Homer's *Battle of the Gods*, which I return to often because it reminds me that it is mortality that gives life its significance.'

There was another low murmur while Lady Davenport blinked at Lord Huntingly in abject wonder, and then he began. Much to her irritation, Josephine found herself entirely mesmerised this time. It wasn't so much that he related the passage without falter, as that his rendition left no one in any doubt that life and love were meaningless without mortality. And when he came to an end, there was a moment's protracted silence before the whole room erupted in applause.

'What a dark horse!' Matilda exclaimed as Lord Huntingly made his way to a footman holding a tray of glasses.

'You have no idea,' Josephine murmured.

Thoughtfully, she watched Lord Huntingly polish off a glass of Burgundy, as Lady Davenport's piercing voice rose above the chatter once more.

'And now I believe there are only the Miss Fairfaxes left to perform, and it will be time to break for refreshment!' she announced in a vulturous tone. 'Come, dears, which of you modest young ladies would like to delight us first?'

Josephine's hopes sank as she realised the gentlemen's performances had not distracted Lady Davenport at all. Another hush fell across the room, before she became suddenly and intensely aware of a heavy pressure on her toes. She rose reluctantly.

'I will play for us both tonight, Lady Davenport,' she replied with a forced smile, 'for Matilda has the headache.'

Immediately, there were several murmurs of sympathy for the afflicted Matilda, who accepted them with the grace of a true rogue, as Josephine made her way towards a harp in the shadows. It belonged to one of the Miss Davenports, but she'd chosen to sing, so it had remained silent tonight.

'This piece is taken from Dussek's "Sonata for Harp in C Minor",' she introduced quietly. Then before she had time to change her mind, she sat down and began to play.

The room fell silent, but Josephine was already unaware. Unlike her sisters, she'd relished her music tuition, and the escape it gave her from illness. And over time, while her sisters and brothers ran wild across Knightswood's rambling estate, it became multiple worlds, filled with light and health. Performing always felt uncomfortably close to sharing this magic, but even she accepted that some moments couldn't be avoided.

The piece passed in a blur, and it was only when she felt the very last string vibrate to a standstill that she allowed herself to look up. His was the first face she saw. He was still in the shadows, holding a drink, but his usual mocking expression had been replaced with something quite inscrutable. She returned his regard for a moment, and then the sound of rapturous applause reached through her haze. She stood up and nodded awkwardly.

'Brava, Miss Fairfax, brava!' she heard Sir Francis call from the crowd. 'You play like an angel!'

'Indeed you do, Miss Fairfax,' Lady Davenport added a little sourly, glaring at her own daughters. 'All that practice has certainly paid off!'

Josephine flushed, so conscious of Lord Huntingly's watchful gaze as she made her way towards the refreshments table at the back of the room. For a second, she thought of the glass-eyed hares hanging from his saddle bag, and swallowed.

'You were wonderful, Miss Josephine, quite wonderful!' a female voice gushed as she began pouring herself a glass of ratafia. 'I found myself transported somewhere else entirely. Indeed, such was your concentration and skill that I wonder if you might not be in need of a breath of fresh air … or a turn around the orangery perhaps? I find the air in here quite … *exhausting.*'

To Josephine's great surprise, she found herself looking directly into the perfectly-ringleted face of Miss Amelia Carlisle. She smiled at her almond-shaped eyes, pert nose and rose-bow lips, and briefly wondered if every Carlisle was blessed with the face of a Renaissance maid.

'And now we will break for refreshments!' Lady Davenport announced. 'During which time, my daughters have prepared something a little *extra special* for your entertainment, so please don't wander too far.

Josephine raised her eyebrow at her companion, and then followed her swiftly out of the room.

Chapter Ten

Lord Davenport's Orangery; Blossom and Thorns
A few minutes later

The first thing Josephine noticed was the ease with which Miss Amelia led the way and fleetingly, she wondered if she too was in the habit of escaping.

'Are you enjoying your stay with the Davenports, Miss Amelia?' she asked, following her guide turned down a succession of corridors until she paused before a wide, lead-framed door.

There was a solid click before she turned back to smile. 'Why, yes, Miss Charlotte Davenport is one of my closest friends,' she replied, before leading the way into the vast and silent glasshouse.

Josephine paused, unprepared for the embracing warmth or intoxicating scent of honeysuckle, entwined with all kinds of citrus blossom. 'I suppose the warmth enables Lord

Davenport to grow more exotic blooms,' she murmured with interest, as she closed the door.

'Certainly, and the scent is enough to make one believe we could be in the middle of some Grand Tour adventure, rather than the wilds of Devon!' Miss Amelia exhaled, her eyes shining. She picked up a nearby lantern. 'Come this way, Miss Fairfax, and I'll show you my favourite spot.'

Josephine smiled, too used to Matilda's dramatic tendencies to be deterred, and she made a mental note to introduce the two as soon as possible. Quietly, she followed Amelia's slight figure along the winding path, through an arbour of flowering jasmine and back around some coppiced fruit trees, before she halted beside a small pond.

'Edward would love this,' Josephine observed, reaching out to touch one of the large water lilies. 'Are there any frogs within? Or fish perhaps?'

'Some goggle-eyed fish, I think,' Amelia replied, 'but don't ask me their name! They are quite frightful to look at and remind me of a governess I once had. Pray, come and sit beside me. I do *so* long to make your better acquaintance.'

Amelia sank down onto a wooden bench, and patted the seat beside her in such a welcoming way that Josephine couldn't help but oblige.

'This is indeed a most welcome escape.' Josephine exhaled as the gentle trickle of water calmed her ruffled spirit. 'And I did so enjoy your singing, Miss Amelia, it was most musical.'

'Oh, thank you! Though I do wish we weren't always required to entertain in such a manner,' Amelia replied, 'for I find my thoughts are not always in an entertaining place.'

To this, Josephine agreed most readily.

'However,' she added after a pause, 'it made for a *very* pleasant and welcome surprise for the gentlemen to partake! Particularly as they both did so with such passion and commitment.'

Again, Josephine found herself nodding in agreement. She'd often wondered at the equity of a society that placed so much emphasis on young ladies being skilled at entertaining, while young gentlemen could be skilled at anything they pleased.

'Indeed, I do not know much of Lord Huntingly, for he is quite recently returned from the continent as I understand it, but I must admit to *a little* prior knowledge of Sir Francis.' Miss Amelia lowered her voice bashfully, even though they were already speaking softly and at quite a distance from the main party. She looked around furtively, as though they might be overheard.

'But how fortuitous!' Josephine replied kindly. 'I am quite in awe of the gallant Sir Francis, who is staying with us at Knightswood presently, and is perhaps the most knowledgeable gentleman of my acquaintance. And I say this, despite possessing four brothers! Do your families know one another?' she continued. 'Or do you have a brother of a similar age? I'm aware you may be related to Lady Aurelia Carlisle, who is acquainted with my older sisters, of course.'

'Oh yes, of course!' Miss Amelia replied, wrinkling her nose in thought. 'But she is married and quite dreadfully old now,' she added dismissively.

Josephine suppressed a chuckle at the infamous Lady

Aurelia Carlisle, now the Baroness Aurelia di Caserta, being called old at the age of four-and-twenty.

'But yes, you are clever to guess that Sir Francis and I know each other through family connections, for his mother has been the bosom-friend of my own mother for as long as we both can recall.'

'That is indeed fortunate,' Josephine replied wisely. 'For, if parents are friends, friendships between sons and daughters have already begun.'

'Oh yes, Miss Fairfax!' Amelia replied, her blue eyes as round as teacups. 'That's it exactly, and I knew you would understand. I could just tell from your face!'

Josephine smiled, mystified her face alone could say anything of real consequence, but content Amelia was happy anyway.

'You see, I have a very *particular* kind of friendship with Sir Francis,' Amelia continued in a confiding tone, 'and I feel I might just burst if I don't tell someone. Charlotte Davenport is quite addle-pated, and to be within such close proximity and have one's *secret poem* spoken aloud like an affirmation ... well, you can just imagine!'

At this sudden and startling confession, Josephine stared, unsure if she'd daydreamed and missed a crucial fact. Yet somehow, she knew she hadn't. The oddest feeling swirled in the pit of her stomach as Amelia's eyes lit up like two moonlit pools, and her whisper softened until it was barely audible.

'One's *shared* secret poem,' she emphasised in case Josephine had missed any part of her meaning at all.

The swirl was replaced by the most curious sense of dread as Josephine forced a smile. Yet she could hardly understand herself. What difference would any romantic confession make to her? She had no agreement with Sir Francis, quite the opposite in fact, and she was betrothed to someone else entirely.

'Are you telling me you have *an understanding* with Sir Francis, Miss Amelia?' Josephine asked, her tone oddly unnatural.

Thankfully, Amelia seemed not to notice. 'Why, yes!' she exclaimed. 'You really are the cleverest thing, Miss Fairfax! And I daresay you guessed by the *longing* expression on his face when he recited our poem? In truth, I knew not where to look through most of it,' she continued without drawing breath, 'as I was sure someone might note his melancholy air when he gazed in my direction.'

Thoughtfully, Josephine recalled Sir Francis's performance. She hadn't noticed his gazing at anyone in particular, or indeed anything less than his usual delight in sharing his knowledge. Yet, she had been distracted.

'I can assure you I did not guess,' she replied honestly, 'and I will say nothing of your confidence, of course – except to wish you well, for I'm sure your families must be delighted!'

At this, Miss Amelia's face fell, taking Josephine's hopes of a speedy exit with it.

'Well, no not quite,' she whispered, looking singularly downcast. 'You see, Sir Francis's family, while entirely respectable, are experiencing *hard times*, and he will not offer for me unless he can keep me in the style to which I am accustomed. Is it not the most romantic thing, Miss Fairfax?' she asked in a plaintiff tone. 'We are doomed, quite doomed, and all we have is a secret love poem which he recites like a dying pledge, and I cannot bear it another day!'

Josephine could think of many things she would find considerably more romantic, but decided against sharing them as Amelia began to sob.

'Dearest Amelia, please do not cry, I beg you!' Josephine exclaimed in an aghast tone. 'Can I be of any assistance perhaps? Speak to Sir Francis and convey a message, or—'

But before she could finish her thought Miss Amelia looked up, as though her heart hadn't just been breaking at all. 'Why, you are the kindest creature, Miss Fairfax!' she replied in delight. 'I thought you might be kind, I can just tell a good soul, and so I have already prepared a little something for *my Francis* here. Oh, and please do not think me forward if I call him that, it has forever been my habit to do so,' she added with a beaming smile.

She pulled a lavender-scented letter from her reticule and waved it triumphantly. 'Here it is!' she announced, much in the manner of a magician producing a rabbit from a hat. 'If you could give him this letter and whisper that I await his response *longingly*, I would be most grateful!' She sighed happily before standing up. 'Thank you from the bottom of my heart, Miss Josephine. And now I must return before my Francis abandons all caution and comes looking for his Amelia!'

Then she was gone, together with the lantern, leaving Josephine in the gloom clutching the perfumed letter.

For a few moments, Josephine stared at the goggle-eyed fish and tried to rein in her own spiralling thoughts. She wasn't in any way beholden to Sir Francis, so why would she feel anything about his secret understanding? Yet she did.

Her chest thumped uncomfortably, and she had the most disconcerting feeling that she'd been woken, quite abruptly, from a delightful dream.

'Am I disturbing you, Miss Fairfax?'

At this fresh intrusion, Josephine sat bolt upright, and nearly consigned Amelia's lovelorn missive to the goggle-eyed fish. 'Lord Huntingly?' She swallowed as his distinctive person emerged from the gloom, starkly conscious this was the first time they'd been alone since the library. 'Not at all,' she replied. 'I was merely getting some air before returning to the drawing room. In fact, I can recommend this seat, it is most ... restful.'

She stood up swiftly, secreting the letter among her skirts.

'Pray do not leave, Miss Josephine,' he urged, moving forward. 'I came to find you as I noticed you'd slipped out. I wondered if you were quite well.'

Josephine gazed at his tall, graceful figure, his chestnut eyes thoughtful, and a faint smile creasing his lips. He'd dressed with care again this evening, and while he could never be accused of dandyism, his Pomona-green evening coat fitted like a glove, his pantaloons accentuated his military gait, and his shoes shone with a gleam that even Thomas would have approved of – in truth, he looked every inch a respectable gentleman, and not wayward Lord Huntingly of Huntingly Manor.

'That is kind, my lord, but unnecessary,' she replied, unprepared for consideration, 'for I am perfectly well.'

'May I?' he asked, indicating Amelia's recently vacated seat as he closed the distance between them.

She nodded, conscious of a rush of warmth through her cheeks, and grateful for the cover of semi-gloom.

'For you,' he added with a small smile, proffering some of the citrus blossom she'd passed on the way in.

She stared briefly before accepting it, certain her cheeks were now brighter than any bloom in the orangery. Was he teasing her again? Should she be on her guard?

'You do not like to perform,' he observed softly, 'and yet you play better than anyone I know. I was quite mesmerised by your performance, and there is little that truly distracts me these days. Thank you.'

Startled, Josephine began mumbling an awkward thank you of her own, just as he closed his scarred hand over hers. His touch was warm and unexpected, and she flinched, making him withdraw instantly.

'My apologies,' he muttered sincerely.

'No ... I'm sorry,' she replied quickly. 'I ... I very much enjoyed your recital too. I haven't studied the *Iliad*, but Fred has told me many of the stories, and the *Battle of the Gods* has always fascinated me.'

'Really?'

'Yes!' She nodded, conscious her flush was deepening. 'Because despite it being a battle between gods, it really is a story about mortal vulnerability and heroism, isn't it?'

Lord Huntingly gazed at her, a curious smile warming his face. 'What a true and refreshing mind you possess, Miss Fairfax,' he replied, his face relaxing so that for just a second, she glimpsed his younger self again. 'It is indeed such a story. And it suggests that our mortality is both a blessing and a

The Proposition of the Season

curse for, while it offers honour to those who are injured or fall in battle, there are many who do not deserve such acclaim.'

His voice trailed off as Josephine listened, wondering if he was alluding to his own story.

'I would have thought anyone who is injured, or falls in battle, deserves some honour,' she offered carefully.

'Perhaps,' he returned, before seeming to collect himself. 'Of course, one should not need to succumb to injury or death in order to become a hero,' he added, with a glint of mischief. 'Take Sir Francis, for example. I'm sure he must have many heroic tales he could relate, should we ask him.'

Josephine smiled and lowered her gaze. It was true Sir Francis was full of such stories, but she'd not quite recovered enough from Miss Amelia's confidence to chuckle.

'Sir Francis is both knowledgeable and talented,' she said fairly, 'though I'm sure even he must know the difference between a literary hero and one who faces a pistol or sword in the hands of a sworn enemy.'

There was a sudden silence then, when the only noise was the gurgle of the water beside them.

'As you did ... in the army, my lord,' she clarified swiftly.

'Yes, I certainly faced many enemies with the army, though that wasn't what you were thinking, was it?' he replied brusquely. 'How much have you been told about my past, Miss Fairfax?'

Josephine flinched, unprepared for his change in tone or the stiffening of his person. She stole a glance at his face in the semi-gloom and was struck by his tighter jawline and narrowed eyes. She swallowed, knowing this was her chance to ask for the truth, yet so conscious that doing so might risk their arrangement, and Matilda's freedom too.

'I'm aware there was a difference of … opinion…with a friend … before you left for the army,' she offered haltingly, Williams's words echoing through her head.

'*Old man Huntingly died in a hunting accident … the young lord discovered Pellham was to inherit part of the estate… The coroner ruled he fell from a bolting horse… I believe his son may have issued the challenge because of his grief following his father's death.*'

'A *difference of opinion* is a very nice way to put it,' he replied caustically, his dark eyes glinting. 'I imagine you must have had many differences of opinion with your sisters which didn't nearly cost you a limb, as well as several years of your life!'

'True,' she replied, stung by his tone, 'and I cannot imagine the pain of your injuries, but you did not have to stay abroad?' The words were out before she had chance to check them, and she flushed instantly. 'What I meant to say was that one of those things was accidental…' she stumbled, trying to find the right words that would lessen the severity of her accusation.

'… while the other was a matter of choice?' he finished harshly.

'No! I was going to say *avoidable*,' she amended swiftly, 'though I know nothing of the details, obviously.'

There was another silence while Huntingly stared into the semi-gloom, hardly appearing to breathe at all.

'You don't,' he muttered bluntly, 'and I can tell you that there is nothing glorious or heroic about violent bloodshed! It's raw and ugly and rarely brings the kind of satisfaction it promises. Then it haunts you, with a savagery that never lets you go…'

Josephine swallowed as she stole another furtive look at the gentleman seated beside her. He looked entirely different from the one who'd held out an orange blossom only moments before. His countenance was tense and dark, while his cheeks were hollowed in a way that only accentuated his words. Without warning, the thorn-choked cherub at Huntingly Manor spun to the forefront of her mind, its stone eyes bulging and body hidden by thick, suffocating ivy. A twist of fear reached up within her – perhaps the rumours about Italy really were true, after all. Perhaps his scars only masked a darker truth.

'I can't imagine the horror of real bloodshed,' she murmured, as he slowly inclined his gaze to hers.

'We all have our ghosts, Miss Fairfax,' he replied coldly. 'The only question is how far we allow them to control our lives – but this I would expect you to understand already...' His eyelids lowered. 'Given your own position over the last three years.'

Josephine's head jerked up, a flare of anger surging through her – how dare he equate her failure on the marriage mart to his failure to clear his name of murder!

'I beg your pardon?' she replied icily, rising to her feet. 'I might remind you that you are the one who asked what I knew of your past, and I do not believe you can compare my marital progress with the rumours surrounding your name, sir! Indeed, my position is not deliberate. I had every hope of making a respectable match, but—'

'Now you have to settle for a disrespectable one instead!' His Lordship interrupted with a scornful laugh.

'Perhaps ... but only you know the answer to that!'

Josephine quivered in anger. 'And perhaps I did fail in the eyes of the polite world, but at least I did not pursue a gentleman abroad and slay him in broad daylight!'

For a second, everything seemed to still as Josephine's words echoed around the humid glasshouse, and then Lord Huntingly stood up. She held her breath, watching the rise of his shoulders before he turned, his amber flares scorching like flames. 'If that is what you truly believe, why do you contemplate a match with me at all?' he demanded furiously. 'It would make you as good as complicit, and by marrying me, your soul would be stained by my sin for all eternity!'

Josephine pressed back into the wall behind the bench, trying to steady her thoughts, though her chest was tight and hammering. 'And leave my sister to such a fate instead?' she reposted. 'In truth, sir, I wonder what sort of woman you believe me that I could damn her in such a way!' She inhaled raggedly, aware she'd given voice to her deepest suspicions, while Huntingly appeared a thousand miles away. A stab of fear reached through her as she conjured Matilda's relief when she was told she no longer needed to marry; she couldn't let Huntingly change his mind now. 'I pray you say such things because you have been wronged beyond what any gentleman could stand,' she attempted, willing her voice to remain steady. 'And I do not pretend to know the full affliction of your past, but I can see you have suffered – that you continue to suffer, because … you do not let it rest there.' She closed her eyes, praying it was enough.

'You are right that you know nothing of what you speak,' he replied at last, his voice oddly formal, as though they were barely acquainted at all. 'But I would rather know your poor opinion of me now, than on our wedding day.' He continued without waiting for a response. 'Now, if you will excuse me, I have been absent for some time, and I am concerned for your reputation. After all, our betrothal is not yet announced, and who knows what everyone will think of you being in the company of a gentleman with such a chequered past! I thank you for your time, Miss Fairfax, and bid you goodnight.'

Then he nodded abruptly, and left Josephine to the heat of her own tumultuous thoughts.

Chapter Eleven

Knightswood Drawing Room; Confessions and Secrets
The following morning

'Oh, do hold still, Henry. I cannot tie it if you continue jumping about like a giant cricket!' Matilda complained, wrapping Henry's arm in a makeshift sling.

'Well, that sounds perfectly reasonable when my arm does not require a sling at all!' Henry retorted, trying to shrug off his sister's determined attentions. 'And why you imagine we are still babes in the nursery I know not – I am a man of nine-and-ten now!'

'Pooh! I don't care how old you are, and this is not a game. I need to practise! When one of your friends is injured on the battlefield, and I am able to dress his wound and save his life, you will thank me.' Matilda grinned, darting behind the long-suffering Henry, and tying another bandage over his mouth.

'Oh, that's much better!' Edward approved, peering over the latest volume of *Curtis' Botanical Magazine*.

Briefly, Josephine thought of her dear, departed Uncle Higglestone, and how proud he would have been to know his nephew shared his passion.

'Don't you two ever run out of energy?' Fred groaned from his favourite armchair.

Josephine looked at her brother thoughtfully. A few sore heads and frayed tempers were normal after a Davenport Derby, but Fred seemed unusually fractious. She drew a deep breath, still not certain what to make of her own disastrous evening. She'd returned to the drawing room moments after Lord Huntingly, but he'd already taken his leave, giving her the rest of the evening to dissect, and overthink, every moment of their conversation.

That she'd spoken unguardedly was without question, but that she'd been provoked was also true. She recalled his dark face inclining towards hers, his eyes dark with memories, his jaw tense with fury. Had she ruined everything? And yet, if the rumours *were* true, didn't she need to know for her own sake?

'It would make you as good as complicit, and by marrying me, your soul would be stained by my sin for all eternity!'

Josephine shivered and gazed out at Knightswood's rolling lawns, picturing her brothers and sisters careering down the soft grass. She'd watched them so often as a child, picturing herself among their joy, and never tiring of their tales of tree-climbing and swimming when they returned. They were chased by faded images of Huntingly Manor, leering at her in the half-light, withholding secrets. Hadn't she sensed the shadows at the outset? And yet what choice did she have when Matilda's entire future was at stake? She could never let her innocent younger sister pay such a price.

The Proposition of the Season

'Energy? No! Sisterly patience – most definitely!' Henry retorted, pulling the bandage off and threatening his laughing sister with it. 'Thank the Lord we are back to Oxford next week. I should find myself fully mummified otherwise.'

'Don't give me ideas!' Matilda snorted, throwing herself on the settle beside Edward and casting an eye across the page he was reading. '"The importance of flora and fauna for native amphibious species",' she read aloud before wrinkling her nose. 'How can you find teeny, tiny, crawly things so interesting?' she complained. 'You're so odd, Edward – you can do anything you wish, whenever you wish to do it, and you choose to study lizards?' She rolled her eyes so dramatically, everyone chuckled. 'If I were a gentleman, I'd do *all* the things that made me feel truly alive, like Lord Huntingly! He leaves one in no doubt that he really has lived – I mean, apart from the whole *dubious duel* thing, of course.' She grinned, ignoring Fred's groan of disapproval. 'You can feel it, even at a recital, which, by the way, was *so* inspirational, wasn't it? It made me realise how *excessively tedious* most of these evenings are, but truly, I shall recall his words for a long time to come. I could almost conjure the battlefield and the fighting between the gods!'

Josephine listened with growing unease as her younger sister described her delight with Lord Huntingly, wondering if her admiration extended further than she knew. Matilda had never expressed any interest in anything but horses and adventures before, but her decided interest in the enigmatic Lord Huntingly somehow made sense. She swallowed. Perhaps Thomas had a point after all? Perhaps Matilda had always been more suited, and yet how could she ever have abandoned her to such a man? It would be like trapping a butterfly with a malign flame.

'Really, Jo, I think things have turned out well for you.' Matilda shrugged. 'And Lord Huntingly made Sir Francis look a hapless schoolboy reciting Byron, which made me very happy...' She trailed off, laughing, dodging a cushion swat from Henry, while Edward rolled his eyes at the pair of them.

'Well, I don't think that's quite fair,' Fred defended from the corner of the room. 'Francis had clearly prepared something he thought the ladies would enjoy, whereas Huntingly sought only to impress. I thought he did splendidly!'

Josephine glanced at her brother as a frown settled upon his sunny features, and felt another twinge of concern.

'Pooh! Lord Huntingly called him a crowing peacock and now I shall never see him as anything else,' Matilda declared airily.

'Matty!' Josephine chastised. 'I do not believe that was intended for our ears, and you certainly shouldn't repeat it.'

'Of course it was, and you're the greater simpleton for not realising it,' Matilda retorted. 'I think he did it for your benefit, Jo. You didn't see the look on his face when you were gazing at Sir Francis, he looked as though he could commit another murder!'

'Matilda!' all four of her siblings gasped this time.

'What? And anyway, I don't blame him,' she continued, winding herself up to a finale. 'There is nothing *remotely* heroic about reciting pretty words, or talking at great length about one's own literary studies... Words should convey colour and emotion and experience – all of which Lord Huntingly has by the wagon-load! I think Lord Huntingly is ten times the

The Proposition of the Season

gentleman Sir Francis is and, if you can't see that, you shouldn't be betrothed to him!'

Matilda picked up her skirts and flounced from the drawing room.

'Well, what on earth was all that about?' Edward enquired, eyeing Josephine over the top of his magazine.

'Girls!' Henry replied knowingly, rolling his eyes. 'Fancy a swim?' he asked in the next breath. 'This is all devilishly dull.'

'Excellent notion! There's far too much talking this morning.' Edward grinned, abandoning the dietary habits of amphibians in favour of fresh air, and leaving Josephine alone with Fred for the first time in weeks.

'Well, that was exhausting.' Josephine exhaled, closing the drawing room door and treading across to the window.

'Some things never change,' Fred agreed with a faint smile which swiftly faded. 'I say, Jo,' he added awkwardly, 'I've been meaning to ask – Matilda's outburst aside, of course – if you're content with your arrangement? With Huntingly, I mean?' He pulled at his stiff collar. 'I can't help but recall our conversations before Thomas confirmed your betrothal, and it's been plaguing me. Anyway, I wanted to say I can talk with him again … if you wish me to?'

Josephine smiled at the only brother who'd ever tried to take care of her.

'Thank you, Fred,' she replied, 'but you and I both know that will change little where Thomas is concerned.' She took a deep breath. 'In truth, I feel I may have changed things myself last night.'

Fred eyed her with concern. 'That sounds ominous, but I know better than to poke my nose in where it's not wanted.

Pon' rep, for what it's worth, Jo, I don't think Francis is thinking of marrying anyone any time soon, anyway.'

Josephine regarded her brother, recalling the letter she'd pushed under Sir Francis's door on Miss Amelia's behalf earlier – and before that, his compliment as they entered the Davenports, and the attention he paid her during his stay at Knightswood. He certainly didn't act like a gentleman who was disinterested in female company, but perhaps that was just his way. She closed her eyes, conscious of a small dull ache, and yet determined not to lose herself to any more daydreams.

'Is his family suffering financial hardship?' she asked, forcing herself to think of Amelia's predicament.

Fred stared in bewilderment, before he threw his head back and laughed in a way she hadn't heard for a long while. She frowned, wondering if he was still partly inebriated.

'Hardship? I hardly think so, the Dashtons are as rich as Midas!' he chortled, wiping his eyes. 'No, it's just there are some gentlemen who are made for marriage, and some who aren't, and, well, Francis is … somewhere in the middle,' Fred explained, a faint flush creeping into his cheeks.

'He's not sure if he's made for marriage?' Josephine repeated, thinking again of Miss Amelia, before shrugging. 'Well, I'm sure Sir Francis is very dedicated to his studies and entitled to live his life how he chooses. He will marry when he's good and ready, I suppose.'

'Perhaps,' Fred replied, eyeing Josephine warily, 'though I'm not sure I will, and who knows, maybe Francis won't, either.'

Josephine stared at her sensitive brother, wondering why he felt the need to obstinately deny the possibility of marriage for either himself or his Olympian friend, just as Sir Francis himself was announced.

'Good morning!' he beamed delightedly. 'I do hope I haven't missed anything?'

Rotherby House
Grosvenor Square

2nd June 1826

Dearest Jo,

I would have written earlier but Harriet, your intrepid eldest niece, decided to dive head first out of a tree while her younger sister, Louisa, continues to have the most dreadful cold, and even though I have been in rude health, I have been trying to rest! The Lord knows it is hard enough on any day with a young brood, but I find these latter months of being with child quite tiring and Dominic's attentions beyond nonsensical...

Josephine smiled at Sophie's new letter, presented by a footman, as she left the drawing room. Her second eldest sister had a distinct knack of writing most directly, with so many anecdotes about her growing brood that Josephine almost felt as though she was in the room with them. Yet this morning her thoughts were distracted, and she could tell by the way Sophie had crossed and re-crossed the letter in a highly animated way, that she had written with some purpose in mind. Swiftly, she scanned the next two paragraphs which described the loss of

Louisa's tooth in a bowl of cherries at the Hamptons' picnic, followed by a long rambling tirade on the difficulty of keeping a governess, while Harriet insisted on bringing her *dear insect friends* to breakfast, before she got to the point:

> *And so, dearest Jo, I understand that you are shortly to wed? I was so delighted when I first heard that Dominic had to repeat everything before I could speak a word! It is truly (thrice underscored) wonderful news, dearest, and Lord Huntingly must be a very impressive gentleman indeed to have won the mind and heart of the most knowledgeable and romantic among us…*

Josephine sighed as she hurried down the flagstone corridor towards the kitchen door. Her sisters had always known of her desire to marry a real fictional hero – but reality couldn't be further from the truth. Despite Matilda's naive protestations, Lord Huntingly couldn't be any less like the heroes in her books, and presently she didn't even know if she still had a betrothal left at all. She turned out of the corridor and into the bright sunshine of the kitchen gardens.

> *Of course, I told Dominic right away that I needed to see you, because who better to advise your bridal trousseau than your beloved older sister with fashionable friends in all the best places? And, of course, Madame Montmartre is wonderful, though I do find she has become particularly revolutionary again of late … but I digress… Oh, do come to London, dearest, for I long to talk of something other than nap times and jelly, and you know I am the most sensible and practical of sisters when it comes to events of consequence.*

Josephine suppressed a hundred ready retorts about Sophie's good sense flying straight out of the window the moment she met Lord Rotherby, as she hurried through the old kitchen archway. Then she scanned the rest of the letter, which comprised of three paragraphs on the absurdities of relaxing one's corsets when not one dress was designed with a mother-to-be in mind, before tucking it in her pocket and focusing on the task ahead.

She knew exactly where Matilda would be and, as she made her way along the narrow path to the stables, she wondered, not for the first time, at a world that had produced eight such different siblings. Phoebe and Matilda had always been the most free-thinking, although Matilda possessed a fire that put Vesuvius to shame. Sophie claimed to be the sensible one, and yet showed herself to be just as impetuous and headstrong when it came to matters she really cared about. And then there were her four, very distinct brothers: Fred was sensitive and thoughtful, the twins spirited, while Thomas … had always been Thomas.

Which left herself, the quiet bluestocking.

'I do believe the day will come when someone will ignite that bluestocking flame of yours, and then we will all have to look out!'

Matilda's words echoed through her thoughts as she crossed the old stone courtyard that led to the stables. She'd never thought herself fiery – most certainly not in the same way as her sisters – and sometimes she wondered at their being related at all. How Matilda could believe Lord Huntingly, with his dubious moral compass, to be in any way superior to Sir Francis, whose only fault appeared to be an enthusiasm for sharing his love of literature, was a mystery of epic proportions.

Without warning, Huntingly's sudden kiss surfaced amid her thoughts. She'd tried to bury it, but this morning it seemed determined to thwart her. A flush of heat crept across her cheeks, before a further memory of the orangery subdued it. She took a breath, her heart hammering: he knew she was a failure, and she wasn't sure if he mesmerised or terrified her more. Yet what did it matter now – she was the only Fairfax to scare off a bridegroom before she even reached the aisle.

Closing her eyes against the spring morning, she passed beneath the stone archway to the stables, unable to think about that night without clenching every muscle she possessed. She couldn't believe she'd spoken her doubt aloud: '*…and leave my sister to such a fate instead? In truth, sir, I wonder what sort of woman you believe me to be that I could damn her in such a way…*' Yet, the thought that he might equate his own shame with hers was almost unbearable.

'Matilda?' she called, the cool of the stable an instant balm on her ruffled feelings.

She listened to the quiet air, knowing it didn't mean her intractable sister wasn't there, before drawing a deep breath and heading to Misty's stall in the far corner. Sure enough, as soon as she rounded the last whitewashed pillar she spied the stubborn tilt of her chin.

'Misty is positively gleaming.' She offered as she reached the stall gate. 'Phoebe is so happy with the way you take care of her, Matty.'

'Ponies over people any day,' her sister muttered,

continuing to brush the patient pony's coat. 'They're far more logical.'

Josephine took a deep breath, wrestling with the impulse to tell her sister she'd only become engaged to Huntingly to protect her, that she was still protecting her.

'Are you well?' Matilda asked suddenly, glancing up mid-rub of Misty's broad back.

'Yes, of course,' Josephine assured. 'You know how the hay irritates my throat sometimes. I just wanted to mention that Sophie has invited me to London, and was wondering if you'd like to come too?'

'And listen to our dearest sister wax lyrical about Harriet's and Louisa's *artistic genius* for days on end?' Matilda rolled her eyes. 'I'd rather wear one of her newfangled French corsets, but thanks anyway.'

Josephine chuckled. Sophie was undeniably one of the proudest mothers she'd ever known.

'I suppose she's offered to help you with your wedding preparations?' Matilda queried after a beat.

'She has,' Josephine replied, carefully monitoring her sister's face. 'If I'm not careful, I may find myself ousted from the entire thing!'

'Ha, too true!' Matilda returned drily.

Josephine steeled herself. There was nothing else for it but to ask directly. 'Have you undergone a change of heart, Matty?' she ventured softly. 'Would you rather not have a season and … marry earlier perhaps? You're entitled to change your mind, of course, it's perfectly natural…'

'What on earth gave you that idea?' Matilda exclaimed as she filled Misty's feed trough. 'Because I have an opinion about the type of gentleman I admire? That's not the same as wishing to enter the wedded state this instant, Jo, even though your favourite novels do often mix the two up!'

Josephine bit her tongue, in part relieved, but also confused by her sister's clear irritation.

'And another thing,' Matilda snapped, 'I cannot abide the way Fred allows himself to be thrown into the shade by Sir Francis! Have you not noticed the way he's tongue-tied around him, when we all know he's just as well-read? You're nearly as bad,' she rattled on without pause. 'Blushing and accepting his arm whenever he is near. It's little wonder Lord Huntingly reacted the way he did at the soiree!'

Josephine swallowed, hardly believing her ears. She'd made no secret of her admiration for Sir Francis because she believed there was little chance of his returning any – but she certainly hadn't intended to appear flirtatious. And, while Fred had always seemed in awe of his knowledgeable, golden friend, she'd spied only derision on Huntingly's face the night of the soiree. Suddenly, she felt utterly exhausted.

'I have no special regard for, or expectation from, Sir Francis, Matilda,' she replied quietly, ignoring the tightening in her chest. 'In fact, I have reason to believe he has been as good as engaged to Miss Amelia Carlisle for a number of years. And if Lord Huntingly looked a particular way at the Davenports, it is probably because I gave him sufficient reason to call our whole betrothal off!' She drew a steadying breath while Matilda stared at her revelations. 'So, if you're quite finished, I'll return to my room and accept Sophie's invitation, for a short break apart may be good for us both.'

Chapter Twelve

Rotherby House; Gigot Sleeves and Looped Knots
One week later

'In all truth, Jo, I cannot tell you the number of times I've asked the nanny to bring them to luncheon *at midday*, but she is so married to the traditional ways! I have, however, insisted that boiled potatoes and mutton belong to yesteryear and Harriet can have as many puffed pastries as she desires, for I do not believe they are bad for a child's digestive system, *or morals*, contrary to what everyone says! The idea! Fortunately, Louisa does not care for them so it is not so much of an issue, though she does like sugared candy, which might perhaps explain the cherry bowl tooth drama at the Hamptons' – mightn't it, dearest?' Sophie rattled in one breath, while reaching forward to tickle her youngest under the chin.

Josephine gazed at her chuckling niece, torn between admiration for Sophie's maternal instincts and an even stronger desire to laugh at the absurdities of her domestic life.

'I'm sure Harriet and Louisa are lucky to have you as their mother, Sophie.' She smiled. 'I'm not sure I'd have half your patience.'

'Oh, nonsense, dearest!' Sophie remonstrated. 'This will be your life soon enough, and you shall be the one delighting me with stories of your firstborn's first word or steps. Oh, what special moments await, dearest. Has Thomas set a date yet? I wager Huntingly won't want to wait long for an heir. He's been out of the country for some time, hasn't he?'

At this easy reference to her impending nuptials, Josephine caught her breath. She'd managed to avoid too much detailed conversation since her arrival the day before, but there was only so long she could hold out against Sophie's infamous inquisitorial skills.

'I imagine Thomas must be delighted to enact stage three of his Monstrous Marriage Masterplan, particularly as Matilda's season is coming up so soon.' Sophie chattered on, entirely unaware of Josephine's shift in mood. 'He will soon be rattling about Knightswood all by himself, for Fred and the twins are hardly likely to live in the country when everyone is in town. Oh, do say you'll keep a house in town, dearest, for we shall be able to see each other *all* the time, and Dominic and Huntingly…' She wrinkled her nose. 'Do you know I've no idea of his given name… shall go to Whites, while we visit fashionable friends and take our children to the park and—'

'Do you know anything of Sir Francis Dashton, Sophie?' Josephine interrupted, hardly able to bear her sister's description of domestic bliss a moment longer. Matilda's criticism had rung in her ears since leaving Knightswood, so that she hardly knew what to think anymore. Sophie could be relied upon to know everyone, however, and to provide candid insights too.

'Sir Francis, Fred's companion?' Sophie replied, clearly surprised Josephine wished to talk of anything other than her impending nuptials. 'Why … he's a very personable young man, to be sure, though I do believe he's developed an understanding of late?' She frowned.

'With Miss Amelia Carlisle?' Josephine returned.

Sophie paused. 'Miss *Carlisle*? Younger sister to Aurelia? Oh no, no, dearest, with *Isabella*! The eldest of the Hamptons? Or so I've been led to understand, anyway. They're well-matched, I'd say, both from old families…'

Josephine stared as Sophie rattled on, wondering if her society queen of a sister could be mistaken for once – ton gossip was notoriously unreliable – and yet she seemed quite certain.

'Anyway, I've accepted an invitation to the Hamptons' last soiree of the season next week, their *Grand Ball*, so you can swap betrothal details then. Before that, I thought we might pay a visit to my modiste here in London. She's not Madame Montmartre, of course, but one must make sacrifices when one is not in Paris. And I did think we could send your preferred designs to my dear friend, once you have quite decided?' she added, her eyes shining at the thought of wedding dress designing. 'I am quite convinced that some of the new Romantic fashions are so well timed for you, dearest, for who could be more worthy of a gown that says Byron or Keats in a single glance, than my own most romantic, novel-obsessed sister? Truth be told, I have just the gown in mind for you, with a nipped-in waist into which we shall pleat yards of the skirt, so it creates the most beautiful bell as you sweep down the aisle. And you shall have the widest gigot sleeves, of course, adorned with small pearls to signify ... well you must choose, of course, dearest, but as you can tell I am SO excited...'

15th June 1826

Dear Fitzwilliam,

No one in the world could be more excited for a betrothal than Sophie, for she has talked of nothing else since I arrived! I have tried diverting her, but even talk of Harriet and Louisa comes back to the same thing and, in truth, I'm not sure how much longer I can last. How do I tell her there may not be a betrothal, after all? That I'm not sure there should have ever been one? I assumed so much – that Thomas was right about Huntingly, that protecting Matilda was all that mattered ... but now I couldn't be less sure.

And there has never been any kind of understanding between myself and Sir Francis, so why am I so affected by news of his 'attachments'? Is Matilda correct? Have I allowed myself to dream too much of a gentleman who seems the living embodiment of every fictional hero I ever read? Indeed, how can I think clearly at all, when my thoughts are determined to replay <u>that</u> moment in the library quite incessantly?!

Josephine broke off to chew the end of her quill, as the tension in her chest intensified. She closed her eyes and concentrated on her breathing before it subsided again, though her anxiety remained. A week had passed without any word from Lord Huntingly. She had no expectation of love letters, of course – those dreams belonged to a previous life – but the absence of any contact at all only confirmed her worst suspicions.

What did silence mean? That the betrothal was over? What if, at this very moment, he was penning a letter to Thomas explaining his withdrawal on the basis of repugnant dislike?

Josephine's face flamed with embarrassment at the thought. Surely, being thought a *bluestocking* or *wallflower* was far preferable to being the one even a shamed lord wouldn't marry? She swallowed, conjuring his wild and nonchalant manner when she arrived at his dilapidated manor. Hadn't Thomas warned her he was looking for a wife to help dispel the rumours, not one who would accuse him of murder herself!

And yet how could she ignore such a likelihood? Had this moment been fated from the moment she asked him to marry her? Was he reconsidering Thomas's offer of Matilda's hand instead?

She exhaled as the oddest ache snaked up from her stomach and dissipated through her taut limbs. Pensively, she drew Thomas's most recent letter forward. It had arrived only yesterday and contained a jubilant description of his win at the races before he reached the real point of his missive:

While celebrating Kingston's win, it occurred to me that a swift wedding requires a swift announcement, and as most families are now considering their withdrawal from town for the summer months, I am minded to keep everything local. I have, therefore, and after much deliberation, decided to resurrect the Knightswood Ball and do the deed then.

Matilda is already aware I intend to write the event off as a singular expense to announce both your betrothal and her presentation, and this to me seems a most efficient use of funds. Furthermore, I am content to leave the bulk of the arrangements to your sisters and have already written to Sophie with this in mind. Of course, I shall notify Huntingly of the date this afternoon.

I trust you are well otherwise and using this time to reflect on your forthcoming nuptials. It will surely be a welcome change from your books!

She didn't bother with the rest of his formalities, which were a clear reflection of his relief at getting rid of another sister, and replaced the letter beneath a small decorative hourglass. She picked it up thoughtfully and turned it over, watching the fine silvery sand trickle through unchecked. Sophie had indeed received a letter from Thomas, and made no secret of her excitement of a real ball at Knightswood, at last.

'It's the greatest honour, dearest! Thomas never did as much for Phoebe or myself – he must be genuinely thrilled!'

Yet the news had only prompted more betrothal conversations, which worsened the hollow inside. More details and decisions would only lead to more disappointment when Lord Huntingly finally announced his withdrawal. Josephine swallowed, wishing she could turn the hourglass of her life upside down and start again. Instead, it seemed only that time was running out.

The Proposition of the Season

The Hamptons' Grand Ball
16th June, 9 o'clock

'I do declare that ivory silk net with embroidery and a satin trim were positively made for you!' Sophie exclaimed as they arrived at the Hamptons' extensive town residence. 'And my blue ostrich feather was such an inspirational moment … you should wear your dark hair in a looped knot more often, Jo. Don't you think, Dominic? Josephine really could be one of Sir Walter Scott's heroines.'

Sophie turned her pretty face up to her tousled-haired, handsome husband who gazed back in a way that made her blush, leaving Josephine in no doubt about exactly who he considered to look a heroine this evening.

Josephine smiled, wishing she had half of Sophie's faith in fashion solving most of life's problems. Instead, she had a plan that she intended to put into action as soon as she could. Lord Huntingly may have disappeared, but he'd also provided her with time to conduct a little research. She might not find out exactly what happened when he and Pellham served in Italy, but someone in a position of military responsibility would have to know more.

'Wasn't Lord Hampton in the army?' Josephine quizzed as they stepped out of the Rotherby coach and up to the Hamptons' colonnade entrance.

'Yes, he was a very respected general,' Rotherby replied.

'Lord, Jo, of all the things I thought you might say!' Sophie chuckled, rolling her eyes. 'Anyone would think you weren't in the least bit excited about your new dress… Oh look, there's Ursula – in lavender! Goodness me, when will the Hampton ladies realise a pale countenance does not do well in pastels…'

Josephine smiled but was already a thousand miles away, scanning the crowded hall for sight of Lord Hampton. It wasn't easy – tonight's affair looked to be well attended, given the Hamptons' imminent removal to the country, and as though every family in town had come to wave them off.

'What a pleasure, Lord and Lady Rotherby!' Isabella Hampton twinkled in a gown of jonquil, trimmed with blonde lace that made Sophie blink.

'And Miss Fairfax too! How delightful to see you again, Miss Josephine! Would you believe we have six tables for twelve in this room, and a long table for sixty in the parlour? I only hope everyone is looking forward to the turtle soup and asparagus, for Mama has been talking of nothing else for weeks!'

She peeled off into polite laughter as Josephine bobbed a curtsey, wondering again if there could be any doubt about Isabella's supposed engagement to Sir Francis. They seemed so very different.

'Might Lord Hampton be in the ballroom, Miss Isabella?' Josephine asked. 'I do so wish to thank him personally for inviting us.'

Isabella stared at her briefly before releasing another peal of polite laughter as she proffered her arm. 'Oh, Josephine, I declare you are too droll for words! Papa was here receiving guests, but he must have slipped away when Mama wasn't looking. I warrant he's in the card room already but let us look together. I'm sure he will be *most* flattered to know you were looking for him. And never fear, Lord Rotherby,' she added with dancing eyes, 'there are no archery plans this evening, so you should be quite safe from any rogue arrows!'

Josephine swallowed a gurgle of laughter, knowing her sister had long ceased finding references to her near-murder of her own husband humorous.

'Thank you, Isabella,' Sophie replied, her eyes glinting. 'I hardly recall the occasion to which you refer for life has been *so* busy, but then that is so often the way when one weds and starts a family. Perhaps you too will discover this joy for yourself when you finally realise that pastels...'

'Let us fetch a refreshment, Isabella,' Josephine interjected as her companion's smile started to fade. 'And you can tell me all about the seating arrangements for supper...'

At this enticing invitation, Isabella's spirits brightened, and Josephine steered her hostess away from Sophie's glare.

'Mama is ecstatic that every family of the ton accepted tonight,' Isabella gushed as they made their way to the refreshment table. 'Every single one! It is her finest moment and she vows, if Ursula and I are not announcing our matches soon, she will eat her new hat! Bearing in mind her new hat is a *monstrous affair* with a Prussian-blue brim, a matching ribbon, silk flowers and three peacock feathers at the crown – *three!* – it's quite the assertion, don't you think?'

Josephine blinked her agreement, wondering what Sophie would make of such a creation.

'Indeed!' she replied, as they made their way through the chattering throng in the vast hallway and towards the open doors of the ballroom. 'And are there any *particular* gentlemen to whom you might be referring?'

They paused just inside the entrance. A hum of chatter and dancing filled the air, laced together by one of Josephine's favourite minuets. She inhaled the colourful scene. She might not have relished her three seasons, but she had missed watching the ballroom, where she where she'd witnessed the start of a few real matches. The ton was littered with marriages of convenience, but sometimes there was a visible spark between two dancers that filled the void in her chest and made her long for her quill to capture it. She told no one of these moments, knowing they rightly belonged to others, but the briefest eye-widen or second glance gave her hope that occasionally, magic could happen outside the pages of a book.

'Well, there might be a *certain* someone.' Isabella blushed, pausing beside a solemn footman holding a tray of ratafia. 'But, as you know, it's not de rigueur to talk of such matters before—' She broke off with a wide smile. 'Aurelia! Or Baroness Caserta, as I should call you now. How well you look!' She held out her hands in greeting. 'And you too, Miss Amelia. Oh, it's been an age since I've seen you both. How is your delightful son, Aurelia? He must be nearing two years of age now, I believe?'

Josephine looked up as Baroness Aurelia di Caserta and Miss Amelia Carlisle paused to greet them and couldn't help but stare. They had identical doll-like eyes, dark lashes, creamy skin, bow lips and small, distinctive chins. Little wonder she'd been so mesmerised at the Davenports' soiree: Amelia was a smaller, softer version of her older sister.

'Oh goodness, how on earth should I know, Miss Hampton?' Aurelia tittered. 'It's quite exhausting enough to recall their particular requirements, let alone the months since they ruined one's body for all perpetuity. I didn't know you were still in town though, Miss Fairfax?' she asked in her next breath, turning to Josephine with her old gleaming smile. 'I thought you'd had quite enough of polite company, and abandoned us for the wilds and your books?'

'Oh no, not at all, dear sister!' Amelia intervened. 'For I had the good fortune to cross social paths with Miss Fairfax in Devon and, not only is her musical talent second to none, but we shared the most wonderful tête-à-tête, did we not, Miss Fairfax? How lovely to see you again,' she added demurely.

'Ah, I do detect a secret!' Isabella smiled delightedly. 'Pray do tell, Miss Amelia, for there's nothing I like so much as a secret…'

Josephine stilled, a wave of sudden realisation drowning out the delightful closing steps of the minuet. If she wasn't much mistaken, both Isabella and Amelia were harbouring exactly the same secret about Sir Francis Dashton, and she had no wish to be party to any conflicting declarations – especially when the gentleman in question was not here to clarify matters.

'Oh, I really cannot be pressed!' Amelia inhaled dramatically, clutching the pearls affixed to her lemon bodice. 'Miss Fairfax is a wonderful friend, and I know she will be loyal until the world is a kinder place to young love…'

'I knew it!' Isabella exclaimed. 'I can see the look of love in your eyes – for I may know a little of its torment myself.' She dropped her voice to a whisper, 'Tell us, Miss Amelia, is it a *desperately romantic* love or a *forbidden parental* love or…' Isabella's eyes grew rounder as she tried to think of all the possible permutations of love that society frowned upon.

'Touching though this display of sentimentality is,' Aurelia interjected drily, 'I would urge you both to remember that most types of *love* are highly impractical when it comes to marriage – indeed, I have found a good circle, better cook and formidable modiste have served me far better.'

'All I will say is that the gentleman in question is *beyond* fault and *quite* remarkable in every way,' Miss Amelia offered as though Aurelia had never spoken at all. 'In fact, we share a *secret love poem* that—'

'You *must not share* for fear he will be identifiable,' Josephine finished swiftly. 'And I believe I've just seen your papa, Isabella. Do excuse us,' she added, curtseying to the Carlisle sisters. 'We were looking for Lord Hampton before this delightful conversation, and I simply must not put off speaking with him any longer – Isabella?'

Without waiting for a response, Josephine grasped Isabella's hand and pulled her around the ballroom, weaving her way around groups of chattering ladies and gentlemen, until she reached the doorway through which Lord Hampton had disappeared.

'Really, Josephine!' Isabella panted, fighting for breath in her tight-fitting corset. 'There is no urgency to thank Papa, for he will be in the card room for the rest of the evening. And I have so little opportunity to talk with anyone about *anything*,' she added woefully.

'That may be,' Josephine replied in a low tone, 'but nothing is undone faster than a love secret, and I presume you do not wish your *understanding* to be affected?'

'Oh!' Isabella replied, her eyes as round as her jonquil bell skirt.

'Exactly,' Josephine affirmed. 'And now your papa is coming over... Good evening, Lord Hampton!' she called with far greater confidence than she felt, as a silver-haired gentlemen in military dress approached them.

'Good evening, young ladies.' He smiled. 'And what brings you to the card room? Unless you have a desire to make up a four with myself and the colonel?' he chortled in a way that made his waistcoat strain alarmingly.

'No, Papa...' Isabella began, looking anxious.

'That would be wonderful, thank you,' Josephine accepted instantly. 'I have only a rudimentary skill, and would so enjoy a game with more experienced players.'

'But Josephine?' Isabella entreated, startled by her friend's sudden desire to sit in a room of portly older gentlemen and cigar smoke, when there was dancing and gossip to be had next door.

Yet Josephine was already halfway to the table, looking more determined than ever.

'I trust you young ladies are looking forward to the supper?' Lord Hampton asked congenially as the game got underway. 'I am particularly fond of Shrewsbury cake and baked custard myself, though you mustn't mention it to Lady Hampton, for she thinks I am rather *too* partial, you see.'

He winked and patted his stomach as Isabella rolled her eyes.

'Your secret is safe with me, my lord,' Josephine reassured, taking another card, 'though it does make me wonder how you developed such a sweet tooth? For you have led a military life, have you not?'

She smiled innocently, though her mind was turning over how to ask about Huntingly without raising suspicion.

'I have,' he replied, 'though I'm retired now, and determined to make up for lost time, for there were few baked custards in France. We were lucky to have our bread of maslin and some bacon, though it all washed down well enough with the right wine.'

At this, he turned to his elderly friend and chortled again.

'And do you recall many details from your time in France, sir, such as … the soldiers in your brigade, perhaps?'

'But of course, Miss Fairfax,' he assured. 'We were soldiers of occupation following Waterloo, and once Louis XVIII was back life was easier than before, but I still prided myself on being able to address every single one of my officers by name, as well as their concerns. It was part of my role as General.'

Josephine nodded as Isabella eyeballed her ferociously, wilting with boredom.

'And what of the gentlemen soldiers who'd been injured? Did they remain with you in occupation?'

'Well, that depended,' the General replied, rubbing his whiskery chin as he considered her question. 'Some were sent home, others healed well and wanted to stay. Injuries can vary a great deal, and I've no wish to ruin your evening with talk of some of the atrocities I have seen.'

'My younger sister is keen to pursue nursing, my lord,' Josephine offered swiftly, 'so I ask partly to help inform her… Were there many who suffered serious injury and yet stayed on to fight, for example?'

Josephine held her breath as she edged the conversation

towards her goal. Thankfully the General seemed not to bat an eyelid, while Isabella scowled behind her cards.

'Plenty suffered in that way, Miss Fairfax, and every single one pained me. Some managed to stay on, others returned home to make the best of it.'

'But, of all injuries, injury to an upper limb has to be one of the hardest, surely?' Josephine pursued. 'For we use them for everything and take them so much for granted.'

'Yes, the injury of a limb is always a serious matter,' he nodded. 'A few of mine had suffered in that way and I greatly admired their resilience. I recall one soldier in particular who arrived with scarring from significant injuries. I was doubtful he'd last, but he proved himself the finest officer and an even better swordsman. In the end, I was sorry to see him go, even though it was clear that he was suffering,' he concluded a little wistfully, staring into his drink.

'How did he prove himself, sir?' Josephine followed up, hardly daring to breathe. Somehow, she knew he was referring to Lord Huntingly.

'Well, he was a quiet one with an air of melancholy. I never quite got to the bottom of it, but there was some family trouble, I gathered... Anyway, he was distinctly honourable, always at the front of a line, and better in combat than any of my other officers.'

Josephine swallowed, recalling Lord Huntingly's scarred chest. *Could he have earned them in battle, and not Italy?*

'So, he returned home after the occupation?' she asked nonchalantly.

The General wrinkled his brow in thought. 'Not directly as I recall. He was discharged with full honours, but there was some damnable incident in Italy in the months that followed. He was accused of murder in some street brawl, and I was asked to provide a reference.' He frowned, re-ordering his cards. 'Which was all part of my job, of course.' He stared at his cards intently. 'Anyway, the investigation was dropped once they discovered the deceased had suffered a family loss and wasn't in his right mind.' He appeared to lose himself in thought before his face lit up suddenly. 'And on a much happier note, I am happy to declare a sixth trick! Now then, who's for another game?'

Chapter Thirteen

The Hamptons' Grand Ball Supper; Turtle Soup and Asparagus
Three hours later

Isabella had not been jesting about the turtle soup or asparagus, or twenty dishes besides, and Josephine's eyes grew round with astonishment as she glimpsed the laden supper table.

'Have you ever seen anything quite like it, Miss Fairfax?!' Lord Hampton smiled as they assembled to be led into the parlour. 'I do declare I can smell the baked custard from here!'

Josephine ignored Isabella's disgusted expression as she took Lord Hampton's arm, and left her to his ancient friend. Ordinarily, the young ladies were escorted into supper by their most recent dance partner but, as Josephine had insisted on spending much of the evening in the card room, there were no young gentlemen left. She threw her friend a swift, apologetic smile as they joined the throng of couples leading the way into the long parlour, though her mind was awhirl with new questions.

Lord Hampton's account had to be as reliable as any, but it could also change things. If Pellham had indeed been suffering with melancholy after a family loss, there might be any number of explanations for his untimely demise. Perhaps the street brawl had even offered a welcome release – yet the only person who knew the full truth was Huntingly.

'We all have our ghosts, Miss Fairfax… The only question is how far we allow them to control our lives… How can you contemplate a match with me at all? It would make you as good as complicit and, by marrying me, your soul would be stained by my sin for all eternity.'

She closed her eyes as she recalled his hostility, the flares in his eyes touching her bones. That he was haunted by his memories was clear, and she suppressed a shiver as a familiar voice interrupted her thoughts.

'Hampton! Your servant, sir! Apologies for our late arrival, we have only come up to town this evening…'

'Fred!' Josephine exclaimed, more delighted to see her brother than she ever recalled. 'I didn't know you were coming!'

'Sir Francis!' Isabella chimed with similar relief. 'How truly delightful to see you! Believe me, the evening has only just begun…'

'Not at all, you young gentlemen are most welcome, and not least of all by these young ladies. Now then, Colonel, I believe we have precisely two minutes to find out exactly where they have placed the baked custards before Lady Hampton locates me. We might have to deploy a covert operation…'

Josephine laughed and curtsied as the elderly gentlemen took their leave, leaving Fred and Sir Francis to make up their four instead.

'Thank you, Alfred,' Isabella murmured as Fred offered his arm, leaving Sir Francis and his sandalwood cologne with Josephine.

Josephine drew a breath, overtly aware that the gaze of every lady in the supper line was lingering on the Olympian beside her. In all fairness, it was difficult not to look. Tonight, he was sporting a velvet green frock coat with broad shoulders and a nipped-in waist, beneath which a mustard waistcoat was buttoned high, leading the eye to a meticulously tied cravat with more folds than Josephine could fathom. His flaxen hair had been styled in the new Romantic way, that required precise short curls to fall around the forehead, and his whole ensemble had been finished with fitted pantaloons and polished evening shoes, in which she could see her own image.

Momentarily, she gazed too, certain that Sir Francis looked the very picture of every hero she'd ever imagined, before Lord Huntingly replaced him, holding a sprig of citrus blossom. She blinked and his image disappeared as the supper line moved forward.

'We meet again, Miss Fairfax,' Sir Francis murmured with his golden smile, 'and I never had the chance to thank you.'

Josephine pushed her glasses up her nose with a faint frown.

'I believe it was you who pushed a letter beneath my door back at Knightswood?'

'Oh ... yes it was,' she replied in surprise, making her way to a seat next to Fred at the long parlour table. 'It was no trouble and I trust it was welcome.' She smiled politely as an army of footmen began filling the table with an impressive array of first- and second-course dishes.

'To be fair, I cannot recall the contents well enough to know if it was welcome,' he replied nonchalantly, his brow wrinkling, 'but I appreciate your part all the same.' He surveyed the table appreciatively. 'Now then, I spy neck of venison, Scotch scallops, boiled chicken, patties and stewed celery among many other delicious dishes,' he observed, oblivious to Josephine's frown. 'It looks like Fred and I arrived just at the right time.'

'Oh, but you did, Sir Francis!' Isabella gushed, craning her neck around Fred. 'And I can personally recommend the turtle soup.'

'Indeed, Miss Hampton? Then I shall make sure to have some,' Sir Francis replied with another dazzling smile that prompted Isabella to turn bright pink.

'Do I look like a sailor, Miss Fairfax?' he quizzed quietly, rolling his eyes.

Josephine coughed on a sip of wine, conscious his comment wasn't exactly what she'd expect of a bridegroom-to-be. 'I'm sure she was just being a good hostess,' she murmured.

'Certainly.' He smiled, though there was a fresh gleam in his eyes.

She tried to compose her thoughts which were already so tangled with Amelia's confidences, Isabella's expectations and her own disordered emotions. He was too well bred to be anything but jesting and yet, for some reason, she wasn't quite sure.

'Do you always say the right thing, Miss Fairfax?' He threw her an amused glance.

'I am quite certain I do not, sir,' she answered with conviction, thinking back to the morning she asked a disgraced lord to marry her.

She flushed at the memory as Sir Francis stared, a flicker of candlelight in his eyes.

'Perhaps you haven't done quite as you should ... once?' he murmured suggestively, a small smile playing around his lips. 'Pray do tell, Miss Fairfax, for I thought I knew the female mind but, indeed, you are proving *quite* the mystery.' His smile widened as he reached towards the scallop dish and seemed to, quite deliberately, brush his fingers against hers.

Josephine stiffened, a surge of indignation replacing her jangled nerves just as they were interrupted.

'What a delight to see you here this evening, Sir Francis, and you too, Mr Fairfax,' Aurelia trilled from further down the table. 'My younger sister was quite in raptures with your recent performance at the Davenports',' she added, as Miss Amelia inclined her perfectly ringleted head.

'Miss Amelia is too kind,' Sir Francis replied with one of his brilliant smiles that mesmerised every other young lady within ten dinner places, 'but the truth is that, apart from the enigmatic Miss Fairfax here, I had very little competition.'

Josephine flushed as the admiring young ladies switched their attention from her companion to herself with far less enthusiasm. Yet she was conscious of a faint stir of injustice too – Lord Huntingly had outshone them both that evening, and to pretend otherwise was wrong.

'Sir Francis is also too kind,' she added swiftly. 'For,

without doubt, Lord Huntingly was the most adept performer of the evening.'

She'd intended to be honest, but the moment she spoke his name aloud a strange silence stilled the air. She glanced around, suddenly aware she'd committed a societal faux pas and that the cloud surrounding Huntingly's name was bigger than even she'd realised. She swallowed, feeling oddly defiant.

'Your defence of Lord Huntingly is to be expected given your forthcoming *event*,' Sir Francis murmured once normal chatter resumed. 'Though you must know his name is far from unblemished?' He selected a cherry from a large platter. 'Indeed, if I were you, I should take a little care before announcing it in polite circles, for you aren't wed yet and, even when you are, your Fairfax reputation will have much work to do to counteract his history. Indeed, might I offer you some advice, Miss Fairfax?' He glanced at her from beneath his long lashes.

Josephine knew he meant well, that she should nod with the usual quiet grace she was known to possess. Yet in truth she felt far from herself and was aware only of a strange chagrin clawing up her throat.

'With marriage to such an individual on the horizon,' he continued, oblivious to her thoughts, 'some might say that now is the time to enjoy yourself.' He popped the cherry in his mouth, reminding Josephine forcibly of a winged god at a Renaissance feast. 'There is plenty of time for fashionable protestations *after* the vows, after all.' He smiled, clearly well pleased with himself.

'Well, that is where you and I differ, Sir Francis,' Josephine replied, finally finding her voice. 'For I've never been in the least bit in vogue.'

Chapter Fourteen

Ebcott Guest Bedchamber; Whispers and Ghosts
22nd June

Dear Fitzwilliam,
I don't know what possessed me, it was certainly the first time I've ever felt our minds to <u>differ</u>…

Josephine underlined 'differ' twice, before closing her eyes to picture Sir Francis's expression. She still wasn't sure if he was irked or amused but, judging by the way he'd turned his attentions elsewhere for the remainder of the supper, she could only assume the former.

And, while I am certain his nature is akin to mine, I simply cannot fathom what he intended. Was he so affected by the wine, or I so misguided in my defence of Lord H? Is it only the start of what he described – a slow darkening of my soul? And what does it matter now anyway – it is three weeks since the night in the orangery...

Josephine gazed out of the guest bedchamber window at Ebcott's pretty gardens sprinkled with golden buttercups, swathes of cow parsley, delicate apple blossom and wild rambling roses. It was just the kind of scene that prompted Sophie to reach for her sketch pad, Phoebe and Matilda their riding boots, and herself a quill. Yet her thoughts were far from quiet enough today.

She'd spent the last few days trailing around the most fashionable London modistes and parks with Sophie, who'd proceeded to talk of little else but the outfits she might need for her betrothal ball weekend which was bound to include at least two suppers, three luncheons and, perhaps, if Matilda got her way, a steeplechase too. And then there were her endless design suggestions for the wedding dress itself, which already filled an entire sketchpad. Josephine closed her eyes as she recalled the number of times Sophie had referred to *Romantic gigot sleeves, full pointed flounces, superb ornamentation* and *yards of silk*, before moving on to such mysterious items as *pelerine capes, mancherons* and *Bavarian straps*. It had all proven to be most exhausting, especially since she was sure there wasn't even a betrothal anymore.

... and he has sent no word.

Josephine swallowed as she stared at the words she'd scrawled on her page. She was certain the General had related

Huntingly's story the night of the Hampton Ball, but struggled to know how she could corroborate any of it, until old Williams came to mind. Viscount Damerel's elderly gardener knew both Huntingly and Pellham before everything happened – their duel, their time in the army, Italy... If anyone could say if there was any truth to the General's understanding, it would be Williams, and the realisation had prompted her to take her leave of London and return to Ebcott Place.

Sketchily, she recalled Williams's story:

'Young Huntingly wasn't exactly the rich landowner lord type, he was a bit of a hothead, happiest with his dogs and horses... Old man Huntingly was a fine sportsman and the coroner ruled he fell from a bolting horse... I believe his son may have issued the challenge because of his grief following his father's death...'

Huntingly was certainly a bit of a hothead, as Williams described, but could Pellham have been responsible for the bolting horse? And the backfiring pistol? But then why would Huntingly not have had his revenge in Italy, tragic news or not?

Josephine closed her eyes as her questions ricocheted through her mind. The heroines in her novels met arrogant gentlemen, seafaring gentlemen and secretly betrothed gentlemen; they rarely had to work out if they were betrothed to murderous ones. And if the General's instincts were wrong, and Huntingly *had* murdered Pellham...? Josephine recalled the moment in the orangery when his eyes had darkened in a visceral way that still sent shivers through her core. She was certain even Thomas might withdraw from the engagement if the bridegroom turned out to be an actual murderer, and yet why did the thought of such an outcome trouble her so?

She exhaled as Phoebe and the viscount came into view along Ebcott's carriageway, pushing a black perambulator, and was conscious of a faint pang of envy. The picture was a stark reminder of how she once dreamed her own life might unfold, and yet she couldn't be further from her sister's present happiness. She hadn't heard from Huntingly in weeks, and there was less than a month until Thomas's Grand Betrothal Ball. She'd vowed she'd protect Matilda, but if Huntingly really was a murderer she also had to consider herself – especially since she'd never been less certain that any gentleman was quite who they seemed at all.

It was a full day before she was finally able to visit Williams. Phoebe, while weak, was overjoyed at her return and had demanded a full and immediate update on all their siblings, and Josephine was more than happy to comply – though she omitted her disagreement with Matilda. Phoebe had been through so much lately, the last thing she needed was to worry about a sibling quarrel. Instead, Josephine gave her a highly animated account of the Davenport Derby, followed by a summary of every childhood ailment that Harriet and Louisa had ever contracted, courtesy of Sophie.

'*Though I warrant you enjoyed every second of it all,*' Phoebe had chuckled.

And while Josephine had given all her attention to the newest Rotherby who, with a head full of wild curls and lungs to rival Matilda, appeared to be in rude health, it didn't prevent her perceptive, older sister noticing something was awry.

'Well, not quite every second perhaps?'

Josephine pondered her sister's gentle enquiry as she walked down through the grassy meadow. She'd reassured her, but Josephine knew she was far from convinced and, not for the first time, she wondered at a world that had given her so many intuitive sisters, yet not one straightforward hero.

Briefly, she paused to admire the hopeful field poppies dancing in a sea of golden grass. She'd been thinking of this moment ever since the General suggested Pellham's death might be linked to family news, but now it had come, she felt her feet slowing. In truth, she was afraid to find out if Williams knew any more – and whether it would make things final. She turned her gaze in the direction of Huntingly's estate, imagining he and Pellham riding out to meet each other before any thoughts of duels and death. Whatever had occurred between the two young gentlemen must have been very serious to result in such tragedy.

'Mornin', Miss Josephine. I weren't expecting you back here so soon?' Williams called, shuffling out from his poultry shack. 'You come to see old Jemima, or the chicks? Most of them have grown like weeds since you been 'ere!'

'I've come to see you, Williams,' Josephine chuckled. 'But it would be lovely to see your brood too, of course. I told Matilda and the boys about them, and they were all envious!'

'Well, they're welcome any time, Miss Josephine.' He smiled kindly. 'But I know life can be very busy at your ages... Now then, would you like to help with their feed and water?'

Josephine nodded gratefully as she took a pail from his outstretched hand, knowing he sensed she'd returned for a reason and that she needed to work up to it too.

'That's it, Miss,' he encouraged as Josephine tipped some of the poultry feed into the old trough. 'Go light on the feed now and let the greedy ones eat before topping up for the weaker ones... You still got the knack. Look, here comes old Jemima now!'

Josephine was content to let all her questions subside for a while, as Williams's oldest, matriarchal duck waddled forward and marshalled some order.

'There's not much that worries Jemima except a fresh straw bed and where her next meal's coming from.' Williams chuckled. 'Think we can learn a lot from her.'

Josephine nodded wholeheartedly. 'Are they loyal to one another?'

'To a point, though it don't mean they don't bicker among themselves, of course. Families are much the same the world over, aren't they, Jemima?'

'Williams...?' Josephine hesitated before forcing herself on. 'Did Pellham have any family that you know about? Family he was in regular communication with?'

'Young Pellham, Huntingly's friend?' William frowned. 'He had no living father. It's why old man Huntingly adopted him, but there was a grandmother and a sister, if I recollect rightly,' he mused, scratching his head. 'Used to live on the outskirts of the village, though they're both gone now.'

Josephine looked up sharply. 'Why so?'

'Typhoid,' he pronounced emphatically. 'There was a nasty outbreak a while back. It affected a good number of local families ... old Ma Pellham caught it first, and then Pellham's sister nursed her and contracted it herself, or so they said. Either way, they both ended up in their graves, God rest their souls.'

A rustle that sounded like the softest whisper stole through the surrounding trees. Josephine suppressed a shiver. She wasn't superstitious, but Williams's mention of deceased family had suddenly made the General's story far more credible.

'Do you know when they died, Williams?' she murmured, reaching down to stroke Jemima.

'Aye, it were some time last year, during the worst of it all as I remember... but this seems a morbid matter for a young lady such as yourself.' He turned and shuffled towards the grouse cages. 'Wouldn't you like to see some hatchlings, instead?'

'Thank you, Williams, I would.' She smiled faintly, recognising he'd reached the end of his willingness to talk about the Pelhams.

It was half an hour later when Josephine finally left and, not yet ready to return, she took the meadow path alongside the estate border. She'd walked it many times when she was younger, and needed time to think over everything Williams had said.

Even though the General had mentioned that Pellham received news of a family loss in Italy, she hadn't allowed herself to hope it might be significant. Yet now she was certain Pellham learned of his grandmother's and sister's deaths while in Italy. If she was right and he was thrown into a melancholy, he might not have wanted to defend himself in any fight – his own demise might have been exactly what he desired and Huntingly a means to achieve it... But it still didn't explain why they duelled with such violence in the first place.

Lost to her rambling thoughts and the gentle warble of summer, Josephine found herself taking the forest path north of the estate before sweeping across the top of the local village. It was the type of morning she'd always loved, full of light and hope – a reminder of the gift of her recovery and of her strength too. On another morning, the dappled trees and birdsong might have sent her to some quiet spot to try and capture the mood and colours, yet today she was too distracted.

She knew Huntingly had a past, but had been willing to trust Thomas's judgement until his reaction in the orangery. Now she wasn't sure of anything. That he was capable of violent emotion she was certain, but murder was an entirely different question. He might have pursued Pellham to France and Italy, but to believe he'd killed his friend in cold blood?

'Who *are* you?' she whispered as she emerged from the forest trail, and onto a hillside on the outskirts of the village. She paused to catch her breath, and while doing so noticed a small local graveyard, sleeping peacefully in the morning sun. It was halfway down the hill and surrounded by a moss-covered stone wall to keep grazing livestock out. Instinctively, Josephine made her way down through the soft grass towards it. She let herself in through a wrought-iron gate, and within moments she'd located the Pellham family graves, marked with small, neat headstones:

Albert Pellham 1773–1815
Martha Pellham 1755–1825

Eliza Pellham 1803–1825

There was no mention of Eliza's mother, and all of the graves appeared to be well tended. Josephine stared down at the neat plots, each bearing a small fresh posy of buttercups, and felt a brief chill whisper through her. Pellham was dead, yet someone still cared enough to place fresh flowers on his family graves. Frowning, she glanced towards the village, wondering if it was too early to make enquiries – which was when she saw a silhouette just beyond the graveyard gate. She drew a sharp breath, unsure if it was real or a trick of the light, before he stepped forward, looking as though he were the one who'd spied a ghost.

'Miss Fairfax?' Lord Huntingly called as Josephine willed her limbs to move.

She swallowed, the drama of their meeting in a graveyard not entirely lost on her, despite everything. She turned to leave as he closed the distance between them, trying to fathom any good excuse why she might be in the village graveyard at such an hour.

'Miss Fairfax?' he repeated, walking towards her. 'Please don't go on my account! What are you doing here? I thought you'd gone to London.'

She stared as he drew to a halt before her, the early sun bathing his face in a soft, translucent light that made his eyes look autumn green. And for a moment he stared back, not in the same, intimidating way he had in the orangery, but wistfully – as though he wished to say something else entirely.

'I came out for a walk,' she replied, picking her words with care, 'and found myself here. I thought I might know some of the families as I spent a few years at Ebcott.'

Lord Huntingly glanced down at the nearby graves, his jaw tensing as he did so. 'And do you...? Know them, I mean?'

There was a pause as Josephine realised he was testing her, wondering if she knew of Pellham and his family.

'You know nothing of what you speak—' his accusation echoed through her thoughts *'—but I would rather know your poor opinion now than on our wedding day.'*

She took a breath. 'No, I don't believe so... I was admiring the flowers. These posies look quite fresh...'

She watched as he glanced again at the Pellham graves, looking for any sign of recognition, but his face was carefully schooled.

'Perhaps I did fail in the eyes of the polite world, but at least I did not pursue a gentleman to Italy and slay him in broad daylight!' She swallowed.

'The village is a close-knit one,' he murmured. 'They take care of their own – much like any family.'

Joephine thought of the way she'd taken matters into her own hands when she'd heard Thomas's betrothal plan for Matilda.

'Do you consider yourself part of the village family, sir?' she asked steadily. 'Were you ... visiting to pay respects today?'

There was a poignant silence, when the only sound was the bleat of a young lamb some distance away.

'Yes, I knew some of those resting here,' he replied, his eyes shuttering. 'Some had care of me as a child.'

'I'm sorry to hear of your losses, sir, and I'm sure the villagers welcome your visits.' She did not mean to sound inquisitive but was aware she might not have another opportunity.

He stared, his eyes reflecting the meadow around them for just a moment before the sun slipped behind a cloud. 'When I was younger, I would visit the village regularly to see old staff and acquaintances,' he replied curtly. 'Less so now.'

'It is always the way as we grow older, unless we have a specific reason to fall out of touch…' She paused deliberately. 'I myself have several friends I've not written to in some years because our paths have led us in different directions.'

'It is common,' he replied, a small frown appearing between his eyes. 'And time changes some paths more than others.' He inhaled deeply before continuing. 'Miss Fairfax, I feel I should say something about the evening at the Davenports'. I am not usually a man of poetry or exhibition, and I was feeling especially … ruffled. Please accept my apology for speaking so harshly. It was undeserved.'

Josephine stared, taken aback. An apology was the last thing she expected, especially after such a protracted absence.

'Thank you, my lord,' she managed. 'I believe we may have both spoken out of turn, and I assure you no apology is required.' She paused, wondering what the protocol was for asking one's betrothed whether their betrothal was at an end.

'You see, you confuse me, Miss Fairfax,' he replied, his eyes flooding with colour again, 'because you are unlike so many debutantes. You come to me proposing a straightforward business match, and then you confound me by making me care what you think. And I haven't cared what anyone has thought for a very long time.'

Josephine frowned, unsure what to think. 'Surely, sir, caring what someone thinks is a good thing? Otherwise we would have a world without conscience or kindness.'

'I am no stranger to that world, Miss Fairfax,' he replied swiftly, 'and I have learned to despise dependency. In my experience, dependency leads only to disappointment – far better to navigate life's path without it, if you can.'

Josephine schooled her face, though her chest was suddenly tight and thumping. Was he referring to her? To their betrothal?

'Is that what you truly believe?' she asked. 'That we are all better off alone? Why, then, do you come here? Surely your presence here bears witness to the strength of past relationships, if nothing else?'

He stiffened, his lips pressing into a firmer line. 'Please do not read into my presence here, Miss Fairfax,' he replied quietly. 'I live nearby and often walk this route. Yes, I pay my respects on occasion, but that is not the same as any kind of familiarity or dependency; something you would do well to note for when we are wed.'

Josephine stared in disbelief as he uttered words she'd assumed to be retracted. 'You still wish us to be wed?' she repeated in an incredulous tone.

'Why, yes, isn't that what we agreed?' He frowned heavily. 'Or have the rumours changed your mind? I must say, our first meeting gave me to believe you were made of steelier stuff than the rest – but perhaps I was wrong?'

'I … change *my* mind?' she challenged, her tone rising in a way she'd heard in her sisters' voices, but rarely her own. '*I* am not the one who abandoned a social soiree, and then disappeared for nigh on a month without a word! Indeed, I have been awaiting confirmation from Thomas that I am the very last debutante you would ever wish to marry!' Her voice quivered with an anger she barely recognised. She stole a shallow breath, wondering how he brought out a side of her she never even knew she possessed.

'If I had my way, I wouldn't marry at all!' he replied in a low and furious voice. 'Why would I inflict my person, my story, on *anyone*, given a choice? But I am the last of my line and my father would not have wanted the Huntingly name to die under such a cloud – I am duty-bound to look to the future of my estate!'

'You, sir, are beyond belief! Not only intent on ridiculing my questions, you assume that my proposition, while lacking in sentimentality, was entirely without any investment at all! To tell me *I* have changed my mind because you have not had the decency or manners to confirm any arrangements is ridiculous! And then to make it abundantly clear that you would vastly prefer *no* marriage to *any* marriage at all is beyond what I can fathom! Indeed, I am beginning to wonder whatever possessed me to believe that this match would ever work!'

'Why are you here, then?'

His brusque question hung on the air while his eyes flared amber-gold in the sunlight. Josephine hesitated, so close to challenging him with the full truth, and yet halted by the shadow in his voice.

'We all have our ghosts, Miss Fairfax ... by marrying me, your soul would be stained by my sin for all eternity.'

'It is all quite settled ... Matilda will marry Huntingly at the beginning of the season.'

She swallowed, knowing she was trapped. 'I am visiting my older sister at Ebcott,' she said quietly. 'But it would do well for you to know that my younger sister would be no more … comfortable a match. She has ambitions to train as a nurse and is well known to be the most headstrong among us.'

There was another silence as his eyes shuttered entirely.

'I am quite aware of the differences between you, and I do not regard the Fairfaxes to be as interchangeable as hats,' he snapped. 'And now, if you are quite finished, Miss Fairfax, I have business elsewhere. Allow me to escort you back to Ebcott.'

'Thank you, sir, but I also have business elsewhere,' Josephine declined frostily. 'I bid you good day.'

Chapter Fifteen

Huntingly Village; Suspicion and Discord
A few minutes later

Josephine waited inside Ebcott's stone boundary wall until her fury had subsided enough for her to talk without grimacing.

'For you cannot make enquiries in the village looking as though you might well murder someone yourself,' she muttered.

Yet she was conscious of so much more than fury too: discomfort, chagrin, a deep ache that threatened to usurp all else. Of all the places to bump into Lord Alistair Huntingly, the resting place of the family of his murdered foe had to take some beating – even by Phoebe, the most dramatic of them all! And then there was the fact he considered their betrothal arrangement stood – despite what he'd said at the orangery, his protracted silence and now this exchange? How could they promise themselves to each other with nothing but suspicion and discord between them? His sudden kiss in the library stole through her mind and she flushed, despite the dappled green of her hiding spot.

Perhaps it wasn't quite all discord? Yet the traitorous nature of her thoughts only made her decision to make enquiries all the more urgent.

Twenty minutes later, she stood in the heart of Huntingly village, feeling more conspicuous than she ever had in her life. Huntingly was a traditional Somerset village with a central square, a busy market and thatched cottages scattered throughout. On any other day, she might have paused to admire the medieval-fronted blacksmith's or allowed herself a pastry from the deliciously scented bakery, but the morning was advancing and she had no desire for Lord Huntingly to discover her a second time.

Swiftly, she made her way to the local schoolroom, a simple stone building with a bell atop its slate roof. Then she pushed back the hood of her pelisse and smoothed her hair before knocking on the thick oak door. Seconds later, it was pulled open with some force and a cross-looking gentleman peered out.

'Yes, what is it?' he asked testily, before realising a young lady of quality stood on his doorstep. 'Oh! Begging your pardon, miss, I thought it was one of the local gut—children playing games. How may I help you?'

Josephine pushed her glasses up her nose and channelled all her sisters' natural authority at once.

'Thank you.' She smiled politely, trying to put the cross schoolmaster at ease. 'I'm here to pay my respects to an old friend – Miss Eliza Pellham? I was saddened to learn of her passing last year, and wondered if she had any family remaining in the village?'

He stared briefly before appearing to collect himself and force a nauseating smile. 'A friend of Eliza's?' he queried. 'I mean, Miss Pellham's? But, of course! You could try her mother? Poor soul was the only Pellham to survive the dreadful scourge of last year. She's still on Rose Hill, last cottage on the right before the grazing field, you can't miss it,' he added in a fawning tone that Josephine was certain he reserved for all his school patrons.

Yet he'd given her exactly what she needed so taking her leave, she hurried through the busy streets, her thoughts whirling. Quite why Williams had failed to mention a surviving mother was a puzzle, and she could not help but think it odd that she'd to discover it for herself. 'Yet, I'm certain Jane herself would be proud,' she murmured, 'for I'm sure her heroines did not have half such a mystery to solve!'

It was in this determined state of mind that Josephine made her way through the heart of the village towards Rose Hill. Smiling at a child in the street, she followed its gentle incline until she reached the last cottage on the right, covered in wild, rambling roses. She trod forward tentatively and knocked, wondering if she'd come this far only to find her quarry had moved on.

'Hello?' she called through the murky gap. 'Is anyone at home? I'm looking for Mrs Pellham?'

She waited, listening to the sound of her own breath, and wondering if she was allowing the mystery to unnerve her. Then a scuffle of slow footsteps reached through the darkness. Josephine took a deep breath, feeling her chest tighten as the footsteps trod closer, certain this was a meeting that would prove or disprove everything – it had to.

'Yes?' came a soft, querulous voice, as the door opened to reveal a stooped, elderly woman, wearing a faded woollen dress and clumsily-knotted headscarf.

'Have I the pleasure of addressing Miss Eliza Pellham's mother?' Josephine asked doubtfully, eyeing the gnarled stick in her free hand.

There was a moment's hesitation before the elderly woman answered with clear effort. 'Yes, my dear, though Eliza's been gone this past year, as have my son and mother too, God bless their souls... It's just me now.'

Josephine gazed into her wizened face, lined by time and heartache, and realised the older woman wasn't looking at her, but straight through her – that she was without sight.

'I am so sorry for your losses, Mrs Pellham,' Josephine replied, suddenly guilt-ridden, 'and for disturbing you at this time.' She sucked in a breath, silently berating herself for trespassing on the poor woman's grief when she'd clearly had enough of her own challenges. 'My name is Josephine. I was a friend of Eliza's and wished only to pay my respects, but I can come again another time.' She gathered up her skirts and made ready to leave.

'A friend of Eliza's, you say?' Mrs Pellham exclaimed in a tone of genuine wonder. 'But then you must come in, my dear ... please ... come in...'

Reluctantly, Josephine followed Mrs Pellham's stooped figure into the sparsely furnished old cottage, feeling even worse than before. She could guess why Eliza's mother might have been spared the wave of typhoid that had claimed the rest of the family: it was unlikely she'd been able to help nurse any of them.

'Tea, dear?' the elderly woman asked, already filling a small black kettle with water and setting it on a small stove.

It was a routine she clearly knew well, and, murmuring her thanks, Josephine took a seat in a rickety chair as the woman collected two cups from a distinctly warped sideboard and washed out a porcelain teapot.

'Of course, you must know my dear mother had care for Eliza and her brother when they were young, as she did for me, but they were the light of my life all the same,' she sighed, before mustering a brighter tone. 'Not that you came here to hear that, my dear. Tell me, how did you and Eliza know one another? And do forgive my asking your age?'

'Of course.' Josephine replied gently. 'I'm two-and-twenty, and I attended Ebcott School,' she added to add substance to her claim. 'Eliza and I crossed paths locally a few times.'

'Oh, you're an Ebcott schoolgirl!' Mrs Pellham replied, her face lighting up. 'Well, that explains it, then! And I am honoured you have come to see me. Eliza was always so headstrong, flying everywhere without heeding any of my advice, rarely told me anything.' She smiled.

'She was certainly ... independent,' Josephine echoed cautiously.

'That she was, dear. I remember the day she was born, my mother called her a *moorland pixie*, with hair the colour of wild berries and skin as pale as the moon. Her brother was just the same, of course. They had such a special bond…'

'Did he look up to her? As a sister?' Josephine ventured, her chest beginning to thump at Mrs Pellham's mention of her son.

'Look up? I suppose so, though there were only minutes between them, mind, and they were as thick as thieves from day one. Always chasing and playing together, even when they befriended others … I expect Eliza probably told you all this already…'

The older woman turned her attention to the teapot as Josephine's thoughts whirled. If Pellham and his sister were twins, Huntingly must have spent time with Eliza as well. She must have known exactly what prompted the duel, and his injuries too. If only she were alive to tell the tale.

'Indeed, Eliza talked of her brother very often,' Josephine replied cautiously, 'and their happy moments growing up together.'

'Oh, there were so many!' Mrs Pellham replied. 'They ran wild! And when one of them befriended another, they fell out a bit, too, as close brothers and sisters are wont to do, I suppose.'

Josephine stared. Williams had mentioned Pellham and Huntingly's friendship – but never that it might have irked Pellham's twin sister. Perhaps he hadn't known himself.

'It must have been hard for Eliza when Pellham left for the army,' she mused carefully. 'I wonder he did not write while he was in France.'

'Oh, but he did, my dear, and often!' Mrs Pellham nodded vigorously before a shadow crossed her face. 'The letters didn't always arrive regularly, but when one did, Eliza would carry it around for days and reread parts to me. But, now then … where are my manners? Let me pour you that tea…'

Seconds later, a cup of hot, sweet brew was being pressed into Josephine's hands. She took a sip and thanked her hostess, though she was aching to know more.

'You were telling me about Pellham's letters to Eliza while he was away?' she prompted when Mrs Pellham had settled back down into an armchair as faded as her dress. 'He must have really missed her.'

Mrs Pellham appeared to collect her thoughts. 'Aye, he did, and she him, though they weren't always the best behaved!' She chuckled, her eyes shining. 'Truth be told, they were a right couple of mischief-makers at times, and I should know, they were my flesh and blood! Some used to ask if I were jealous of their bond, but they were like one person, see, and it didn't surprise me that they departed together in the end, too...' Mrs Pellham trailed off thoughtfully before drawing a deep breath. 'Eliza probably told you they grew up living with my mother, but they visited me whenever they could. Then Eliza came more when her brother left for France, to tell me all the news... I do so miss her voice,' she added, her voice lowering. 'Though I still keep them both nearby, even now they're gone.'

She stood up again as Josephine watched, mesmerised, but this time she crossed to her dusty mantlepiece and felt along, before gently lifting down an old, cracked vase. Then she returned to her seat and withdrew a thick bundle of yellowed envelopes tied with a frayed scarlet ribbon. Mrs Pellham pressed the bundle to her lips before untying it and offering a letter to Josephine.

'I wonder if you might read me a little, my dear ... while you're here?' she asked, her pale eyes misting.

Josephine stared, dumbfounded, at the thick bundle of old letters resting in her lap. They were in matching yellow envelopes and addressed in the same flowing hand, with foreign, military-looking postal stamps. She couldn't have hoped for as much. If Pellham's letters to his own sister didn't offer an insight into the truth, she wasn't sure anything could.

'It would be my sincere pleasure,' she whispered, taking the letter and waiting as Mrs Pellham settled back in her chair.

She opened it nervously and spread the single sheet out on her skirt before clearing her throat.

'*My dearest Eliza,*' she read by a stream of light through a small, latticed window. '*I trust this letter finds you, Mother and Grandmother in good health. I am well and finding life in the regiment to my liking. The rations are fair, the quarters are decent, and the weather has been kind for the most part. I haven't spent much time with the other men, there isn't the opportunity between shifts, and I like to keep to myself. In truth, I have not felt entirely comfortable, for you know I did not enlist alone and a meeting is inevitable.*

'*I do hope, however, dear sister, that when this letter finds you, the rumours surrounding my departure will have subsided. It pains me to know you must have endured so much in my absence and I entreat you to bear it with Pellham fortitude, until such time that I can return and do so for you.*

'*Your affectionate brother, George.*'

Josephine paused when she reached the end and stared at the careful lettering. It was the first time she'd seen Pellham's name in his own hand, and somehow it made him so much more real. She could tell there was much he wasn't saying explicitly, that only Eliza would have understood his full meaning, but it was clear that the bond between them was significant.

'Yes, they were very close, my dear,' Mrs Pellham

confirmed as though she could read Josephine's thoughts. 'And even though there was all that business with young Huntingly, it never divided them, even at the end. He always swore he'd protect her in life and death, and he did.'

Josephine looked up, startled by Mrs Pellham's direct mention of Lord Huntingly.

'Business with young Huntingly?' she repeated softly.

'Aye, Eliza must have told you, even if you didn't hear of it at Ebcott – it were all over the county at the time! But I don't care what they said, George wasn't the type to go hurting anyone. He were a caring boy, brought up with respect, and when it happened, well, it changed him.'

'I understand,' Josephine assured her, somehow knowing her testimony was more than the words of a loving mother, that she was speaking the truth.

She drew a deep breath, her mind whirling with a very different George Pellham from the one she'd expected to encounter, together with a succession of new questions that cast all her previous assumptions into shade. Yet, she was certain his thick bundle of letters would somehow contain the answers. 'Did you ever discover the truth?' she ventured, wondering how his mother seemed aware of her every thought.

Mrs Pellham slowly turned her head towards Josephine. 'It were a bad business,' she replied in a low voice, 'and the only people who knew the truth were themselves. I thought they might have time, all of them, to work it out and find a resolution, but after Lord Huntingly's accident there was the duel—' she paused to shudder '—and … Italy.'

'Please don't upset yourself,' Josephine intervened swiftly. 'It really is none of my—'

'He didn't do anything dishonourable!' Mrs Pellham interrupted fiercely, catching hold of Josephine's wrist. 'He weren't the type, I'm telling you!'

'I believe you,' Josephine whispered. 'Whatever happened to Lord Huntingly, George was innocent.'

At this reassurance, his mother relaxed her hold. 'Yes, you know it, I can tell. They were good children and always tried to take care of me. Even old Lord Huntingly could see that. But when he passed—' she drew a deep, wracking breath '—it changed everything. No one believed it was an accident ... and there was such talk in the village. Eliza tried to stem it, but then they only turned against her... It were all a terrible time, Miss Fairfax, and that's no lie.'

'Pray, do not upset yourself, Mrs Pellham,' Josephine entreated again. 'I should not have asked such a question, it was thoughtless of me.'

'No, my dear, I am grateful, for you have brought George's voice back, and now I can sleep. The letters are all I have left, you see?'

'I am more than happy I've helped,' Josephine whispered as Mrs Pellham drew a breath. 'Would you like me to replace the letters in the vase for you? It's no trouble.'

'Please, take them with you, my dear,' Mrs Pellham muttered, lifting her head wearily. 'I am not long for this world, and I worry they will fall into the wrong hands. Take them because you cared. Take them because of your friendship with Eliza.'

She smiled and pressed the bundle into Josephine's hands,

her expression so hopeful that Josephine couldn't refuse her, despite her burning conscience.

'I will treasure them, I promise,' she replied in a hollow voice, rising to take her leave.

'Don't treasure them, *read* them, my dear,' Mrs Pellham said softly, 'and discern the truth for yourself, for that is why you're here, isn't it? And when you are done, perhaps you can do the one thing I couldn't?'

Josephine waited, unable to say anything.

'Burn them.'

Josephine hurried back to Ebcott, feeling as though she'd fallen between the pages of one of her gothic novels. She'd set out looking for answers, but had hardly dared hope for a living relative, let alone a mother with a tragic story. She traced the outline of the letters concealed within her reticule, and felt the oddest shiver run through her. Mrs Pellham had guessed her real purpose, yet it hadn't stopped her gifting the letters. Had she sensed her need for the truth? And now it could be truly within reach, which was tantalising, and yet she was conscious of a stir of fear too.

If Pellham wasn't the wicked character she'd assumed, then where did that leave Lord Huntingly? Had the second meeting in Italy been as the General suggested? Or was there something she didn't know about Eliza? Her mind darkened as it conjured all the mysterious ways a wild twin might complicate a close friendship. Could Lord Huntingly have been close to her himself? It would certainly explain his dark and melancholy turn of mind…

She hurried back along the woodland trail lost in thought, wondering if the answer had been under her nose all along.

She'd so wanted to believe in Huntingly's innocence that she'd convinced herself it was simply a case of proving Pellham's guilt. But if Pellham was as honourable as his mother claimed, Huntingly couldn't be innocent too.

She closed her eyes briefly, wondering if Phoebe had dispatched a search party for her yet, just as a shrill whistle permeated the air. Startled, she glanced down the trail, certain it wasn't Willams, which was when she saw him, coming from the direction of Ebcott itself.

Josephine caught her breath, unable to believe her ill luck. 'My lord?' she questioned stiffly, as he drew near on the dappled forest path.

'Miss Fairfax.' Lord Huntingly frowned heavily. 'I came to enquire after your safe return, only to find you had not yet returned.'

Josephine stared at his chestnut eyes, flaring with suspicion, together with his long, tousled hair that somehow suited the woodland setting so well. He looked a respectable country gentleman in his walking cape, fitted coat, cream breeches and Hessian boots, yet all Josephine could see was someone whose scars told only part of the truth, that there was so much he kept hidden, even from a grieving mother.

'I had business elsewhere, as I mentioned,' she replied coolly, feeling the weight of the letters even more now.

'In the village?' he challenged.

'Yes,' she returned, holding her ground. 'And what of it? I used to go to school here, so why shouldn't I walk into the village, if I choose?'

'Who did you see?' he demanded, striding up before her, his glinting eyes searching hers.

'I'm sure that is none of your business, sir,' she snapped.

'Don't tell me it is none of my damned business, when we are to be wed,' he hissed.

'Really? And is that a promise or a threat?' she retorted furiously, as he caught her around the waist and pulled her so tightly against him that she was forced to catch her breath.

'You can make it whatever you wish it to be,' he ground out savagely, before crushing his lips to hers.

For a moment, Josephine was too startled to do anything except absorb the heat of his fierce kiss, to return it with a mad fervour, and then acknowledge the cold seep of reality. Summoning all her strength, she thrust him away with a growl unlike any she'd heard from her own throat before.

'How *dare* you!' she accused furiously, gathering her skirts. 'You are in every way insufferable!'

Then she stalked away, cursing every wild and unapologetic nobleman who'd ever insulted a girl, and made her burn for more.

Chapter Sixteen

Ebcott Place; Olympians and Mortals
Three days later

Truly, Fitzwilliam, never were any of Jane's heroines treated so, particularly by a suspected murderer, betrothed or not...

Josephine lifted her quill and stared at the blot of outrage she'd created just beneath her scribbled words. It had been three whole days since she felt calm enough to write in her diary. And now she'd related the whole affair it seemed even more scandalous. To be suddenly kissed by anyone was startling enough, but to be suddenly kissed by a suspected murderer-bridegroom was downright confusing.

For how am I supposed to maintain any consistent thought when he is adopting the habits of an irrational Romeo, who was also, incidentally, a murderer twice over.

Josephine had already written to Thomas. It was the first thing she'd done on arriving back at Ebcott, despite Phoebe's complaints about her missing Alexander's first real chuckle. Privately, Josephine thought it far more likely to be a complaint about Phoebe's incessant peek-a-booing but refrained from saying so.

I have entreated Thomas to delay announcing the betrothal on the basis on new information I will impart directly...

She broke off to eye her mahogany writing box, containing the pile of letters from George Pellham to his sister. She'd scanned them all the day she'd returned, yet while she'd learned a lot about the regiment's occupation of Paris after Napoleon's banishment, there had been little mention of the reason he'd joined in the first place. Now she was slowly reading them again, convinced George and Eliza must have communicated through scant references that could still reveal the truth. It was the most tantalising situation – the promise of a few words that could prove or disprove Lord Huntingly's innocence once and for all.

Momentarily, she thought back to his discomfort in the graveyard, and then his reappearance on the trail, when he kissed her with all the zeal and fervour of her beloved fictional heroes. She had no idea what to make of him and, while she couldn't ever claim that theirs had been anything but a business proposition, she had so many questions now.

'*We all have our ghosts, Miss Fairfax, the only question is how far we allow them to control our lives...*'

She swallowed as she recalled his words in the orangery –

had he been telling her some of the truth then? Was the marriage a way to conceal that his scars reached further than it appeared? He must have known Eliza as well as George: could he be hiding a broken heart as well as a murder?

Josephine sighed, and laid down her quill, before tucking her diary away beneath her mattress. Phoebe had suggested a morning walk with Alexander, and the fresh air could only help to clear her thoughts. Swiftly, she caught up her shawl and made her way down the grand formal staircase that led to the library and garden doors.

'Why, Miss Fairfax, how truly delightful to see you!' a familiar voice exclaimed, as Josephine descended the impressive Damerel staircase lined with the viscount's ancestors and hunting trophies. Phoebe's presence had done much to soften Ebcott, but there were certain areas that would always reflect her husband more.

'Miss Carlisle?' Josephine replied, genuinely surprised to see Aurelia's petite, pert-nosed younger sister standing in the large entrance hall of Ebcott Place.

Momentarily, her gaze travelled over Amelia's attire which comprised a cornflower muslin dress and matching pelisse, all set off by a significant lemon bonnet with a wide halo and several fluttering silk daisies. It was a truly eye-catching ensemble, and she immediately memorised it for the tragic heroine in her current novel, who was increasingly infuriated by the hero.

'Oh, I do hope I'm not intruding, Miss Fairfax?' Miss Amelia entreated. 'Only they said you were staying with your sister, and I simply had to see you. You see, there have been some ... *developments*.'

The stubborn tilt of Miss Carlisle's small chin made Josephine's heart sink into her sensible, everyday slippers. She'd already passed on Amelia's letter; the last thing she wanted were more confidences and secrets to keep – especially regarding Sir Francis. Their last conversation at the Hampton Ball supper still made her flush, and she couldn't help but regret their parting. Yet she still couldn't understand why he'd chastised her for praising Huntingly's performance at the recital – as well as encourage her to do what exactly?

'...With marriage to such an individual on the horizon, some might say that now is the time to enjoy yourself. There is plenty of time for fashionable protestations after the vows, after all.'

She was certain he was far too sophisticated to waste time on improper dalliances, and Fred was equally certain he'd never marry; yet, with both Isabella Hampton and Amelia Carlisle claiming understandings, there now appeared to be significant evidence to the contrary. She swallowed a rise of disappointment that even the fictional hero of her dreams did not appear to be wholly perfect ... and yet hadn't she thought the same of Sir George before Sophie's whirlwind adventure through Paris? She drew a breath, hoping she was not destined to be disappointed by the nature of gentlemen forever.

'Oh, not at all, though I am impressed you found me,' she replied, greeting Miss Amelia with a light embrace. 'In fact, I was just stepping out for a turn with my sister and nephew, but if we head to the garden now, we can have some time alone before they join us?' She smiled at Miss Amelia's long-suffering abigail, before ushering her mistress through the library and into the garden.

'Oh, it's so beautiful here!' Amelia exclaimed as they

stepped outside, though Josephine could tell she was even more distracted than at the Davenport soiree.

Amelia sighed wistfully and her hopes sank further, as they made their way along the path above Ebcott's rolling lawn.

'It is, and I will always be thankful for the school years I spent here,' she replied honestly. 'I trust you and Lady Aurelia enjoyed the Hampton Ball? It seems an age ago now, but of course it was only two weeks. Have most families started to leave London?'

'Yes, the heat has persuaded most of them to remove now,' Amelia replied, wrinkling her nose. 'In truth, it makes the streets so nauseating, I've no idea how anyone stays longer.'

'Perchance they do not have the means to leave,' Josephine replied gently.

'Oh yes, I'm sure you're right.' Amelia nodded, though it was clear her mind was elsewhere entirely.

'Well, we are quite alone now, so why don't you tell me what is on your mind?' Josephine said, resigning herself to the inevitable.

Amelia brightened perceptibly. 'Oh, Miss Fairfax, I have come in such a state of nerves and anticipation,' she whispered, 'and I dared not share with anyone else, but really it is … *so hard* not to…' She broke off to stare entreatingly at Josephine, her large lower lip wobbling dramatically. 'Then I thought to myself, 'But dear, kind Miss Fairfax is so especially my friend, and the *only* person in the world I can trust never to repeat the words that are presently … carved into my heart…' She broke off again, waiting for Josephine to nod her agreement before drawing another deep breath. 'Which means, at last, I can tell you … Sir Francis has asked me to run away with him!'

For a second, all Josephine could hear was the soft chirrup of the garden birds living their perfectly contented lives. Then she drew a ragged breath, recalling the golden Olympian at the Hampton Ball, encouraging her to behave as she pleased. A wave of confusion arose within her, followed by something else entirely. She had wanted to believe him the most noble and honourable of gentlemen, who valued books and ideas above mere beauty and charm. Yet, how could both Isabella and Amelia be so misled, unless there was some truth to their claims? And how could she think him above others, when his actions were so very mortal?

'And he has asked you this directly, by reply of letter, perhaps?' she asked, trying to keep her tone neutral.

'Oh no!' Amelia replied aghast. 'That would be far too dangerous! With his family so impoverished, he wouldn't dare commit such words to paper. No…' She glanced behind to ensure they were quite alone. 'He came to find me after the Hampton supper and, although that bird-witted creature Isabella plagued him for not one but two dances – one of them a pirouette waltz, too – he paused beside the chaise longue and asked if he could share my seat. Don't you think that was a sign? Not to be asked to dance with twenty other couples, but to be singled out for conversation!'

Privately, Josephine thought it could mean several very different, much less flattering things, but refrained from saying so.

'Anyway, the moment Aurelia was occupied with several of the other matrons, he turned to me directly and said: "Are you looking forward to escaping town, Miss Carlisle?"' She paused to look at Josephine in triumph. Josephine returned her gaze blankly. 'Don't you see, Miss Fairfax? We have to talk in code!'

Josephine smiled weakly, praying she didn't look as doubtful as she felt.

'So, of course, I said I was very much looking forward to it and asked him the same, and he said he was ... "counting the days because the country is where my heart lies" ... *where my heart lies*, Miss Fairfax! Was there ever any greater protestation of love?'

Josephine inhaled, certain she could think of several more convincing protestations without blinking, but bit her tongue instead.

'So I asked: was he considering an escape any time soon ... and do you know what he said, Miss Fairfax?'

'I can't imagine,' Josephine replied wryly. 'Pray, do tell.'

Miss Amelia leaned forward, her pretty china-doll eyes wide with intrigue. 'He said ... "imminently"!' She caught her breath before glancing around again, almost as though she expected Sir Francis to spring from the bushes. 'And then he said he was "expecting a ball invitation from Sir Fairfax shortly and was looking forward to seeing me there". Which is *the plan* ... isn't it!' she whispered triumphantly.

Josephine felt her eyes widen almost as much as Miss Amelia's. 'The plan ... for what?' she repeated.

Amelia stared as though she couldn't believe Josephine could be so dull, before letting out a little sigh. 'Why, you are so very noble and proper, Miss Josephine, it's little wonder you cannot immediately see it, but you shall wonder how you didn't, when I explain!'

Josephine waited with no such expectation as Amelia drew a breath, ready to impart her winning shot.

'We are to elope from the Knightswood Ball!'

'Well, the Ball part is accurate anyway, dearest,' Phoebe mused after Miss Amelia left and Josephine had related her tragic entreaties. 'I had a letter from Thomas this morning saying he'd fixed a date and invitations had been dispatched. I don't think he's mentioned the betrothal announcement, just given notice to the great and good, but it is uppermost in his mind, of course. As for Sir Francis's plans—' she frowned '—who knows for certain? But Miss Amelia wouldn't be the first young lady to have misunderstood a gentleman's intentions. The Lord knows I hardly understood this one's father for most of the first six months of our acquaintance!'

She paused to lean forward and tickle her baby son with the most doting expression, making Josephine wonder at the dramatic effect of motherhood on her trouser-wearing, highwayman-fighting rebel of an older sister.

'Where has Miss Amelia gone now? Is she staying locally?' Phoebe added as an afterthought.

'With some maiden aunt, who knows the *most divine modiste*, apparently,' Josephine replied, taking Thomas's letter from her sister's outstretched hand. She sighed at his scrawl, written and overwritten to save paper, as was always his way.

Swiftly, she scanned the formalities to reach the part Phoebe had mentioned.

The Proposition of the Season

> *...You will be interested to know I've fixed a date for the Grand Knightswood Ball and invited all the usual families, of course. A handful of guests will stay with us, and I'll depend on yourself and Sophie to help host the occasion.*
>
> *Matilda has also requested I organise a steeplechase for the following morning, which I've refused, naturally. One event is costly enough and will serve to announce both Matilda's forthcoming season and Josephine's betrothal. Indeed, I hope the occasion will also serve Matilda's betrothal, for what other social event could she possibly need to secure an eligible offer? As such, I flatter myself I have handled both matters most efficiently...*

'He flatters himself he's got rid of the last of his sisters, more like!' Josephine scowled, passing the letter back to her sister. She suppressed a rise of anxiety as she recalled her own recent letter, which entreated her brother to delay any betrothal plans until she'd had time to speak with him. She'd not yet had the opportunity, but if Ball preparations had begun, there was very small chance of Thomas changing anything.

'You can't let Miss Amelia's account of Sir Francis upset you, dearest,' Phoebe advised. 'She must learn for herself that gentlemen speak in riddles they barely understand themselves. And I know Lord Huntingly isn't a love match for you, but you seemed quite settled on the matter the last time we spoke. Has something changed your mind?'

Josephine eyed her sister carefully. While Sophie's offspring often distracted her from reading her younger sister too well, Phoebe was an entirely different matter. And yet how could she tell her most protective sister that she now suspected Huntingly *had* murdered Pellham in Italy, and hidden the deed, even from Pellham's own mother? She had no proof and was far from safe herself. If she told Phoebe her suspicions, and Thomas refused to release her from the betrothal, she would tell Viscount Damerel and the Captain, and there was a very good chance one of them would take matters into their own hands. For a moment, she recalled the viscount's clash with Lord Rotherby, Sophie's husband, at Versailles, and closed her eyes. Far better she try to speak with Thomas directly.

'Just pre-betrothal nerves,' she assured her sister. 'I always imagined I'd marry someone more…'

'Heroic?' Phoebe filled with a chuckle. 'So did I, dearest, but heroes can be a little de trop when it comes to everyday matters. Far better to catch a real gentleman who cares to behave nobly, than a noble gentleman who does not care to behave at all. Lord Huntingly is kind and gentlemanly when you spend time together?'

Briefly, Josephine thought of Lord Huntingly's unpredictable behaviour every time they crossed paths.

'Oh yes,' she replied with a tight smile. '*Quite* gentlemanly.'

Chapter Seventeen

The Grand Knightswood Ball; French Lace and Moorland Hair
Two weeks later

'I honestly cannot believe that all three of you sold your souls in such a way!' Matilda exclaimed heatedly. 'You spent years telling me how modern and independent you are, and then willingly incarcerated yourselves in one of these? A literal cage!' She huffed at the looking glass as one of the housemaids pulled her new corset even tighter.

'It's just a corset, Matilda,' Sophie chastised, closing her eyes. 'You've worn one before, and this is one of the newer designs Madame Montmartre sent from Paris – at no small expense too, I can tell you!'

'Yes, but mine are comfortable! I don't cinch them in so I can't even sit down, and I always have ribs left at the end of a day... Indeed, that's it! Let me out! It's bad enough that I have to go through with this charade, let alone be tied into the underbelly of a whale.'

All three of her older sisters, who were sprawled across her bed, began to laugh.

'Matilda, I swear you are the most dramatic of all of us,' Phoebe chuckled. 'I've never heard such a fuss about a coming-out gown! Just wait until you get to The Queen Charlotte's Ball, which involves more pomp and ceremony than any girl can reasonably bear; you just have to keep telling yourself you can tear the wretched thing off as soon as you get back to your bedchamber.'

'I don't think that's quite the right attitude either!' Sophie exclaimed, heaving herself on the bed cushions and staring down at her considerable bump. 'And, quite honestly, I miss having a waist. There's no allowance in any of the new Romantic fashions, so I would make the most of yours while you still can, dearest sister.'

'Pooh! If you think I am in any way subjecting myself to your present condition, you can think again, especially after Phoebe's considerable, attention-seeking experience…'

Josephine raised her eyebrows at her outspoken younger sister, who trailed off sheepishly. She and Matilda had made up almost the moment she'd returned to Knightswood, but she was also conscious Lord Huntingly hadn't yet come up in conversation.

'Oh Jo, if you think I'm going to be *mawkish* about my impending confinement because Phoebe ran into a spot of bother, think again!' Sophie exclaimed. 'This one will be no trouble, just like all the rest.' She patted her stomach affectionately. 'The midwife believes it a boy from the way he's challenging my dress fastenings, and I know that would delight Dominic, but I'm so very weepy I think it must be another girl. Anyway, it'll be your turn next!' She smiled mischievously. 'And I do hope you take baby Huntingly to the park a few times before you start them on the entire works of William Shakespeare!'

'It's never too soon,' Josephine retorted, pulling a face as they all laughed.

She gazed around at their animated faces, wishing she could bottle the afternoon before the weekend celebrations were upon them. Her return to Knightswood had been beset with failure – both to persuade Thomas to delay the betrothal announcement, or to discover any evidence in George Pellham's letters. They made frequent references to the *unfortunate* or *regrettable* circumstances that had led to his situation, but nothing more – though she was still slowly making her way through her second read. All of which had left her with an approaching betrothal ball and an impending sense of doom.

'You expect me to throw away the first decent offer you've had in three years, a match you yourself secured, because of a suspicion?'

Thomas's words echoed in her ears as she watched her sisters chat. None of them knew how much she suspected, and now the rumours about Huntingly had somehow been lost amid talk of betrothal gowns and coming-out announcements.

'I told Thomas I'd suffer through this whole affair if he would but reinstate the steeplechase,' Matilda interjected sulkily, 'but he was just … churlish.'

'Dearest, you know Thomas will only spend where he deems entirely necessary,' Phoebe placated. 'As it is, Sophie was lucky to obtain a dress allowance for you both which must have been like—'

'Getting blood from a stone,' Sophie muttered, rolling her eyes. She pushed herself onto her feet before treading across to the armoire. 'But this Parisian lace will be so worth it! Madame Montmartre worked through the night on yours, Jo,' she added wistfully, letting the fine material run through her fingers. 'It really is the loveliest betrothal dress I've seen, with sleeves worthy of any romantic heroine!'

'Well, I need all the help I can get,' Josephine laughed, 'unlike our dear, lovely Matilda who could wear riding breeches and a shirt, and still have a dozen suitors fighting over her first dance.'

'Don't tempt me!' Matilda growled, making them all laugh.

'You're perfect just as you are, Josephine Fairfax,' Phoebe chastised in her old way, 'and Lord Huntingly is extraordinarily fortunate to share a future with you. The stars don't always shine clearly but that doesn't mean they aren't there, and I pray your union brings you every blessing, for the Lord knows you deserve them.'

'Hear, hear!' Sophie applauded admiringly. 'You haven't delivered a speech like that since we produced *Frankenstein's Monster* with an all-female cast.'

'The peak of my career,' Phoebe laughed.

'When you all told me being the monster was the best part,' Matilda grumbled.

'Well, you're no monster today, dearest,' Sophie chuckled, taking over from Betsy, who was attempting to fasten a row of tiny silk buttons on Matilda's dress.

'There!' she exclaimed as her experienced fingers made

light work of the fastenings. 'Now you look like the most sophisticated debutante of the season!'

Josephine smiled at Matilda's scowling reflection, all ivory silk, French lace, gigot sleeves and wild moorland hair – some things would never change.

'Which means you must be the most sophisticated bride!' Sophie smiled, turning back to Jo.

3rd April 1825

My dearest Eliza,

Thank you for your letter and news of our grandmother, which I read with a truly heavy heart.

Life with the regiment is far from easy, but it is nothing compared with the pain and worry you must have endured over these past few weeks. Indeed, my only solace is that you were with our grandmother throughout her fever, and at her passing. There is so much I wish I could say to her, but instead all I ask is that you mark her resting place with a bunch of spring buttercups. They were her favourite, and when she looks down, she will know I am thinking of her now and always.

I pray the typhoid sweeping the village spares the lives of any more friends and family, and that the angels bless you and Mother with strong, good health. Trust me when I say that I cannot imagine how I would live without you, Eliza. You have always been my guide and strength, even through the darkest times, and I know that, like me, you regret it all.

I beseech you take care until such time that I can return.

Your fondest brother,
George.

Josephine sat bolt upright in bed as she reread one of George's last few remaining letters to Eliza. Her first rapid read had elicited nothing consequential at all, indeed most had read along very similar lines, enquiring about the health of his sister and family before sharing a little about life in the regiment. She certainly hadn't noticed any mention of Eliza's culpability, until now.

'*Trust me when I say that I cannot imagine how I would live without you, Eliza. You have always been my guide and strength, even through the darkest times, and I know that, like me, you regret it all,*' she repeated to herself, her chest suddenly tight.

She looked up at her betrothal gown, hung with care on the front of her armoire by Sophie. The Knightswood Ball weekend had arrived faster than anyone expected, and most of the guests were arriving today, including the rest of the family, Sir Francis, the Carlisles, the Hamptons and Lord Huntingly. She scowled: she'd heard nothing from him since Ebcott, despite sending two letters requesting he call off the engagement, and now … this.

She cast her mind back to the day she'd first heard about the duel, and snatches of conversation with Fred, Williams and Captain Damerel reached through her whirling thoughts.

'*As far as I know, it was some dispute over old man Huntingly's will… Pellham's father was as thick as coves with old man Huntingly… Old man Huntingly died in a hunting accident with only Pellham there, and afterwards, when the will was read, the young lord discovered Pellham was to inherit part of the estate…*

Huntingly's weapon backfired, and they were Pellham's Flintlock pistols...'

Josephine's chest began to pound – what exactly did George mean when he wrote of Eliza's *'regret for it all'*?

'Aren't you dressed yet?' Matilda exclaimed, bursting in and running to the window. 'We're losing enough of this weekend being paraded like peahens, so I thought we might sneak in a ride before breakfast?'

Josephine smiled as she stuffed the letter beneath her pillow. 'How about a walk instead?' she asked hopefully, knowing her younger sister too well to try to dissuade her.

'Pooh! Who wants to walk the grounds when the *whole* moor is so very near? And besides, Misty needs exercise and fresh air!'

Josephine was certain it was Matilda who needed the exercise and fresh air, but refrained from saying so. All week, Knightswood Manor had been slowly transforming from the faded country home they all knew into the polished seat of a respectable family of the ton. Thomas really was as good as his word, and ensuring Knightswood shone at the prospect of getting rid of the last of his sisters.

'Is that more food supplies?' Matilda asked, pressing her nose up against the window. 'It's not quite six, the pre-Ball supper isn't until eight, and have you seen the flowers? Seriously, Jo, I think Thomas thinks he *is* actually marrying us off from this event and he'll never have to spend a groat on us again!'

'Groat?' Josephine gurgled with laughter. 'Don't let Thomas hear you saying that.'

Matilda grinned. 'I like words that say so much more than

the ones we're supposed to use ... like isn't it a *top of the trees* morning, and I really am feeling quite *corky* and I'd love to *kick up a lark* rather than—'

'Enough!' Josephine conceded, groaning. 'Let me get dressed and we'll go for a short ride, there's only so much Bertie Briggs I can take before breakfast.'

Half an hour later, Josephine had to concede that Matilda was right. The fresh air was like a tonic, clearing her head and brightening her mood, though her chest still felt unusually tight.

'How are you feeling about the weekend, Matty?' Josephine asked as they slowed to a trot along their favourite trail. It was framed with moorland heather and wild, flowering gorse, and briefly she recalled their last breakfast picnic, when life had seemed so much lighter.

'Oh ... fine.' Matilda shrugged colourlessly. 'I mean, it's not a formal presentation, just Thomas's notice of my coming out. And Henry and Edward will be there, so I can always rely on them to rescue me should anyone get too boring – like Sir Francis.'

'Is he really so very boring?' Josephine raised her eyebrows, mostly to cover her rise of mixed feelings.

'Sir Francis is boring before he even arrives!' Matilda retorted with a grin.

'Hmm,' Josephine murmured, recalling Miss Amelia's secret plans for the weekend. 'He may surprise you.'

'What do you mean?'

'Oh, just that we shouldn't assume we ever really know people,' Josephine shrugged knowing Matilda was hardly likely to be reliable when it came to confidences involving gentlemen to whom she'd taken a vehement dislike.

'And what about you, Jo?' Matilda returned after a beat. 'I take it you resolved any differences with Lord Huntingly when you went to Ebcott?'

Josephine shot Matilda a sidelong glance, wondering whether to tell her fieriest sister that, far from resolving anything, their differences were a hundred times worse. That, in fact, she was increasingly suspecting him of murder, of a secret attachment to Pellham's sister, and perhaps even of dishonouring Pellham's mother too. Yet, what good would it do except encourage Matilda's fire over a weekend that was already beset with challenges?

'I have given Lord Huntingly the option to withdraw from the betrothal,' Josephine replied tersely, 'and he hasn't so ... here we are.' Her tangled thoughts suddenly conjured his passionate kiss on the trail around Ebcott, and she looked away so Matilda wouldn't see her blush.

'You really are the oddest creature, Jo,' Matilda mused. 'You spend an entire lifetime dreaming about wild, impossible heroes who only appear in wild, impossible novels – and then the moment one appears, you refuse to wake. You could be happy, I think, if you just ... allowed it.'

Josephine stared out at the summer moorland, wishing she could tell Matilda everything. Instead, she drew a deep breath. 'Do you ever imagine yourself in my place, Matty?' she asked gently. 'Because I'm sure that, if you were, you might wish yourself elsewhere entirely.'

'Lord, no, whatever makes you think that!' Matilda snorted

decisively. 'I'm more than content, and intend to turn down every suitor Thomas presents until he washes his hands of me!' She chuckled before glancing at her sister. 'It's your decision, anyway,' she added with a faint shrug. 'Only you know if you want to take a chance.'

Chapter Eighteen

The Knightswood Pre-Ball Supper; Truth and Regrets
That same evening

'There you go, miss, and you look a real picture too!' Betsy murmured, stepping away from the looking glass so Josephine could fully admire her supper ensemble.

'Thank you, Betsy,' Josephine replied, barely recognising the fashionable young lady regarding her back.

'The pale blue taffeta really is special, miss, especially with the lace flounces and ... *rouleaux*, was it? Miss Sophie really does have a good eye.'

'Yes, I believe that's what she called it.' Josephine looked down her lace bodice to the firm fabric roll at her dress hemline. 'Apparently, it's all the rage in Paris, so Knightswood is officially ahead of London now!' She raised her eyebrows and smiled.

'I wouldn't expect anything else, miss.' Betsy handed

Josephine a pair of matching gloves. 'And your ball dress is going to have all the young ladies swooning tomorrow too.'

Josephine glanced at the ivory betrothal dress Sophie had herself designed for the Grand Knightswood Ball. It was the sort of dress everyone should wear at least once in their lifetime, with a fitted bodice, glistening pearl decor and a sheer gauze stitched over, to create a shimmering effect when she moved. She'd spared no pains, and Josephine only wished she felt worthy of wearing it, instead of a consummate fraud.

'I believe Madame Montmartre would be happy,' Josephine murmured, watching the candlelight flicker in the sapphire hair pins Betsy had placed in her curled hair.

'She would indeed, miss, especially finished with the Apollo knot as Miss Sophie suggested,' Betsy replied, shaking out a discarded chemise. 'The curls frame your face beautifully.' She smiled as she made her way to the door. 'It's so exciting, miss, the beginning of a whole new chapter.'

Josephine frowned at her dark eyes and ruby lips, stained with a little rouge, before pushing her spectacles firmly up her nose.

'Or the end,' she whispered to herself.

Josephine was reassured by Benson's kindly smile as she made her way downstairs. He'd accepted a retirement position at Knightswood when Rotherby and Sophie wed, and his very proper, steadfast ways had swiftly endeared him to the rest of the family.

'Good evening, Miss Josephine,' he called, nodding his

head more regally than royalty. 'Sir Thomas is gathering everyone in the library tonight.'

Josephine forced a smile. The library was usually her favourite place of escape, but tonight felt very different.

'Thank you, Benson,' she replied.

'And this arrived a little earlier, Miss Josephine.' He paused to withdraw a package from an inside pocket of his livery. 'One of the kitchen maids brought it up.'

Josephine looked down at the thin paper package which was addressed only 'Miss Josephine, Ebcott School', before frowning and sliding it into her pocket. Then she nodded, and Benson opened the door.

'Sister!' Thomas proclaimed instantly, striding forward to take her arm. 'I declare you look the very image of our dear Mama tonight, which seems so very fitting for this weekend of celebrations. He smiled to acknowledge a ripple of agreement while leaning closer. 'And I applaud you for having the good sense to know when family duty must prevail,' he whispered, leading her forward.

Josephine swallowed, taken aback by the chorus of greetings from her siblings, their spouses and selected family friends, including the Hamptons and their guest, Miss Amelia Carlisle. It had been a long time since such a group was gathered under Knightswood's roof, and for a few minutes it was as much as anyone could do to stay afloat in the overlapping conversations. Yet, she was conscious of one gentleman's regard from the back of the room, all the while.

'Oh, my dear!' Aunt Higglestone gushed, the first to secure Josephine's sole attention. 'How very lovely you look this evening, *and what exciting news too*!' she added in a loud whisper, looking fit to burst with pride. 'I could barely believe my ears when Thomas confided in me, but, oh dearest, it is the very thing I dreamed of throughout *all* your seasons, and I knew you'd do it in the end…'

'Thank you, Aunt,' Josephine intervened, before everyone was treated to a very plain account of her outstanding failure. She was also aware that most of those assembled had been apprised of her news, but had strict instructions not to speak of it until Thomas made the official announcement.

'Did you know Sophie sent to Madame Montmartre for this taffeta?' she continued swiftly, in the hope of distracting her loquacious aunt. 'Indeed, she designed all of our ball—'

'Do excuse the interruption, Miss Fairfax, but I wonder if I might have the honour of escorting you into dinner?' His voice was charming, and disarmingly near.

'—dresses, and they are quite the latest fashion…' Josephine clenched her fingers in her skirt, aware it was the first time they'd spoken since Ebcott, and that Lord Huntingly's request made them seem the most ordinary betrothed couple in the world. She looked up with a million conflicting thoughts, while her aunt looked on indulgently.

'Why, yes, of course, Lord Huntingly,' she mustered with a hollow smile. 'I should be honoured … thank you.'

He nodded, giving nothing away, and yet lingering all the same. Josephine willed herself not to recall their last encounter in painstaking detail, but it filled her thoughts all the same, sending a heat to her cheeks that fanned out like a telltale whisper. A faint smile creased his lips and she gritted her teeth, knowing he was recalling the same.

'And have you been well?' she asked in a brittle tone,

ignoring her aunt who was making the greatest drama out of slipping away unnoticed. 'I must admit, I am growing quite used to sending letters out into a great big silent void.'

A frown flickered across his face as he took her arm and guided her further from the chattering group. 'I have been away from home these past three weeks, so please accept my apologies if I have missed anything. Believe me, it is not my intention to ignore anything you say. Why don't you tell me what you wrote instead?'

Carefully, Josephine studied his expression, but his eyes were heavily guarded. She suppressed a frown, also aware that the efforts he'd made with his appearance were at peculiar odds with his absence. His claret evening coat was cut away to a nipped-in waist and fashionable narrow tails; his silk cravat was tied in the hunting fashion and secured with a single diamond pin; and his dress shoes shone with a gleam that put the silverware to shame.

And yet there was a wariness between them that no outward show could breach.

Josephine took a deep breath. 'You can guess at what my letters said, following your assertions at our last meeting,' she whispered rapidly. 'You stated your position about marriage very clearly, that you marry for duty. But to be told you'd rather do anything but marry, and then be subjected to such *monstrous* behaviour? It is beyond everything! More importantly, it is quite clear, sir, that you keep many secrets.' She tried to gain control of her quivering voice, aware those closest were glancing at them. 'It is your choice, of course, except they mask a truth that could free others from heartache. And I might guess at your need to travel,' she concluded icily, 'when you keep such old friends abroad!'

For a moment Huntingly stared, his jawline tightening at her reference to Pellham, yet the letters had all but convinced her of George's innocence, and Huntingly's unpredictable turn of mood seemed more suspicious with every passing second.

'And now, dear brothers, sisters and close friends,' Thomas boomed at that precise moment, 'it is time for us to go in to supper, but I do have something of import to say, as many of you already know, and I see no reason not to confirm the happy news ahead of the Grand Ball announcement tomorrow!'

Startled, Josephine swung her head back to her jubilant brother, who was standing at the drawing room fireplace, a glass of champagne in his hand. Then he smiled in a way that extinguished every hope that she might put this fateful moment off any longer.

'Some of you will know I had some reservations about this day ever occurring, but it goes to show that none of us should ever make assumptions based on history,' he began. 'What matters is the future, and I'm delighted to confirm with you all that Josephine, our beloved sister, has lately agreed to become the new Lady Huntingly! Yes, it is wonderful news!' He nodded at the low murmur of congratulations. 'And I'm sure you'll agree with me when I say that they make a very handsome couple indeed!'

He beamed widely at the select company, as Josephine gazed at them all. There were so many animated reactions to the confirmation of her news – delight, curiosity, relief – until she reached Phoebe and Matilda. Both were in the shadows near the window and looked as serious as she felt. She swallowed. 'Now then,' Thomas continued, holding forth his glass, 'I believe Benson has brought around some very good *Piper-Heidsieck* that I selected on my last trip to Reims, and it would be a terrible shame not to put it to good use!' He paused to acknowledge the murmur of agreement. 'So, without any further ado, I ask you all to raise your glasses to Lord Huntingly and our own dear Josephine! Congratulations to you both and may your union be blessed!'

Josephine had no choice but to accept Lord Huntingly's arm amid the fresh blur of congratulations, yet it was only as they turned to follow Thomas that he inclined his head to reply.

'I had hoped your brother might temper his enthusiasm tonight,' he murmured as they turned into the dining room, 'so we might enjoy a little time without attention, but clearly it was not meant to be.' He nodded at Aunt Higglestone, who was dimpling with pride from a seat further up the dining table. 'But I would like to answer your earlier charge, if I may, Miss Fairfax, and clarify that I *keep* very few friends, as I'm sure you have already guessed, and it was business that took me away, not pleasure.' He paused beside Josephine's chair, while she took her seat. 'In truth, while I accept your admonishments and apologise for them,' he added intently, 'I hope to nurture one very particular friendship in the future, with far fewer secrets.'

He made his way to his seat then, between Matilda and Captain Damerel, while Josephine awaited the first course feeling even more confused than before.

How could he talk to her of fewer secrets when he kept

more than anyone she knew? And why did he think that she would be remotely interested in friendship, when he couldn't even be honest with himself?

'You are certainly very quiet for a newly betrothed young lady,' Sir Francis murmured beside her. 'I hope you are contemplating new beginnings ... or perhaps missed opportunities?'

Josephine glanced across at his athletic figure, his eyes reflecting the deep Prussian-blue of his evening coat, and wondered again why the universe seemed so intent on putting them in the same space.

'I'm not sure why you might imagine I am considering either,' Josephine replied tersely, nodding to a footman bearing a tray of crayfish, 'when there are so many delicious entrées for the first course and my favourite pastries among the puddings.'

Sir Francis's eyes danced with amusement. 'As I said many weeks ago, Miss Fairfax, I believe you are the enigma of the family. Every other Fairfax says what they think when they think it – you, however, are like an untitled book, and I do so like to know what I am reading.'

Josephine suppressed a frown, conscious of both Miss Isabella's and Miss Amelia's misty-eyed gazes from the bottom of the table.

'Do you believe every young lady should be available for perusal, Sir Francis?' She smiled politely. 'Or should they be entitled to choose their own readers?'

'Smart, Miss Fairfax! Very smart! I don't believe even your dear brother has your presence of mind, but my question is coloured by my experience, you see – I've never met a young lady who hasn't wished to be read *a little* ... until you.'

Josephine paused, noticing the same gleam in his eyes as the night of the Hampton Ball. 'Then perhaps, sir, it is beneficial that you have found a favoured book with whom you yourself are contemplating *a new beginning*,' she replied, accepting a slice of roast pigeon pie.

Sir Francis looked quizzical as he took a sip of wine, yet was prevented from responding as Sophie's light voice suddenly rose above the rest.

'Do you plan to reside in Somerset, Lord Huntingly, once you and Josephine are wed?' she asked brightly. 'Or will you reopen your townhouse? I understand it is but a stone's throw from Grosvenor Square.'

'What our dear sister is actually asking is whether Josephine will be on hand to babysit her fair charges whenever she is in need?' Henry chortled from further down the table, his cheeks a little too pink.

'Henry!' Matilda chastised like an old maid. 'You're in your cups already and we don't even have our puddings!'

'Matilda Fairfax!' Aunt Higglestone remonstrated in turn, her eyes wider than Josephine thought was probably good for anyone. 'What would your dear mama say! She'd say I hadn't taken enough care of you all, that's what!' she lamented.

'Thank you for your kind enquiry, Lady Rotherby,' Lord Huntingly replied smoothly, coming to Matilda's rescue. 'You are kind to ask, but the truth is that I am keen to restore Huntingly Manor to its former state now I am returned, so I imagine much of our time in the foreseeable future will be spent in Somerset – with your sister's agreement, of course.'

Josephine watched his attention swing back to herself, his eyes guarded as they flickered past Sir Francis to meet her own.

'So, you don't plan to hold any fashionable parties, or venture to the continent for your honeymoon?' Phoebe enquired. 'Alexander and I had the most wonderful honeymoon in Rome and Florence when we visited, and I'm sure Josephine would very much enjoy all the history and culture there.' She smiled at the Viscount Damerel affectionately. 'The view from the top of the Duomo really is quite something,' she added.

'Don't give away all my secrets!' Viscount Damerel exclaimed in mock alarm. 'It took me years to compile a list of exciting locations with which I could impress my dear, headstrong wife!'

A ripple of amusement echoed around the table as Josephine glanced at Lord Huntingly.

'Parties and honeymoons are not terribly high on my agenda,' he replied, after a beat. 'And Italy does not hold any great romance for me. I prefer the moorland on our own doorstep, truth be told.'

'Oh, so do I!' Matilda exclaimed impulsively. 'There is nothing better than a dawn ride with the sun just reaching over the hills. It's always my favourite time!'

'You are to be commended, Miss Fairfax,' Lord Huntingly smiled. 'There are few who would exchange the comfort of their slumber for such a view, but I am in hard agreement.'

'Well, you wouldn't catch me riding at that time – unless I hadn't gone to bed at all!' Fred chuckled.

'And I wager it would be the last thing on your mind, even

then.' Sir Francis grinned, ignoring a melting look from Miss Amelia.

'Lord, don't wager a Fairfax, Sir Francis,' Sophie chimed. 'You really should know better than that, it can lead to all sorts of trouble.' She glanced at her charismatic husband, who raised an eyebrow questioningly.

'I think we all know who needs to learn to resist a wager,' he replied drolly, setting everyone laughing again.

Josephine laughed with everyone else, but was conscious of the tightness returning to her chest. The rapport between her sisters and their husbands was heartwarming, yet it only accentuated the gulf between herself and Lord Huntingly. And then Sir Francis seemed so intent on teasing her that, by the time the ladies withdrew, she was longing for the peace and solitude of her bedchamber.

'Lord, isn't anyone coming to the drawing room tonight?' Matilda complained as she, Phoebe and Sophie all made their excuses at the bottom of the staircase.

'You can't really blame us, Matty,' Phoebe smiled. 'We're old married ladies now – well, nearly all of us – and tomorrow is going to be busy. Besides, the gentlemen will only lay each other a pony they can put out a candle with a flintlock or *some such thing*.'

'Put out a candle with a flintlock?' Sophie echoed, wrinkling her nose in disgust. 'I certainly hope not! I may be a Fairfax, but I'm still in a delicate state.'

'Oh hush, there's nothing delicate about your state, Lady Rotherby!' Phoebe teased affectionately. 'Come on, old lady, I'll walk you to your bedchamber.'

'And what's your excuse?' Matilda demanded mulishly, as their elder sisters turned to go.

'Nothing other than the headache,' Josephine confessed, 'and a desire for my bed.'

'Don't worry, Matilda, we will keep you company!' Miss Amelia cooed as she and Charlotte Davenport emerged from the dining room. 'Josephine has an important day tomorrow, and, if the gentlemen wish for music, Sir Francis can play the pianoforte and I can help turn pages! Oh, I'm sure we will all be well entertained, and your sister will gain great comfort from a good night's sleep.' She turned her pretty smile towards Josephine, who had no doubt that her real delight lay in the prospect of turning pages for Sir Francis, with half the female party out of the way. Yet the thought of joining them for more baffling conversations and questioning looks was more than she could endure.

'Thank you, Amelia, that is most kind,' she nodded. 'I'm sure I will benefit greatly from the rest ... I bid you all good night.'

Then she climbed the stairs to her bedchamber where, at last, she was able to empty her wild and tumbling thoughts onto paper.

Dear Fitzwilliam,

> *I have never felt so lost. Having entered this betrothal with the clear purpose of protecting a most beloved sister, I must conclude that sustaining it is not straightforward at all.*
>
> *In truth, were I to have no misgivings about the bridegroom's character, I might welcome his inclinations towards my sister,*

and yet my misgivings have never been graver – and so I must go on with this charade...

Josephine sighed and reached forward to ink her quill just as a faint rustle made her pause. Frowning, she pushed her hand into the pocket of her skirt and withdrew the slim package Benson had given her earlier. She'd been so distracted by the evening, she'd completely forgotten about it. Swiftly, she untied the string, and opened the paper to find two yellow envelopes, bearing military stamps, inside. A strange excitement laced through her as she turned them over. She knew exactly who they were from for they weren't fresh correspondence at all, but two more letters written in George Pellham's distinct hand. And while there was no note, she knew that Mrs Pellham had sent them for her to read, that somehow they'd been separated from the main bundle.

Her gaze flickered briefly to her writing box containing the rest of the letters. She'd read them all twice and, aside from the brief line about Eliza's regrets, they'd provided no firm evidence at all. But perhaps all that was about to change now, perhaps she was finally to learn the truth.

The truth. Wasn't it the truth that she'd begun this believing she was sacrificing her heart, and now feared she no longer knew it?

She turned the first letter over in her hands, almost afraid to open it, and yet the barrage of conflict within her threatened to dull all else. How was she to proceed at all without knowing what happened in Italy?

'Huntingly's name is far from unblemished. If I were you, I

should take a little care ... your Fairfax reputation will have much work to counteract his history.'

'I cannot imagine how I would live without you, Eliza, you have always been my guide and strength, even through the darkest times, and I know, like me, you regret it all...'

Trembling, Josephine opened both letters and smoothed them out before her. They were dated three weeks apart.

2nd May 1825

Dearest Eliza,

I am beyond worried to read the contagion is sweeping the village, and pray your strength and constitution will bear you through the next few weeks. I also write in some haste for the inevitable has happened... Although in separate battalions, we have finally crossed paths here in Paris, and I could tell immediately that there has been no change on his part. He intends to know, one way or another, and so I have but one choice... It is extremely fortuitous that my time in occupation has recently come to an end and I can disappear – for that is my intention. I shall write again when I reach my destination, but for now please know that I remain

Your doting brother,
George

The Proposition of the Season

17th May 1825

Dearest Eliza,

Your last letter struck a chill into my heart, and all my prayers and thoughts are with you. Look to yourself at this time and know that I am right beside you, as always.

You should also know that he has discovered me in Rome, and I've only just managed to slip back to my lodgings alone. I fear I will not be able to do so forever, and I am so tired.

Promise me, Eliza, that should anything happen you shall not be emboldened to speak out, for our mother's sake, if not your own. And I entreat you, with the love of a brother who has cared for little else, to keep faith.

George

Chapter Nineteen

Josephine's Bedchamber; Books and Their Readers
Midnight

Josephine stared at the letters long after the last tinkling notes of the piano had died away and Knightswood fell quiet. It was the kind of blanketing quiet that always comforted her as a child, but tonight it only felt oppressive.

Again and again, she read the lines that could mean so many different things '... *He intends to know, one way or another, and so I have but one choice ... I can disappear – for that is my intention... Promise me, Eliza, that, should anything happen to me, you shall not be emboldened to speak out – for our mother's sake, if not your own...*'

Josephine drew a ragged breath. It seemed evidence, at last, that Pellham was innocent, and protecting Eliza, but why? And where did that leave Huntingly?

She looked from the yellowed sheets to her ball dress of Parisian silk hung on the front of her armoire, feeling as though every breath she took was a conscious effort, until she could bear it no longer. She had to confront him, betrothal or not.

Resolutely, Josephine climbed to her feet and reached for her robe, which was exactly the moment that a soft knock sounded at her door. She frowned and glanced at her window; the night was dark, and the moon higher than she'd thought: it had to be after one in the morning. Picking up her candle, she crossed the room to inch it open, expecting to find Matilda or one of her other sisters, but instead she found a very tall and distinctive silhouette.

'Sir Francis!' Josephine exclaimed in astonishment, her gaze travelling over his stockinged feet, pantaloons and open-necked shirt. 'Are you well?' She frowned. 'Do you require any assistance?' She thought briefly of Miss Amelia, and wondered if he'd come to enlist her support again.

'Assistance?' Sir Francis smiled enigmatically. 'How very thoughtful you are, Miss Fairfax, I was hoping you might say that.'

'Why, whatever do you mean?' Josephine frowned, suddenly conscious she was in her nightwear and he barely dressed at all. Her chest started to thump: she was no stranger to the games of gentlemen when they were in their cups, and there was a lingering scent of bourbon about his person. She'd witnessed her brothers wagering the most ridiculous challenges when so affected, but somehow this felt different.

'You see, I am in rather a quandary, Miss Fairfax... You are to marry Lord Huntingly, but I do not believe he knows what a prize he wins.'

'That, sir, is between myself and Lord Huntingly,' Josephine replied tersely. 'As are your private arrangements with Miss Amelia Carlisle, Miss Isabella Hampton and perhaps others too!' She took a deep breath. 'Now if you will excuse—'

'So, it would be wonderful if you could assist me to understand why, given all the books I have at my disposal, I cannot read the one I desire most.'

Then he leaned forward and brushed his moist lips over hers in a way that made Josephine recoil, her stomach churning. Lord Huntingly's passionate kiss beneath the trees at Ebcott flew through her mind yet, despite all her protestations, he'd never made her feel so violated. Her face darkened as she wondered why she'd ever put Sir Francis up on a pedestal. Matilda had been right the whole time: he really was a crowing peacock, and an entitled one at that.

'Keep your hands to yourself, sir!' she forced through gritted teeth. 'I have not given you leave to address me thus, and this conversation is at an end!'

Then she started to close the door, only to find its path blocked, and Sir Francis advancing into her bedchamber. Furiously, she snatched up her letter opener and brandished it at the smiling nobleman, who stood over six feet tall in his stockinged feet.

'Come come, Miss Josephine, there is no need to be melodramatic, or to play the schoolroom chit with me,' he crooned. 'We are both aware you are quite old enough to be married and widowed again. Who knows, you might be wishing the same once you've spent a month with that undeserving dog!' He smirked unattractively while Josephine swallowed a rise of nausea, wondering what she ever saw to admire in him.

'On the other hand, we have known each other for some time now,' he continued silkily, 'and I'm quite aware of your *admiration*. In truth, I must own to feeling a little the same way. We are a plane above most others in wit and charm, and what a pity it would be were we not to—'

'Enough, Dashton!' a low voice hissed from the doorway. 'Stand aside this instance or, so help me God, I'll make you!'

Shocked, Josephine's gaze swept from a confounded Sir Francis to a furious Lord Huntingly, also standing in the doorway of her bedchamber. Had he heard something from the gentlemen's wing?

'Huntingly!' Sir Francis sneered, whirling around. 'Did you follow me? Or were you lurking in the shadows – again?'

He laughed then, but to Josephine it sounded thin and nervous, despite his towering frame.

'How dare you!' Huntingly growled. 'Not content with insulting my betrothed, you now seek to disrespect me! You will meet me for this impudence. Now!'

To Josephine's further astonishment, Huntingly then produced a sword that he levelled directly at Dashton's chest. 'And believe me when I say I am not a patient man.'

'Oh now, do consider, Alistair,' Sir Francis wheedled, visibly paling. 'Think of the scandal… It's the Ball tomorrow, and we are both guests of Sir Fairfax, who would not thank us for a scene…'

'Thunder an' turf, Ed, look! A duel! A duel in Jo's bedchamber! Told you I heard something!'

Josephine gazed, in further disbelief, as both Henry and Edward appeared in her bedchamber doorway, looking suspiciously bright-eyed and dishevelled.

'Lay you a monkey Huntingly wins!' Henry said, crossing the bedchamber and establishing himself on her window seat with a happy sigh.

'Of course he'll win, he's the only one with a sword!' Edward admonished, joining him.

'Is he, by Jove? Well, that's easily fixed – here you are, Dashton, have mine!' Henry replied, withdrawing his sword from his robe and offering it in a most sportsman-like way.

'You brought a sword?' Edward whistled. 'Beneath your banyan?'

'Why, yes, of course.' Henry scowled. 'Don't tell me you didn't? I could have been facing a band of ruffians single-handedly! You're lucky it's only Huntingly looking fit to murder Dashton,' he added severely before turning back to the duellers. 'As you were, gentlemen, as you were. Please don't let my brother's lack of forethought affect your matter of honour,' he advised, before settling back down.

Josephine closed her eyes in pained denial, as Edward continued to watch with the look of one who'd come close to losing a ringside seat.

'No, this is very much *not* a duel,' Josephine forced through gritted teeth, just as Huntingly raised his sword in a salute.

'I said outside, but if you're too pigeon-livered, we'll sort it right here and now!' he seethed. 'You were a silver-tongued snake at Oxford, Dashton, and time has done you no favours at all. I ought to run my blade through your rumour-mongering throat this very second and be done with it,' he hissed as Sir Francis brought up his own shaky sword.

'Never have I ever been so insulted or rudely spoken to!' Sir Francis replied, his eyes bulging in a way that cast his

Olympian looks into sudden shade. 'I can think of nothing I would like to do more than give you a good dressing down!' he added. 'However, as we are in a lady's bedchamber…'

Yet whatever raft of social nicety he was about to cling to was lost as Lord Huntingly lunged, forcing Sir Francis to meet his sword with a pronounced gasp. Josephine sucked in a sharp breath at the clash of silver, amid her brothers' delighted calls of *'en garde!'*, *'plant him a facer!'* and *'pon rep, he displays to advantage!'*, while the duellers ignored them all.

It was clear from the outset that, despite his old injuries, Lord Huntingly was by far the finer swordsman. He broke through his opponent's wavering defence time after time, a faint smile creasing his lips, while Sir Francis's distinct lack of courage felt telling too. Then, after several very near misses that made Josephine consider throwing the contents of her flower vase over them both, Lord Huntingly executed a lightning thrust that glanced along Sir Francis's forearm, ripping the delicate lace of his sleeve and leaving a short red scratch. Instantly, Sir Francis turned the colour of porridge and swayed.

'Oh, *will* you desist!' Josephine hissed furiously. 'At no point have I asked for any determined attentions or noble defence! You are both mad! I have no desire for bloodshed, and even less for a betrothal, if it means subjecting myself to—'

'Francis … no…!' a new voice shrieked loudly enough to wake the rest of the household.

Josephine spun round in despair to spy Miss Amelia standing in the doorway of her bedchamber, her eyes as round as saucers, before she expelled a dramatic gasp and slunk to the floor.

The Proposition of the Season

'Unless you wish to join my post ... out of my way this instant!' Josephine growled, brandishing her letter opener and forcing the gentlemen to step aside.

'What the deuce is all the noise about?' a calmer voice complained as Josephine reached Miss Amelia's slumped body. 'Why is Miss Amelia on the floor? Oh, is it a party?' Fred added innocently, glancing around his sister's bedchamber. 'I say, Jo, you're a dark horse! Phoebe and Matty holding a private party, yes, but yourself or Sophie...'

'It is *not* a duel and most definitely *not* a party!' Josephine declared, making Fred wince. 'In fact, everyone is leaving this instant! Perhaps you can see them out?'

Unfortunately, at precisely the same moment, Fred happened to spy Sir Francis's scratched arm and let out a shriek to rival Miss Amelia's.

'I say, tone it down, Fred,' Henry admonished, rolling his eyes. 'No need to enact a Cheltenham tragedy just because you weren't invited. Can't be invited to everything. A man must invite who he wants to his own duels.'

At this, the drooping Edward nodded wisely, just as Matilda appeared in the doorway.

'Honestly, Fred!' Matilda yawned. 'Why are you shrieking like you're being forced to gallop, right outside my bedchamber door?' She peered curiously at the number of people in Josephine's bedchamber. 'Is it a party? Why is Amelia on the floor, and *why* is Sir Francis the colour of your nightgown?'

At this fresh intrusion, Josephine felt her last remaining shred of patience dissolve. 'Henry, Edward and Fred, kindly escort Sir Francis from my bedchamber this instant!' she ordered. 'Matilda, please tie up Dashton's scratch before we have a second fainting invalid, and Lord Huntingly, I would be grateful if you would help me to take Miss Amelia back to her bedchamber? She is recovered but would undoubtedly benefit from being in the comfort of her own bed.'

This time and to her intense relief, no one objected, and even when Henry wrung Lord Huntingly's hand and thanked him for the best fight he'd seen in a very long while, he didn't linger.

Finally, Josephine was left with Lord Huntingly and Miss Amelia, who was sitting bolt upright with a look of stark bewilderment glued to her face. It was only then that Josephine noticed she was dressed for a journey – and felt her low opinion of Sir Francis sink even further.

'Put your arm around my shoulder,' Josephine instructed, 'and Lord Huntingly will assist on your other side… That's it, and now let's find your bedchamber, shall we? I'm sure you'll feel perfectly well once you've had a rest…'

'But I was supposed to be…' Miss Amelia paused and bit her lip. 'I heard a noise and thought perhaps … Sir Francis had been fatally wounded,' she finished in a whisper.

'I would he had. He has taken up valuable space for far too long,' Lord Huntingly muttered, steering the wilting Miss Amelia down the corridor.

'Not at all!' Josephine reassured, throwing Lord Huntingly a dark look. 'Sir Francis scratched himself with my letter opener, and the gentlemen were merely jesting, as they will. Now,' she smiled kindly as they reached her bedchamber door, 'do rest, dearest, and I will convey your warmest wishes to Sir

Francis.' Then she closed the door firmly on Miss Amelia's dazed face.

'Congratulations, Miss Fairfax, impressively done,' Lord Huntingly murmured as they retraced their footsteps back to her own bedchamber door. 'I trust you are not too unsettled by your ordeal?' he added.

Josephine turned to look at him in the moonlight, reading every tiny muscle in his face.

'What did Eliza do?' she asked quietly.

The question had been haunting her since George's mention of regrets, and she could no longer ignore it any longer. Huntingly's face shrouded instantly, darkening with a pain she could almost feel.

He inhaled. 'Miss Fairfax, I came tonight,' he muttered, 'to give you this.' He reached into his pocket and withdrew a letter which he pressed into her hand. 'I cannot pretend to be rehearsed in matters of the heart,' he swallowed, 'but you were correct in much of what you said in the library, especially in your accusation of secrets.' He pressed her fingers again as she made to interrupt. 'I hope this letter goes some way to explain my caution, and that perhaps, one day, you will forgive me.' He paused as a shadow flickered across his face. 'And as for Eliza … she cared too much.'

Josephine waited until Lord Huntingly's footsteps had receded before making her way to the window seat, where the moonlight was still bright enough for her to read. Then, ignoring the thump of her heart, she unfolded his letter.

Dear Miss Fairfax,

You gave me much to think on tonight, and I hope this letter goes some way to answer some of your charges.

Firstly, I know I should begin by offering a sincere apology for my behaviour at Ebcott Place, but I cannot bring myself to regret it all and, in truth, I hope you do not either.

On that day, you also claimed that I abandoned the Davenports' social soiree and disappeared for a month. You are correct that I was angry, and for that I apologise, but please let me offer some explanation that will help explain my absence.

You are aware of the duel that prompted my decision to leave the country a few years ago, but not that it was the result of my father's death. My opponent was my best friend of many years standing, and that morning will always be the worst of my life. I will not go into the circumstances that led to my challenge, except to say they were ill-founded, as I discovered in Italy.

I will never forgive myself for his death, which was at his own hand and yet, I believe, my instigation. It is for this reason that I have been endeavouring to secure his inheritance on his mother, which should go some way to honouring my father's wish. In truth, Mrs Pellham has been my priority since Italy. She refused my direct assistance when I returned, so during my more recent absences, I have been attempting to find a distant cousin. Fortunately, I have now discovered him and he has secured a living on Mrs Pellham, which should take care of her needs for the rest of her life.

Lastly, at our meeting at Ebcott I asserted that 'if I had my way, I wouldn't marry at all'. Believe me when I say this is only because I would not inflict my history on anyone, given a choice.

Yet, the truth is you changed me at our very first meeting, and I have found myself feeling differently – selfishly perhaps – and of desiring a life that is lost. And still, I am increasingly mindful of your happiness and will not impose a union that is so clearly as unwanted as ours.

It is therefore with a heavy heart, but noble intention, that I release you from our engagement. I will seek an audience with Thomas first thing in the morning, and hope the knowledge that I will not pursue a Fairfax match <u>under any circumstance</u> will bring you some much deserved peace.

Above all, I wish you a future as bright and blessed as you deserve.

Your devoted servant always,
Alistair

Chapter Twenty

Josephine's Bedchamber; Duels and Broken Hearts
The small hours

Josephine read and reread the letter several times before finally crawling into bed. It had been such an exhausting evening, and all she could think was that she'd finally got what she wanted – a release from the engagement without threat to Matilda – and yet it felt far from right.

Lord Huntingly's letter had been entirely unexpected, and now it seemed that, while he had pursued Pellham abroad and witnessed his death, he'd also realised his friend was innocent of his father's death. And then there was the fact he'd been searching for a male relative to secure Pellham's inheritance and take care of his mother – the actions of an honourable gentleman, not a villain. Finally, there was his claim that he'd been desiring a lost life, which could mean so many things and was difficult to reconcile with the dark character she'd assumed.

Which left Eliza.

'And as for Eliza, she cared too much.'

His words whispered through her thoughts like petals catching the light from a dying sun. Were they the words of an enemy? A friend? *A lover* perhaps?

And why did the thought that he might yet harbour feelings for Pellham's sister fill her with such despair? Hadn't she wanted this?

Her questions tumbled endlessly until she fell into a restless sleep, dreaming of duels, secrets and broken hearts.

The following morning

'Lord, you should have seen Henry's and Edward's faces as I patched Dashton up,' Matilda chuckled, helping herself to an extra-large ladle of scrambled egg from the breakfast table. 'They were so disappointed he hadn't been fatally wounded! Can't say I blame them, though,' she added merrily. 'I've often wished I could run him through, myself!'

'Oh, Matty, hush!' Josephine warned, sipping her chocolate and taking comfort from its warmth. 'Someone will overhear you.'

Matilda looked up as Sophie, Lord Rotherby and their noisy young daughters entered the breakfast room.

'No matter! I lay you two ponies your party is all over Knightswood by now,' Matilda retorted, buttering a warm roll while eyeing up a pound cake brought in by a footman.

'What ponies? What party?' Louisa called, running to the

table and climbing on Josephine's lap as Phoebe and Viscount Damerel also entered the room, followed by Miss Amelia and the Davenports.

'Oh!' Amelia flushed immediately, busying herself with some chocolate.

'No ponies for me, thank you!' Sophie exclaimed, nodding at the footman with the pound cake. 'My plan is to sit very still until this evening, praying Mini Rotherby doesn't decide to put in an appearance! You don't look as though you've had a great deal of rest, Jo?' She frowned, declining her husband's proffered coffee with a look of stark revulsion.

'Just not awake,' Josephine dismissed, turning to her eldest niece. 'Have you brought an extra guest for breakfast, Harriet?'

'Oh no, not the grasshopper again,' Sophie groaned. 'Dominic, it's your turn!'

'Not a jot!' her husband protested, halfway through a pastry. 'You decided to bring our intrepid daughters to breakfast when they could have traumatised Alexander in the nursery, so I say their insect friends are welcome too.'

'I'll take her,' Josephine offered, keen to escape the chatter now it was getting busier.

She'd risen early, determined to waylay Lord Huntingly and thank him for his letter, but no-one had seen him yet. She swallowed, though her chest felt caught in a vice, telling herself he wouldn't have left before breakfast or saying goodbye. Yet, as she accompanied Harriet through the library and into the garden, she couldn't help but notice Thomas's study door was firmly closed.

'That's it, carry him over to the grass,' Josephine encouraged her small niece, who looked very reluctant to set her new friend free on Knightswood's vast rolling lawn. 'With a little luck, he'll still be here after luncheon.'

'Which is more than I can say for honoured guests!' Thomas interrupted caustically.

Startled, Josephine glanced back to spy her brother, standing just inside the garden door with an expression of thunder. She took Harriet by the hand and swallowed.

'Take the child back and return directly,' he growled. 'It seems we must talk.'

Josephine closed her eyes, wishing she was Harriet's grasshopper with all her heart.

'I actually thought you understood!' Thomas berated from behind his gleaming study desk. 'That you were different from the rest! I even reassured Damerel that you were *more* sensible than your sisters, that your sense of duty had prevailed you to proposition Lord Huntingly in the first place. Because that is what you did, Josephine, you *propositioned* him!'

He paused to let the full meaning of the word sink in, while his face put her in mind of the bulging-eyed fish in the Davenports' orangery.

'So to sit here this morning, and listen to Huntingly relate some *banbury tale* about your *feelings* and how he didn't believe it was fair to pursue the matter further makes me conclude one thing: you never intended to marry the fellow in the first place! I'm right, aren't I? It was all some … *ruse* you planned with Matilda! Do you know how much I've spent on this little event because of your prank?' he ranted. 'More than your yearly allowance! Have you any idea how hard it is to acquire that kind of money, let alone throw it away on something that has no worth!'

'It wasn't a ruse…' Josephine tried to protest.

'Don't even try to defend yourself! I've already heard whispers about some sort of inappropriate soiree on the ladies' corridor last night, and I am shocked, Josephine! Most certainly to hear that one or two *non-family* members were in attendance, too? Indeed, if I hadn't been assured it was swiftly dissipated, this would be an entirely different conversation!'

'It wasn't what you…'

'And what am I supposed to tell people now?' he continued to bellow. 'We have a hundred guests coming tonight, enough food to feed twice that number, and they will all know of your disgrace, of the tarnish to the Fairfax name, and all because you decided—'

'Enough!' Josephine yelled, jumping to her feet.

For a moment, it was quiet enough to hear the ticking of the library clock.

'I have spent twenty-two long years being told what to think and do!' she seethed, trying to catch her breath. 'All you consider is the Fairfax name and washing your hands of us as fast as you possibly can. But we are all different, Thomas! I no more want to climb trees than I want to design pelisses, or ride in a thunderstorm, and that does not make me more sensible than my sisters, it just makes me *me*!' She drew a ragged breath, aware her eldest brother was speechless for the first time in her life. 'And as for *inappropriate soirees*,' she scorned, 'please credit me with a little more intelligence than to arrange a party in my own bedchamber the night before a

Knightswood Grand Ball! There was a misunderstanding, but it was swiftly dealt with by Matilda and myself!'

Josephine swallowed and lowered her voice. 'And if Lord Huntingly has had the decency to break off what he considered was not fully desired, I believe that deserves respect, not an assumption of guilt!' she added icily. 'I am truly sorry you consider your family's worth in marriage contracts, Brother, but at least you have the assurance that I am unlikely to plague you so again. And I wouldn't worry about our guests, I am sure they will be comforted by news of Matilda's season, and the twelve trays of buttered crayfish!'

Josephine didn't wait for an answer: the incredulous look on Thomas's face was enough to know it would never be positive. Yet, as she left his study with her head pounding and her chest so tight she thought her heart might take flight, she also felt a lightness she'd never experienced before. She'd done the unthinkable: she'd told Thomas exactly what she thought!

'Are you all right, Jo?' Fred asked as she hurried back through the library gloom, trying to catch her breath. She glanced up to spy his quiet figure, just inside the door, a mixture of fear and concern on his face. 'Harriet said Uncle Thomas was being a *troll*, so I thought it best I check everything was in order?'

And for once, Josephine didn't try to hide her feelings or say the right thing but burst, quite unapologetically, into tears.

'It is ... unexpected.' Fred frowned, resting his head back against the oldest, gnarled tree in Knightswood Park.

Josephine cast a sidelong glance at her brother, their childhood haunt was an instant balm and yet she was conscious of treading carefully too. She'd not forgotten their conversation about Sir Francis, and could sense that revealing the truth about his friend's advances might hurt in a way she didn't fully understand. So, she focused on Huntingly's letter and departure instead.

'I mean, he was always a bit wild at Oxford, but with friends enough,' Fred mused. 'Even he and Francis had a friendship for a time,' he added with a wry smile, 'and went hunting and shooting at each other's places before we all lost touch. But a lot of the fellows did that, and I was the odd one out, really. I wasn't into that sort of thing.' He shrugged.

Josephine squeezed her brother's hand. It was no secret that Fred had a violent dislike for bloodshed of any kind, but he'd surprised her with the knowledge that Lord Huntingly and Sir Francis had ever been friends, even so many years ago.

'How odd,' she murmured. 'They seem so very unsuited.'

'They are, but I suppose we care less at that age.'

She closed her eyes, trying to recall all the occasions they'd crossed paths in her presence: the Davenports' soiree, the pre-Ball supper, their duel last night… She hadn't questioned their ready dislike because they seemed so different, but at Oxford they would have been younger, idealistic gentlemen with money and position. Perhaps it was naive to assume they couldn't have ever been friends - and yet last night had spiralled so quickly and venomously, it suggested something else entirely. The oddest sensation slid down her spine.

'Do you know why Huntingly and Dashton … *stopped* being friends, Fred?'

'Not sure I do.' Fred scrunched up his eyes against the sun. 'My last year was so busy with exams and rowing, and they seemed jolly enough then. I suppose they fell out of touch afterwards and grew apart.'

Josephine nodded, knowing he was most likely right, and yet growth apart wouldn't account for the intensity between them.

'He did seem devilish cavy this morning,' he mulled.

'Sir Francis?' she asked, wondering if he was regretting his behaviour now the cold light of day had arrived.

'No, Huntingly!' Fred frowned. 'I rose early and saw him go to Thomas's study and ask for an audience. He looked so grave, I asked him if it was the thought of tying himself up with you... Didn't realise then I was putting my great big Wellington boot in it!'

'Oh, Fred!' Josephine sighed, closing her eyes and picturing Lord Huntingly's dark eyes. She might not know why he and Pellham had duelled in the first place, but she did know he was haunted by his friend's death. And there was still the question of Eliza...

I have found myself feeling differently ... and of desiring a life that is lost.

'I think he might be harbouring a lost love, Fred,' she said wanly, finally saying the words she hadn't wanted to utter. She swallowed, not expecting the pain they brought either.

There was a brief silence when it was Fred's turn to squeeze Josephine's hand.

'I know that feeling,' he murmured. 'It's like a sickness, only worse, because there's no prospect of it getting any better. It lodges itself deep inside, and slowly erodes everything you ever believed because of the hopelessness of it all. Then sometimes you burn hard enough to cry, but only when the moon is watching, and you weep for the life you might have had.'

Josephine regarded her brother, feeling as though she was seeing him properly for the first time in her life.

'They might not deserve it, Fred,' she whispered, 'and that perfect fictional love might be a figment of our imagination.'

'It might be,' he replied, dropping his gaze. 'Or we tell ourselves the same, and accept being a spectator in our own lives... Though that doesn't really explain why Huntingly took flight, of course,' he continued in a gruffer tone, picking at the grass at his side. 'I thought he had more sense than to go getting all worrisome at this stage of the race. It's not like either of you ever claimed a love match, after all.'

'Pooh! Love matches are overrated anyway!' Matilda chimed as she rounded the gnarled tree and hoisted herself up into her old seat in the lowest bough. 'Far too much *beholdenness*, if you ask me, not that anyone does ever ask me. Anyway, Sophie said you're both to come back now because, betrothal or no betrothal, her Parisian silk is not going to waste!'

Josephine closed her eyes, unwilling to think about the Grand Ball that evening while knowing there was no way Thomas would excuse her attendance. As it was, it was highly unlikely he would ever forgive her outburst in his study, and any further breaches of propriety would probably be met with the most severe consequences. But Fred's recollections had started a chain of thoughts she couldn't ignore.

'Do you think Dashton knows more about Huntingly's duel than he shares?' she asked suddenly.

There was a startled laugh from Matilda, as Fred swung his gaze back to his sister. 'What on earth do you mean?'

Josephine drew a breath, knowing she was crossing a line, but also that she needed their help. 'Well, he and Huntingly detest one another, yet you mentioned they were friends back at Oxford... So, what if their dislike stems from more than natural growth apart? If there was a fall out, it would have had to occur just after you all left Oxford, a time period that also happened to feature Huntingly's infamous duel...'

Fred stared, as Matilda whistled.

'That's good, even for you, Jo!' she called admiringly from her tree perch. 'In truth, I've always thought him a pompous peacock, but a criminal? I don't think he could spare the time from his vanity mirror!'

Josephine couldn't help but laugh, despite everything.

'Have to say I'm with Matilda on this one,' Fred chuckled, rolling his eyes at his youngest sister. 'Dashton can be a little pompous and self-important, I know, but mixed up in a duel? He just hasn't got the right stuffing, if you know what I mean...'

Josephine understood and yet couldn't rid herself of the memory of Dashton's advance, either, when she'd seen an entirely different side to him.

'I cannot understand why, given all the books I have at my disposal, I cannot read the one I desire most.'

Her thoughts hardened.

'You do not know anyone until you have seen their whole library,' she mused darkly.

Chapter Twenty-One

Knightswood Manor; Sir Francis's Whole Library
Midday

It was the most hare-brained scheme she'd ever come up with, rivalling Phoebe for daring, Sophie for cheek and Matilda for downright devilry. Yet as Josephine dashed off the note, she felt more purposeful than she had in a long while. And Sir Francis's response, despite a report of a headache that required he kept to his bedchamber, was swift.

Dear Miss Fairfax,

I must admit to some surprise when your solicitous note arrived. I had rather assumed Huntingly's misunderstanding, and interference, would lead you to draw the wrong conclusion about our last meeting.

I am most reassured this is not the case, and accept your invitation to a companiable walk in the spirit it is extended.

Until 3 o'clock at the folly,

Yours,
Francis

Josephine stared at Sir Francis's loopy, self-important handwriting wondering how she ever thought him admirable. She had no doubt he'd encouraged both Isabella Hampton and Amelia Carlisle to believe they were special, perhaps even her brother too, yet his pompous response only emphasised the fact that he had no conscience whatsoever. Her lips curled. Well, he had better have a care about which books he *desired most to read*, because some were not predictable at all. And, if her suspicions were correct, she might be able to clear Huntingly's name once and for all, which would go some way to appeasing her own conscience too. As well as something else she didn't quite understand.

At precisely ten minutes to the hour, Josephine hurried along the front lawn, towards the shrubbery that concealed the way to the folly. The old colonnade temple had been a present from Papa to Mama, Thomas said, though in truth it had been built a long time before any of them were born. Today, its path was bathed in dappled sunshine and bordered by a haze of sky-blue hyacinths, wild roses and blushing peonies, but Josephine paid them little heed as she made her way along. The folly had always been one of her favourite reading spots, yet reading couldn't have been further from her mind.

'Good afternoon, Sir Francis,' she called as soon as she spied him loitering just inside one of the stone pillars. 'I am so very grateful you have come.'

A thin smile reached across Sir Francis's golden face as he stepped out from the folly and executed a low, flourishing bow.

'But of course, Miss Fairfax!' he replied, with a flick of his flaxen hair. 'It felt the very least I could do after that ruffian interrupted our tête-à-tête last night! Truly, I am relieved he had the good sense to depart,' he added, his duplicitous eyes alight with a gleam she was starting to recognise. 'It would have been most awkward had he chosen to remain, I would have been forced to settle the insult with my own sword, which isn't so badly weighted as your brother's, I can assure you!'

'Oh indeed, I believe you showed great sportsmanship, given the circumstances, Sir Francis,' Josephine flattered, safe in the knowledge both Fred and Matilda were in place by now.

'In fact, I'd go so far as to say I was much awed by your courage and your ... conviction! You have opened my eyes to truly honour, and I too was quite reassured by the news that Lord Huntingly left this morning. I'm only sorry that I have not seen this clearly before.' She fluttered her eyelashes, trying not to give in to a rise of laughter. 'Oh! Does your injury still pain you?' she added in her next breath, channelling Miss Amelia's pout.

'This?' Sir Francis replied, shrugging his arm out of Matilda's homemade sling. 'It would trouble most, but your company and perceptive wit have soothed it beyond the reach of any balm or compress. Allow me, Miss Fairfax?'

Then he proffered his arm in such a way that Josephine knew her plan was working. He believed they were on the best of terms again.

'I have to say, Miss Fairfax, you truly are a breath of fresh air!' he went on. 'I pride myself on knowing the female mind rather well, and while I've always known you're not one of the *silly, fanciful* types, your presence of mind and logic are quite inspiring. In short, Josephine – I may call you Josephine, mightn't I? – I believe you may ruin my perception of the fragile sex forever!'

His flattering tone had slunk lower and softer as they walked further from the main house, and Josephine had to steel herself not to wrench her arm out of his. Never had she been more aware of the cunning nature of his words, flattering her so she might be distracted from his predatory nature altogether. She'd no doubt he'd used such tactics on both Isabella Hampton and Amelia Carlisle, while his audacity at using her given name when he'd insulted her no less than a day ago made her boil with rage on behalf of them all. Yet it was a sweet smile she turned upwards, knowing she had the part of her life to play if she was ever to know the full truth.

'You are so worldly wise,' she sighed, suppressing an image of Matilda's vomit face. 'I feel as though you are the only gentleman who has ever truly seen me. And please do call me Josephine...' She glanced up coquettishly, wishing Phoebe could witness her epic performance. 'I reserve it for quite my *best* friends.'

He smiled his blinding smile then, the one Josephine had watched him use on so many others with clear success, yet it only fuelled her fire. She burned to wipe it off his face with a few choice words, to put him wholly in his place, but she forced herself to smile instead.

'As I adore the sound of my name on your lips, Josephine,' he whispered, leaning closer.

A wave of nausea threatened, but they were so close to her destination she gritted her teeth and sighed wistfully instead.

'It is such a warm day to be enjoying each other's company, don't you think? I wish I'd known this afternoon was going to be so delightful, I would have brought a parasol and perhaps even a bathing gown for the lake!' She trilled off into laughter that sounded very fake, and hoped Sir Francis was too far wrapped up in his own growing expectations to notice.

'Bathing gown?' he mused suggestively. 'Why you ladies burden yourselves with such layers I will never know, especially within the privacy of your own grounds.'

'Oh truly, Sir Francis, you will make me blush!' Josephine replied with her finest attempt at an arch smile. 'We *may* have broken the rules a few times in the past, but only in truly *trusted* family company.'

They rounded the curve in the trail then to emerge on the side of Knightswood's large lake, which glistened quietly in the summer sun. It was one of Josephine's favourite spots, not because of boisterous swimming fun with her sisters and brothers, but because of her many happy hours as lookout bookworm in case any family members ventured this far. She swept her gaze around and was reassured by a flash of colour halfway down the trail, which gave her the comfort she needed. Fred and Matilda were in place, which meant she could continue.

'I hope I am starting to feel like a "truly trusted" family friend, Josephine,' he replied, turning and catching hold of her hands. 'It is really *quite* important to me.' He lingered over his words before lifting one of her clenched hands to his lips. 'It was what I was trying to say last night – rather clumsily, I fear, for true matters of the heart are always the hardest to articulate, are they not?' Then he trailed a fingertip down her cheek in a way that made her want to push him straight into the lake.

'Oh, Francis!' she gurgled instead, feeling sure Matilda would have a fit of hysterics if she could hear her. 'I have never met anyone like you. You make me want to throw all caution to the wind! How I wish we had our bathing suits. I vow it would be the finest way to celebrate our friendship on this glorious summer's day!' Then she sighed again as Sir Francis's eyes gleamed in a way that made her shudder. She steeled herself: just a little longer.

'Well, we *could* take one *tiny* little swim?' he whispered. 'No one need know, and it would be such a wonderful way to celebrate our friendship, as you say. It could also be a sign of the trust we place in one another, a trust that could grow into something much more special...'

'Oh!' She feigned a gasp at the suggestion. 'But how could we possibly do so, when we don't have so much as a bathing suit between us?'

His eyes gleamed again, and for the first time Josephine noticed how closely set they were.

'You are wearing your petticoats, are you not?' he murmured, standing so close his cologne overpowered the nearby wild jasmine. For some reason, this irritated her more than anything, but she mustered all her self-control. 'I could wade into the water before you?' he added. 'And turn away when you come in?' His fingers reached to play with hers in a way that turned her stomach. 'Of course, I give you my word you will be *quite* safe.'

'Oh, Francis, I do declare you are far too wild for me, and yet my heart is aglow with the idea!' she replied, rattling off a line from one of the worst novels she'd ever read. 'I will undress behind the willow tree over there, while you do the same behind that oak, and when you are in the water, call me?'

At this, Josephine thought Sir Francis's eyes might pop out of his head, but she continued to smile and dimple becomingly, as he caught her fingers to his lips.

'Your word is my command, Josephine,' he breathed heavily, 'and neither of us will ever forget this day of … friendship.' Then, tugging at his silk cravat, he backed away towards his appointed tree, looking as though all the gods had smiled on him at once.

Fluttering her eyelids as though her life depended on it, Josephine made her way behind the willow, where she pressed back against the gnarled bark, her heart thumping fit to leap out of her chest altogether. Yet this was the moment it had all been about. Craning her neck, she glimpsed another flash of colour further down the lakeside – Fred and Matilda were on the move.

She swallowed, never more aware of the outrageousness of her plan, and never more committed either. Then there was the sound of a faint splash.

'Are you ready, Francis?' she called, suppressing a smile at the thought of Matilda's grimace now she was within listening distance.

'I am, my love,' he cooed, 'and already in the water. It is as refreshing as we imagined, and time for you to join me.'

She drew a deep breath before rounding the tree and looking out at the cool rippling water, where a very naked Olympian gazed back.

'But soft! What light through yonder window breaks? It is the east, and Juliet is the sun—' He broke off. 'Yet my sun is still clothed?' he quizzed playfully.

'Your sun is a little shy!' Josephine called 'But she will join you, if you turn like you promised?'

Within seconds, Sir Francis had spun in the water, giving Josephine a clear view of his golden back. It was a sight that might have mesmerised her once, but now it only made her roll her eyes. Turning, she made her way to Sir Francis's tree, behind which she found a neat stack of clothing, together with a dancing-eyed Fred and Matilda. With a swift smile at her siblings, she scooped up the clothing, and re-emerged lakeside with a far cooler air.

'You may turn, Sir Francis!' she called with a reversion to her previous formality.

Then he turned with a smug smile that faded as he realised his sun was still clothed.

'I don't understand.' He smiled again, though with less certainty as he spied his clothing in her arms. 'Have you changed your mind, my love? Do you wish me to come out and help you, perhaps?' he added flirtatiously.

'Not at all,' Josephine returned flatly. 'But you *can* help me, Sir Francis, beginning with telling me *exactly* how you knew Eliza Pellham.'

At this utterance, his expression changed completely.

'Eliza Pellham?' he repeated, and for the briefest of moments it seemed as though her name was whispered on the breeze. 'Never heard of her!' he declared with his next breath, though his smile had disappeared and he looked a little pale around the mouth. 'Listen, why don't you join me for a bathe, and we can talk afterwards?' he wheedled. 'This was *your* plan, remember?'

'It was,' Josephine conceded, her lip curling, 'and it has worked beautifully. So, if you wish to leave the lake and regain your clothing with any degree of self-respect, I suggest you start by telling me how you knew Eliza.'

'I told you, I don't know the name!' he snapped. 'And you forget we are quite alone, Josephine. I can leave this lake whenever I—'

At this precise moment, Matilda stepped out, halting Sir Francis mid-flow. Josephine passed her his neat stack of clothing, before she left with a cheeky wave.

'Hey!' Sir Francis roared. 'Bring back my clothing! It's my property!'

'It is,' Josephine agreed, 'and, quite aside from the theft of your clothing, Knightswood Lake is notoriously cold, so unless you wish to suffer with severe chills later, I suggest you listen carefully. You are going to tell me exactly what you know about Eliza Pellham, the death of Lord Huntingly's father and the subsequent duel, and, *if* you satisfy my questions, I will permit you to leave the lake and tell you where Matilda has hidden your clothing. However, if you don't, I shall tell Sir Thomas that you brought me here, removed your clothing and tried to entice me to do the same. Do you understand?'

At this, Sir Francis emitted a noise which sounded something like a cross between a cackle and a charging bull elephant.

'And who's to stop me leaving now?' he repeated scornfully. 'Your sister was hardly a threat and don't be fooled into thinking I have any consideration left for your so-called innocence—'

'I will,' Fred replied seriously, emerging from the trees. 'So I suggest you co-operate, and swiftly too, for Josephine was not jesting about the cold. I also believe my eldest brother would be extremely interested to know about your behaviour towards his sister, given the circumstances. It's not looking good, Francis.'

'B ... but Alfred!' Sir Francis appealed. 'Do consider that a swim was your sister's idea. She brought me here!'

At this, Fred tipped his head back in unbridled laughter. 'Try telling anyone that!' he jeered in a tone Josephine barely recognised. 'Jo never learned to swim! Now answer her questions or I'll wade out there and choke the answers out of you myself, so help me God!'

Sir Francis's face contracted in visible shock, while Josephine felt she'd never been prouder. Then there was a moment's silence where he opened and closed his mouth repeatedly, putting her in mind of the actual fish in the lake, before he finally forced out some words.

'I met Eliza ... once or twice,' he muttered with effort. 'Huntingly knew her. Her father was his steward, or something. She was ... not like us. That's all I know, now kindly return my clothes, please.'

'But that's *not* all you know, is it?' Josephine challenged, finally airing the suspicions that had been fermenting since Fred mentioned Sir Francis's friendship with Huntingly. 'You built a friendship with Eliza, didn't you...? In fact, something more than a friendship?'

Sir Francis's expression darkened, and Josephine knew she'd touched a nerve.

'So, what if I did?' he threw sullenly. 'She was different ... wild ... always in the wood ... met her there a couple times.' He shrugged. 'There's no law against it, is there?'

'No, but there *is* a law against murder,' Josephine replied coldly.

At this, Sir Francis baulked, before laughing in a distinctly unconvincing way. 'I most certainly did not murder Eliza Pellham,' he muttered scathingly. 'The typhoid did that. You really should read fewer novels, Miss Fairfax.'

'I'm not speaking of Eliza,' Josephine replied unflinchingly, never taking her eyes off Dashton. 'I'm referring to old Lord Huntingly – Alistair's father.'

Fred took a sharp breath while Sir Francis fell silent, his eyes narrowing to shards.

'Clever Miss Fairfax,' he replied softly, making Fred curse before Josephine shot out a steadying hand. 'I always said you had all the Fairfax brains. No, I did not kill Lord Huntingly ... Eliza did.'

His accusation seemed to ripple across the lake and whisper into the rustling trees, before he started to move forward. 'You wanted to know the truth, and now you do, so...'

'Wait right there, Dashton!' Fred challenged with a heavy scowl. 'It's very convenient to blame someone who can't defend themselves. What do you mean, Eliza killed Lord Huntingly?'

Dashton considered his friend carefully, before drawing a deep breath. 'Exactly what I said.' He shrugged coldly. 'She ran out into his path, his horse reared, the rest you know.'

'Except the reason she was running was you!' Josephine accused, knowing he'd subjected Eliza to the same attentions he'd tried to foist upon herself.

Sir Francis scowled. 'She was wild, I tell you! Spent days and nights in the woods… She ran from everything and everyone.'

'You mean you scared her with your *attentions*, and then you let George Pellham cover for his sister.' Josephine enunciated slowly, never more certain of Sir Francis's guilt. 'Huntingly then discovered the gift to Pellham in his father's will, and assumed the worst… You let them duel, knowing neither was responsible! Which leads me to wonder about Huntingly's pistol *accidentally* backfiring too.'

'Well, that *was* Eliza, if you must know!' Sir Francis blustered. 'She was odd, a wild cat. Never cared for anyone but her brother – tampered with Huntingly's pistol so it backfired.'

Josephine stared as the final piece of the puzzle slotted into place. 'So, Eliza tried to protect her brother … in a duel that would never have taken place if old Lord Huntingly hadn't tragically died … because she was running from you,' she concluded, feeling Fred's open-mouthed admiration.

'What … no! You can't blame me for everything!' Sir Francis objected furiously. 'It wasn't my fault! She seemed interested, and then she changed her mind. I didn't do anything!'

'On the contrary, Sir Francis,' Josephine countered, feeling as though a great weight had finally shifted. 'You started it all.'

Chapter Twenty-Two

The Knightswood Grand Ball; Heroes and Heroines
Several hours later

'Well, there's your gothic novel idea, anyway!' Matilda exclaimed, throwing herself back on Josephine's bed. 'I mean, who needs misted graveyards and poets when you have Knightswood Lake and Josephine Fairfax!'

'Mary Shelley might disagree. And Lord Huntingly isn't a bridegroom any more, Matty,' Josephine replied, fastening the buttons on the sleeves of her Parisian silk ballgown.

She tried to ignore the stab of pain every time she recalled that Huntingly had left Knightswood believing her wholly indifferent and his reputation damaged forever, when both were so far from the truth.

Matilda rolled over to eye her older sister. 'That's *his* loss,' she murmured loyally. 'That French silk is perfect on you, by the way. You know I don't set stock by such matters but I don't think I've ever seen you look so beautiful. Sophie was right!'

'I am always right about fabric and birth dates.' Sophie sighed from the doorway. 'I told the midwife she was wrong about Mini Rotherby arriving this weekend, and guess what happened? Absolutely nothing! I've unbuttoned my stays, relinquished all my corsets and given up on anything but muslin, and yet, here I am, a human post-chaise and four!' she concluded mournfully.

'You couldn't look less like a post-chaise and four, dearest,' Josephine reassured affectionately. 'A rose in bloom, if anything! But shouldn't you be lying down? Or lying in? Or at least resting?' she added in concern. 'You haven't long to go now.'

'Pah! I did that for the first two, and much good it did, I was just bored!' Sophie huffed. 'I might be with child, but that doesn't mean I'm an invalid! Far better to keep to the same old routine I say, and at least I've sisters to live through in the meantime. By the way, Matty isn't wrong: I knew Madame Montmartre's silk would complement your complexion – you look positively ravishing tonight! Just a little rouge, I think, and we'll have every gentleman fighting for your hand, never mind old Lord-no-parties-or-honeymoon-grumpy-face!'

Matilda let out a peal of laughter that brought Phoebe to the door, while Josephine realised her hope of a few quiet moments before the Ball started was looking increasingly unlikely.

'He had his reasons,' she reminded her sisters, quietly buoyed by Matilda's lack of concern for Huntingly's departure. Perhaps she'd allowed herself to worry too much, after all.

'Who had reasons?' Phoebe smiled, settling into Josephine's window seat in a fetching new gown of violet taffeta.

'Lord Huntingly,' Matilda replied, when she'd recovered sufficiently. 'Lots of them! How much do you think he knows, anyway?' she added, watching Sophie apply rouge to Josephine with practised ease. 'About George covering for Eliza, and Sir Francis's involvement, I mean?'

Josephine waited for Sophie to finish and start inflicting the same torture on Matilda, before answering. She'd spent the hours since her return from Knightswood Lake sharing the whole story with her sisters, who'd been shocked and furious in equal measure.

'I believe George Pellham may have said something in Italy that implicated Sir Francis in it all, but without evidence' she replied. 'It would explain why he and Sir Francis could never meet without feuding. It must haunt him…'

She trailed off as Lord Huntingly's dark eyes and scars surfaced amid her thoughts. He'd lost a father, two best friends and his reputation before she even arrived and started treating him like a criminal.

'It is quite clear, sir, that you keep many secrets… It is your choice, of course, except they mask a truth that could free others from heartache … and I might guess at your need to travel when you keep such old friends abroad…'

She swallowed, recalling her whirling accusations that had prompted his departure – they must have felt like salt in an open wound. Had he considered telling her his suspicions then? He must have been sorely tempted, given Sir Francis's continued stay at Knightswood. Perhaps she would never know – and yet she was determined to clear his name now. What was the worth of her sisters moving within the best circles of the *haute* ton, if she could not ask them to spread a few well-placed truths, after all?

'You could write to him, dearest,' Phoebe suggested, 'to let him know Sir Francis has confessed his part? I'm sure he would appreciate the truth from your hand, though I wish Sir Francis all the luck in the world once Lord Huntingly knows.'

They all chorused their agreement, before Matilda grinned, and then chuckled, and then finally rolled onto her back to give in to her mirth with large body-wracking gasps.

'I wish … you … could have all seen him,' she gasped. 'Naked in the lake … with Jo quizzing him … like he was facing … a justice of the peace!'

At this, they all began to give in to her infectious laughter, until even Josephine was holding her sides with tears running down her cheeks.

'And then … Fred … muscled up … like he'd read one too many hero novels too!' Matilda howled.

'Oh dear, darling Fred!' Phoebe exclaimed, mopping her eyes.

'What on earth happened to Sir Francis, anyway?' Sophie gurgled, grabbing Josephine's dress hook to undo the back of her ballgown and sigh with relief. 'Where did you hide his clothes?'

'Oh, Lord, that was the absolute best part. They were right where he left them all along!' Matilda snorted. 'I simply placed them back and listened to Jo give him the most wonderful grilling. Don't think I've never heard her quite so brilliant, or Sir Francis so furious. I will never forget it!'

'Oh, Matty,' Josephine murmured, quite pink by this point,

'you know it was Fred, really. He mentioned their friendship and then it all started to slot together.'

'Pooh! You're sharp, Josephine Fairfax, and don't you forget it! Anyway, we suggested he look for his clothing in the vicinity after we left, but instead he ran straight into Amelia and Charlotte who were both so shocked, they needed their smelling salts and a lie down!' She groaned and started to laugh again. 'So, I'm not sure if he found them, or if he's still naked and running around in the shrubbery – though he'll have left by the quietest exit, if he has any sense.'

'I still can't quite believe it,' Phoebe chuckled, shaking her head. 'He seemed so very proper in every way.'

'Too proper!' Sophie replied, wrinkling her nose. 'Everyone knows fictional heroes *do not* exist in real life. The most any of us can do is find a gentleman who tries to behave heroically for our benefit.'

'Are you speaking of Rotherby?' Phoebe smiled. 'He does seem suited to aspiring hero status.'

'Well, I do not see why we cannot be our own heroes and be done with it!' Matilda exclaimed, rolling her eyes. 'All this talk of wanting gentlemen to adopt fictional hero behaviour for our benefit makes me want to vomit!'

They all started to laugh again, while Josephine thought of Fitzwilliam and flushed: she'd so yearned for a fictional hero she'd written to one every day. Should she have had more contentment within herself, like Matilda? She closed her eyes and Huntingly's haunted eyes swam before hers, tightening her chest and stealing her breath until her senses swam.

'Lastly, at our meeting at Ebcott, I asserted that "if I had my way, I wouldn't marry at all!"… Yet, the truth is you changed me at our

very first meeting, and I have found myself feeling differently – selfishly, perhaps – and of desiring a life that is lost. And still, I am increasingly mindful of your happiness and will not impose a union that is so clearly unwanted as ours.'

It seemed he wasn't referring to Eliza after all, yet what did it matter that she had *changed* him, when she was certain he had stolen her heart entirely? She swallowed, watching her sisters laugh together in the reflection of her mirror. And how could she expect any of them to understand? She herself had called the match a practical arrangement and made no secret of her admiration for Dashton. She'd worn her indifference for Huntingly too well, so why would any of them understand that she *had* found a real-life fictional hero? That he'd been hiding in plain sight?

Except now he was gone.

She caught her breath silently, the thought of never seeing Lord Huntingly again too painful to contemplate. Swiftly, she stole a glimpse at Matilda, her burnished hair already escaping, and a flicker of warmth stole through her limbs. She knew what she had to do. Just because she was the author of her own downfall didn't mean Matilda couldn't hope for happiness. She might not be betrothed, but she was still a sister, and above all, she was a Fairfax.

She stood up and turned to face her sisters. 'I think it's high time we all made an appearance.'

It seemed Thomas's claims really did had some foundation, for Knightswood shone like a jewel tonight. Gone were the threadbare carpets, dusty silverware and homely scent of Cook's shortbread; and in their stead was a sparkling Knightswood that Josephine had only ever glimpsed through family stories. The floors gleamed with polish, the silverware flickered in the candlelight and the scent of roasted joints, exotic sauces and rich, sophisticated puddings reached into every corner and crevice. Matilda sniffed the air hungrily, as they paused on the grand staircase landing to watch the mingling crowds below.

'Well, Thomas wanted a crush,' Phoebe observed.

'Told him gilt-edged envelopes never fail,' Sophie mused. 'I used them for all my invitations until Lady Hampton started doing *exactly* the same! Of course, I stopped immediately,' she added, her eyes narrowing.

'Lord, what a cheek!' Matilda chuckled. 'I wonder you didn't urge Dominic to call the General out!'

'Oh, just you wait, Matilda Fairfax.' Sophie grinned. 'You have all this to come, and how I shall laugh then!'

'Wager you my fringed parasol I don't worry about it then, either!' Matilda smirked.

Phoebe and Josephine groaned.

'Done!' Sophie nodded with a gleam. 'And, now my dearest sisters, I shall depart before my distinctly unheroic husband discovers I have not been resting at all! Enjoy yourselves … and have a waltz for me, all of you?' she added wistfully, before gathering her skirts and disappearing back upstairs.

'Poor Sophie,' Josephine sighed. 'She does so love a ball.'

'She does.' Phoebe smiled. 'But she should rest while she can. Birthing an infant is not easy, no matter what she says.

Now, it must be nearly announcement time so I'll go and find Thomas. You two wait here and try to be prepared, I doubt he'll wait too long…'

Josephine nodded and watched their eldest sister part the crowds with her authoritative stride, before turning back to Matilda.

'Good luck tonight, Matty.' She squeezed her sister's gloved hands. 'It's *your* night now and, truly, you deserve it. I will be right here until the announcement is over, and then I'll find you, I promise.'

'I would you were still sharing this night, Jo,' Matilda replied in a small voice. 'We've always done things together, and I can't help but think that soon enough we'll change, just like Phoebe and Sophie.'

'And become old ladies?' Josephine teased softly.

'No … become part of a new family,' Matilda replied.

Josephine gazed for a moment, before embracing her sister tightly, knowing at last that this was the reason Matilda had seemed particularly fiery around Lord Huntingly. She'd never mourned a husband: she'd been mourning her sister.

'Well, I'm not going anywhere,' Josephine reassured, though her heart ached. There was little doubt Matilda would marry and leave Knightswood, while she remained alone, a Fairfax spinster until her dying day. It was she who would be left behind in the end.

'Ladies and gentlemen!' Benson bellowed in a statesman-like tone from the bottom of the stairwell. Instantly, the crowd fell into a respectful hush. 'Sir Thomas Fairfax!'

A trickle of applause spread through the crowd as Thomas

The Proposition of the Season

made his way through the crowd and onto the bottom step, before turning and smiling congenially.

'Esteemed guests,' he began in the tone he reserved for non-family members, 'what a pleasure it is to watch Knightswood Manor come to life tonight, and for such a special occasion too. Those of you who have known the Fairfax family for longer than you care to admit—' he paused to acknowledge a tinkle of laughter '—will recall we *always* hosted the biggest and brightest Ball at the end of the season! Well, I am delighted to reinstate that tradition this year in honour of one very particular young lady: a Fairfax who knows her own mind, never fails to inspire me and I am proud to call my sister. Ladies and gentlemen, may I present to you…'

'Miss Josephine Fairfax!'

A ripple of gasps reached through the crowd as the crisp utterance rang out from the shadows inside the main doors. There was a hushed pause and then, slowly, the swathes of guests parted to let a lone figure through. He was tall, with wild and tousled hair and a riding cape streaked with mud as though he'd just jumped down from his horse. Yet, to Josephine, he was the only gentleman in the room.

Speechlessly, she watched him make his way through the crowd towards her brother at the bottom of the stairwell, where he executed a short bow.

'My apologies for the interruption, Sir Fairfax, but, as your friends and family are already aware, I am known to be rather impetuous.' He turned to look back at the crowd, who chuckled uncertainly. 'In truth, I have never concerned myself too greatly with the opinion of the ton,' he continued. 'My father taught me long ago that idle tongues will always make mischief and the only control we have is our response.' He paused as the crowd muttered, before continuing. 'So, I ignored the whispers about my past and remained silent, because of my grief, because of my scars … and because of my guilt.' At this, a fresh mutter reached through the guests, many of whom were looking increasingly suspicious. 'But, in recent months, I have become acquainted with someone who was willing to look past it all for entirely selfless reasons… And when I gave her even further reason to suspect the worst, she didn't run, she looked for the truth – with more courage than I've seen in a very long time.'

Josephine caught her breath, barely aware as Matilda pulled her towards the balustrade, prompting those nearest to glance up, including Lord Huntingly. His face softened instantly while his amber flares burned, and in that moment, Josephine felt as though they exchanged a thousand words.

Before he turned to Thomas with renewed purpose. 'That willingness was one of the truest acts of selflessness I've ever known, but you see, we are talking of Miss Fairfax…'

Thomas cleared his throat noisily as though he might reclaim the floor, but Huntingly only held up his hand while Josephine watched as though caught in some intoxicated fever dream that took the world and inverted it, until it became a fictional version of itself.

'Miss *Josephine* Fairfax,' he clarified, turning back to smile in a way that made Matilda squeeze her sister's hand all the harder. 'Yet, despite my deepest … respect and admiration, I've realised that, in allowing such a sacrifice, the whispers would claim someone new … someone who possesses one of the truest minds, keenest wits and kindest hearts I've ever known, someone I ... care about immensely – and I cannot allow that.' He paused as a fresh mutter of understanding rippled through the crowd. 'You see, the truth is I cannot tell you when I began to love Miss Fairfax, only that I refuse to hurt her, now or ever.'

Josephine felt the hall begin to spin as Huntingly gazed up with an expression that took her back to the wooded trail at Ebcott in a heartbeat.

'Which is why I have returned tonight, not with hope or expectation that my hand will ever be enough, but rather to say that among us there is a rare and modest jewel who deserves this celebration more than any other. She has won my heart.' He paused as the crowd murmured again. 'And, while I might not yet have her hand, I will spend every minute of every day of the rest of my life endeavouring to deserve it.'

Then, tearing his gaze away, he nodded at an open-mouthed Thomas before making his way back through the crowd.

'Jo ... Jo ... breathe ... Jo!' Matilda hissed as the main doors opened and Lord Huntingly exited. There was a moment's silence when the air seemed to still, and then Matilda's glare finally stirred Josephine from her frozen state. Picking up her skirts, she bolted down the staircase, past Thomas, through the stunned crowd, and out of the main doors into the cool night air.

'Lord Huntingly has just left, Miss Josephine,' Benson offered as though a declaration of undying love was a most regular occurrence at a Grand Knightswood Ball. 'He had a horse waiting.'

Josephine nodded as she gazed down the pathway, fighting

to steady her whirling thoughts and conscious some of the crowd had spilled out behind her. She'd only ever dreamed of such a protestation and had no idea how to think normally, let alone return to the evening. She swallowed, her chest burning and her thoughts scattered, but her feelings never so clear. Yet he'd already slipped away into the darkness without her.

'Oh no you don't!' called a familiar voice through the gloom.

Startled, she glanced up to see Matilda astride a horse she'd loosened from one of the waiting carriages and extending her arm. 'You don't get to cry, Jo, not tonight, not on my watch. Come on!'

Without hesitation, Josephine gripped her younger sister's outstretched hand and swung herself up behind. There was no saddle, but the horse felt steady and Matilda appeared to have breeches on beneath her ballgown.

'I was planning on my own dawn steeplechase anyway!' she grinned as a shout went up from the doorway. It was Thomas, and by his tone it sounded as though the shock of Lord Huntingly's proclamation was beginning to wane.

'Won't be long!' Matilda called cheerfully, seemingly delighted by the turn of events. Then she guided the horse around and set off into the darkness.

If there was anyone who knew Knightswood blindfolded, it was Matilda, yet Josephine hardly dared breathe as they navigated the rolling lawns and shrubbery by moonlight. She leaned closer to her sister, listening to the shallow thump of her heart, until they emerged near Knightswood Lodge. Then, finally, she exhaled a long shuddering breath for there was a lone figure just ahead, passing through the estate gate. And whether it was the sound of another rider, or simply the velvet beauty of the night, he glanced back.

'Thank you, Matty,' Josephine whispered as she slipped down, never more aware of the scent of the moor.

He dismounted in a heartbeat, and suddenly nothing was as important as reaching him, as telling him he'd won her heart and soul, that to her he was the most noble of gentlemen. But as he strode to meet her, his eyes afire with the last of the titian sun, there was no time for words before he caught her to him and kissed her with a fever that stole the world away.

'I thought I was a monster to you,' he whispered, when they finally drew breath, 'that you no longer wished to marry me.'

'There is nothing I want more!' Josephine breathed, the tightness in her chest suddenly easing. 'I was wrong about everything ... about George ... Eliza... Sir Francis, most certainly. I know he started everything.'

'You know?' Huntingly swallowed, his eyes never leaving hers. 'Then you must tell me how? In Italy, George only said that Dashton caused my father's accident, that he himself had tried to protect his sister, which sounded so very ... George, but he didn't say how, and I had no way of proving anything. And then, when I learned he'd ... died in some street brawl... I felt I'd run a sword through him myself...' He ran his fingers through his wild locks, the extent of his inner scars clearer than they'd ever been.

Her heart burned protectively. 'Sir Francis terrified Eliza, she ran out into the path of your father's horse and ... you know the rest,' she whispered gently. 'Then George heard Eliza had died from the typhoid and, I believe, lost the will to live.

His own mother said they were extraordinarily close…' He nodded, swallowing. 'But from what I've learned of his nature, he would not wish you to suffer for something Dashton started… And that's where a few Fairfaxes can help,' she added in a steelier tone. 'In fact, they're already hard at work.'

'A whole pack of Fairfaxes?' Huntingly whispered in wonder. 'What chance does anyone stand against such a force? You are truly unique, Josephine Fairfax,' he said softly, 'and I'm not sure if it is your formidable wit, your moorland eyes or your ferocious heart that I love most … but I intend to spend the rest of my life trying to find out.'

At this, Josephine blushed so furiously that a tender smile crept across his strained face. 'I know I should apologise for making you blush, but in truth I adore it, so I won't,' he whispered, trailing kisses down her neck that somehow pooled in the pit of her stomach.

She fought to marshal her thoughts. 'It's just … no one has … ever thought…' She stumbled: there was good reason why she had never been admired above her sisters.

Huntingly captured her hand and brought it to his lips. 'You, Miss Josephine Fairfax, have eyes that take me to a moorland glade every time I look into them,' he murmured intently. 'And the very first day I saw you, I knew I belonged there.'

She reached up and cupped his cheek with a tenderness that finally chased the shadows from his eyes. 'In the real world … without armour?'

'Wholly so,' he promised without pause.

Then he drew her in and held her while the nightjars churred in the woods.

Chapter Twenty-Three

Josephine's Bedchamber; Endings and Beginnings
Two weeks later

Dear Fitzwilliam,

So much has happened since the night of the Ball that I hardly know where to begin –
I thought I knew myself, that no gentleman would ever rival a fictional hero, but I was wrong...

She paused, savouring the words which had felt such an impossible dream for most of her life.

...And now Alistair and I are to be wed. I know what you must be thinking, but I've never been so certain in my life that magic can happen outside the pages of a book. Even Thomas observed there appeared to be some sort of 'tiresome draw' between us when we returned on the night of the Ball. And I

made sure we told the whole story this time, including George, Eliza, Italy, and Sir Francis's interrogation, which shocked my brother long enough for Alistair to exclaim we wished to be married 'as fast as damned near possible'!

A distinct heat stole across Josephine's cheeks as she recalled her betrothed's fervent appeal. She exhaled to steady herself, glancing at the pearl-satin wedding gown Sophie had fashioned from her own in the vain hope that the exertion would prompt some interest from Mini Rotherby. It hadn't, but the result was breathtaking.

In the end, he put up little objection, stating that 'two people with such ridiculous notions clearly deserved one another', which left one other person we needed to ask…

Quietly, she recalled the day she and Alistair went to see George and Eliza's mother.

Mrs Pellham welcomed us both and, when at last she knew the whole, she asked us to keep the letters. She said the truth would live on through us, and that we owed it to George and Eliza to be happy…

Josephine closed her eyes and pictured herself and Alistair walking along the driveway towards a restored Huntingly Manor, light and life where there were only shadows and doubt before. She pictured the amber flare in his eyes, the warmth of his embrace and the urgency of his lips, before blushing rosily, wondering at the waywardness of her thoughts ever since he'd proposed 'just to level the tally'.

She took a breath and forced herself to finish.

And so now I must say farewell, for it seems that, sometimes, a living hero can be even more noble than one found within the pages of a book, and our story is only just beginning.

Yours affectionately,
Josephine.

Glossary

Addle-pated – Regency slang for air-headed
Apollo Knot – very fashionable hairstyle c. mid-1820s for formal occasions, consisting of tall loops of hair rising straight up from the crown, while sausage curls were arranged at the temples
As lief – if someone had / would *as lief* do something, they would *prefer* to do it
Banbury tale/story – Regency cant for a falsehood
Banyan – an informal knee-length dressing gown for gentlemen in the Regency period
Blandy's Madeira – wine. Blandy's was one of the largest Madeira producers in 1826. Old Madeira is one of the treasures of the wine world
Blonde lace – not a colour but a type of lace made with satin stitch on a mesh background
Bread of Maslin – a mixture of wheat and rye and part of a typical ration for a soldier of occupation following the Battle of Waterloo

Cephalic Version – some midwives and male practitioners practised various forms of version (turning) to bring the baby into a deliverable position. Cephalic version would turn the baby into the normal head-down position

Chateau Margaux – a red wine from Medoc, Bordeaux, France

Corky – Regency slang for bright and lively

Corinthian – athletes, sportsmen who excelled in most sporting activities of the day including fencing, boxing, hunting, shooting, driving and riding in addition to being well dressed and mannered gentlemen

Displays to advantage – Regency cant for fights well

Ergot of rye – a fungus long known by midwives to speed up labour and beginning to be adopted by accoucheurs in Regency times

Kick up a lark – Regency slang for get up to mischief

Monthly Nurse – whenever a lady from an aristocratic household planned to give birth, she would likely engage a monthly nurse whose duty was to care for the mother (not the child) after birth. She was also trained to deliver the child if the 'accoucheur' did not arrive in time

Piper-Heidsieck Champagne – Champagne house founded by Florens-Louis Heidsieck in 1785 in Reims, France

Pirouette Waltz – name sometimes used for the Regency Waltz

Plant him a facer – Regency cant for a punch in the face

Pomona Green – the green of the Regency era. Apple

green by the name, but dark and rich (made by overdying yellow with blue). Name used from 1811/12 when it became fashionable

Pon' rep – multi usage regency exclamation to express surprise or emphasise a point, similar to 'oh wow' and 'I promise'

Purchase of commissions in the British Army – between the 17th and 19th centuries, officers' commissions in infantry and calvary units of the English and British army could be purchased. This avoided the need to wait to be promoted for merits or seniority and was a usual way to obtain a rank in both armies

'Roy's Wife' – a popular song of 1826

Skeleton suits – the well-dressed Regency boy wore one of these – a long-sleeved, trousered suit made of heavy cotton or linen and white cambric shirts with a ruffled trim. The pants had high waists and were buttoned on to the long-sleeved jacket

Tap-hackled ne'er do well – Regency slang for drunk, irresponsible person

Top of the Trees – Regency slang for someone/thing of high esteem

Wellington Boot – a type of hard-wearing gentleman's boot (from 'battle to the evening') based upon Hessian boots, popularised by the 1st Duke of Wellington. Considered fashionable and foppish in the best circles, and worn by dandies such as Beau Brummell, they remained the fashion until the 1850s, although the name continues today

Acknowledgments

Some of my happiest teen memories are of being curled up with a regency novel, making this series very much a full-circle moment. Josephine is the bookish heroine of my heart, and her band of unruly siblings are the characters I needed while growing up in my own large and chaotic family of eight.

Yet, while the Fairfax sisters have been a joy to write, they've also felt a challenge because of the legacy of the authors I've always loved, and their many readers. The result is this series: regency stories with modern heroines and a big family heart.

I'd like to extend my special thanks to:

My editors, Charlotte Ledger and Helen Williams, for believing in my feisty heroines from the outset.

My illustrator, Chloe Quinn, for the most perfect covers – I will never be over those eyebrows!

My agent, Marissa Constantinou, for her belief and support.

My writing buddies Bex Hogan, Katharine Corr, Serena

Molloy and the original Scribblers for solidarity and the journey.

All the readers, bloggers and Instagrammers who've taken the time to read and review – so important and very much appreciated!

And finally, my Mum and Dad, who somehow raised a whole netball team (+1 reserve) and managed to make it look easy – my heroes, always.

READ ON FOR AN EXTRACT FROM
THE MISMATCH OF THE SEASON

'ENEMIES TO LOVERS WITH A BRIDGERTON STYLE TWIST! FUNNY, POIGNANT, INSPIRING … IT'S A MUST READ!'

☆☆☆☆☆

Miss Phoebe Fairfax dreams of being as free as her four brothers. When she discovers she is to be wed to a repugnant earl who is old enough to be her grandfather, she decides to embark on a real adventure…

Enter the insufferable – and insufferably gorgeous – Viscount Damerel.

AVAILABLE IN PAPERBACK, EBOOK AND AUDIO!

Chapter One

DEVON, 1820

Three months until the wedding

It was the perfect morning for a duel.

Or, at least it would have been had Miss Phoebe Fairfax lived between the covers of a novel where the heroine actually *did* things, as opposed to watching her brothers do them all instead.

The chief offender among them was undoubtedly her eldest sibling, Sir Thomas Fairfax, currently snoring in his bedchamber after the devil's own luck at the races, followed by an even worse run at faro. Which only made her own betrothal all the more vexing. To be betrothed by one's eldest brother was bad enough. To find oneself promised to a gout-ridden old goat more than twice one's age, and without so much as a by-your-leave, a downright outrage.

All of which had left her little choice but to embark on her current course of action – a dramatic yet highly essential dawn flight through the misted grounds of Knightswood Manor.

'Papa wanted this match and you're in no position to object, I'm head of this family now.'

A ready scowl descended as she hastened through the frost-bitten grass of her childhood home. Head of the family or not, it seemed Sir Thomas Fairfax, twelve years her senior, and her legal guardian for the last two, had little regard for anyone or anything, except washing his gambling hands of his siblings as fast as possible.

'The earl is an old family friend, and the match will help to re-establish the Fairfaxes among the ton. Even you have to see that there is no discussion to be had; you will be the Countess of Cumberland in the spring and make the best of it!'

In truth, while becoming a countess didn't *sound* too terrible, she would challenge any young lady to remain in the same room as the crusty old earl for longer than two minutes without concluding it to be the very worst fate to be inflicted on anyone at all.

Phoebe conjured the image of his overstuffed waistcoat and moist, purple lips before shuddering. Quite apart from the fact that he couldn't recall her name, their first meeting last week had only confirmed all the reasons why she should never become a countess.

'Step forward into the light girl! Where I can see you!

'Well, well, your brother could do with feeding you up a bit, but you'll do... Nothing worse than a skinny countess, I say!'

She shuddered again, recalling the way his gaze had rested on her, making her feel the best prize calf her brother could offer after a long, hard winter. Except she had always been the Fairfax least expected to marry, let alone marry well.

Read on for... The Mismatch of the Season

Not that she couldn't understand Thomas's perspective, of course. No one had expected Papa's sudden demise from a pernicious toe the year before and, despite being a veteran of the Napoleonic Wars, Thomas was still only thirty years of age himself. Mama used to refer to it as *a gentleman's dangerous age*, the time when he either married, drank himself into oblivion, or became a confirmed rake. Since Thomas had never made any mention of entering into domestic bliss, Phoebe could only assume he intended to embrace one of the latter two options, while subjecting the rest of his long-suffering brothers and sisters to his *Monstrous Marriage Master Plan*, as her sister Sophie put it.

Phoebe stole a glance back at her bedchamber window, just visible in the pale clutch of dawn, and suppressed her rising guilt. Sophie was more than capable of keeping an eye on the Fairfax brood for three months, and she needed this time. She might not be able to escape Thomas's master plan forever, but she could escape it for three months. *Three precious months* in which to live a lifetime of dreams; it was ambitious enough for any heroine.

She drew a steadying breath and hurried onto the carriageway through Knightswood's famous avenue of oaks.

Thomas's Monstrous Marriage Master Plan had begun the moment they lay dear Papa to rest. Phoebe's four brothers didn't feature of course, they were all in varying stages of education, and would have as much freedom as they wished, leaving all of Thomas's unwanted attention directed at herself and their three sisters: Sophie, seventeen, Josephine, sixteen – and Matilda, twelve, who was already on her third governess this year.

Phoebe frowned at a burst of hopeful snowdrops, trying to escape the frost.

Even if Papa's will *had* contained a request for his first-born daughter to make a match with his closest friend, the Earl of Cumberland – who was nearing sixty and alarmingly purple – it was a brother's duty to protect her from such a fate, wasn't it?

Or at least, give her a fighting chance.

Instead, he seemed more than happy to write off a London season as an expensive and unnecessary prelude, and go straight to the main marital event, which seemed just a little unfair when her younger sisters would have ample time to find suitors of a less gout-prone age.

Indeed, the more she'd thought on it, the more it seemed she'd been dealt the largest slice of ill luck since she'd won the hoopla at Knightswood Fair and Alfred, her second-eldest brother, made off with the candy floss. Yet, it was her fate all the same, unless she did something about it. And since she couldn't imagine any of her favourite literary heroines marrying a crusty old earl without a dramatic adventure or two to sustain them for the rest of their days, she really had little choice but to embark on her current course of action.

A flicker of a smile flitted across Phoebe's face – if only Fred could see her now, stealing away from Knightswood Manor in his old frock coat, breeches and boots, her dark copper tresses pinned up beneath a rotund country hat that had seen so many better days. Not that Fred's lack of fashion bothered her. She was quite certain that the more *bourgeois* her appearance, the less likely she would be to attract attention and the sooner she would be mistress of her own destiny. Plus, she was quite

Read on for... The Mismatch of the Season

certain breeches could be the work of actual goddesses, and was in no mind to trade them for a skirt any time soon.

She paused as the bushes ahead rustled suddenly, and a juvenile doe stepped out on the path. They locked eyes briefly, before the doe bolted towards the rest of the herd in the park. Wistfully, Phoebe watched her darting path through the silver grass towards a waiting buck, his majestic antlers glinting in the amber light. She sighed. Papa used to tell stories about their elusive herd granting wishes, yet none of her siblings had ever been stolen away by moorland fae, leaving her little choice but to conclude that, at best, they were unreliable indeed.

Resolutely, she pushed on, drawing comfort from the sway of her reticule beneath her frock coat. She wasn't such a ninnyhammer as to keep all of her pin money in one of her marvellous new pockets, now that she'd decided to board the common stage, and she still planned to write to dear Fred about a loan the moment she reached London.

A brief smile flitted across her face.

Dear Fred was the least vexing of all her brothers, as well as the one least likely to squeal to Thomas about her whereabouts once he knew the truth; plus he still owed her from the Hexworthy Races two years before. Briefly, she recalled the traditional Dartmoor horse race Fred had dreaded, while filling every bone of her defiant body with envy. Ladies weren't permitted to compete, of course, but with the aid of his riding shirt and breeches – as well as another miraculous hat – she'd not only managed a very credible pass, but also brought home a highly coveted third place in his name. And now he could return the favour.

Phoebe inhaled brightly. She'd never travelled by stage before and was considerably excited by the prospect. Her old governess used to mutter about springs and padding for days after a journey, but she also had a taste for hogs pudding, which Phoebe found most suspicious. Besides which, she really had very little choice; the mail coach would be the very first place Thomas looked, and she could hardly take the Fairfax family chaise, or his favourite racing phaeton to London – there were some things even she wouldn't do.

Humming, Phoebe diverted off the carriageway, and headed towards a discreet estate gate. On reflection, she was quite satisfied she'd managed things reasonably well enough for any girl hoping for a heroic adventure or two. She'd even settle for *marginally unheroic* if it didn't involve being told exactly what to do and think, by someone who'd been absent for most of her life. She would be as free as any of her brothers, or favourite fictional heroines – and even if the latter had rather more important matters to consider than clean stays and lodgings, she was certain her many years imagining adventures with her siblings would stand her in good stead.

'I'm not sure a headless ghost would escape in a chintz curtain, Phoebs – what about the settle throw instead?'

A faint smile flickered across her face. Fairfax Theatrical Company had been a part of their family for as long as she could remember, as well as her only reprieve from a life of corsets and cotillion practice. She never once thought she'd ever actually escape, and yet somehow, at this very moment, she was embarking on a *real* adventure. She had a change of clothing, coin enough to secure a private bedchamber, and she was more than certain she could imitate dear Fred's gentle manner when it came to ordering luncheon, or some such similar refreshment. There was, after all, nothing worse than an empty stomach – it got in the way of plain, sensible thinking. This was a sentiment that had proven quite the bone of contention for her poor, deceased mama, who had given up on her eldest daughter ever contenting herself with just one slice of cake, when Cook had clearly intended her to eat three.

Phoebe's smile widened as she climbed the estate gate, quite certain that breeches were a male conspiracy, too. For years, she'd been inched and cinched into suffocating layers of petticoats, creating a rise of heat she could only equate to one of Cook's rice puddings, and even Sophie had to admit that a hoop and petticoats were a positive disadvantage when it came to *that time* of the month, which must never be mentioned in polite company.

By contrast, Fred's attire felt like utter freedom, and she was never more convinced that ladies' clothing had been designed with canaries in mind, which only fuelled the importance of the next three months. She had this one utterly unique chance to forego all the rules and chase every dream she'd ever had – which was so much more inviting than Sophie's parting accusation.

Briefly, her sister's words echoed through her head. But the more she considered them, the more she was persuaded she wasn't actually running *away*, but rather *towards* the opportunity to discover her own inner heroine.

Because everyone had one of those deep down inside – didn't they?

She was also more than certain she had to have at least one bareback-horseracing-at-midnight kind of adventure waiting for her, despite Sophie's considerable doubts. Why else would she have been blessed with such a lively imagination and, as Mama would say, *hoydenish ways*, if there wasn't some master plan at work?

She nodded briskly at a chirruping robin before turning into the country lane. It had ever been the same. Most of the young ladies of her acquaintance seemed as prone to fits of the vapours, as she was to ravenous hunger; and it was certainly one of Mama's greatest regrets, that she had the most practical head, when needed.

'Really Phoebe, you have the fortitude of an ox!' she complained, the day Phoebe dragged Matilda from Knightswood lake after a skating incident.

From this, Phoebe could only conclude it would have been far more ladylike to let her younger sister drown while she herself expired from shock, which felt a stretch – even for Mama. And while she had nothing against oxen in particular, they did seem quite banal creatures when all was said and done.

Still, Mama had always been somewhat of a stickler when it came to matters of propriety.

'*A young lady needs a certain air of … fragility about her person,*' she would say reprovingly, whenever Phoebe was sighted scaling one of the many trees around the park.

'*Not ruddy cheeks and splinters!*'

Considering an air of fragility seemed synonymous with a life of impressive dullness, Phoebe was certain she would never meet Mama's exacting expectations. It was one of the reasons she'd escape on Misty whenever she could. On the moor, she could ride until she believed she really was Mary

Queen of Scots; or a time traveller from some distant, trouser-wearing age that finally treated men and women as equals – if such a thing were ever *really* possible.

She sighed. For the most part, she also knew better than to rely on any sibling support, despite being considered an all-round *good egg* when it came to quarrels. She no more ratted on the brother who snuck off to a prize fight, than the sister who spent all her pin money on ribbons; and while this loyalty had earned her admiration and reproof in equal measure, there was no lack of genuine affection between them all.

She had *still tried* to call on these affections when challenging Thomas's Monstrous Marriage Master Plan, but as he controlled the purse strings, and therefore every whim and wish of the Fairfax brood, they'd fallen to the wayside quicker than even she'd expected.

'You've got to see it from our perspective, Phoebs,' Fred pleaded, after Thomas threatened to cut off his allowance. *'Tom has us over a barrel until we come of age. And the old earl isn't that bad really... You'll have a fine house, your own carriage ... and just think of all the climbing trees in his grounds.'*

Phoebe's face darkened as she strode down the last section of country lane. Fred could try to placate her as much as he liked, but how he, or any of her brothers and sisters, could expect her to willingly tie her life to an old man who made her feel like a skinny pullet trussed for the Sunday roast, was beyond her. Let alone the fact that when he walked, a decided scent of onions wafted about his person.

Onions! Phoebe wrinkled her nose just thinking about it.

Matilda was first to notice, and had levelled the accusation when Phoebe refused to buy her a second macaroon on a village outing. But her youthful nose had a sound point, and it was one of the reasons Phoebe knew she had to act – that and the *unfortunate incident*.

Phoebe closed her eyes briefly. In truth, if it wasn't for the *unfortunate incident*, Thomas probably wouldn't have felt quite so compelled to enact phase one of his Monstrous Marriage Master Plan. But Sophie had laid a wager and Thomas, above all people, should have known a wager was a matter of honour.

'*I cannot believe Knightswood's church organist intended to create a scandal with Miss Kettering,*' Sophie had mused. '*In fact, I would even go so far as to wager that any impoverished, romantic young gentleman would have little choice but to offer elopement if his liaison is discovered. It's either that or die of a broken heart – don't you think, Phoebe?*'

Phoebe was quick to concede that any church-organist-turned-disgraced-eloper was very deserving of her sister's empathy, but also that Sophie's assertion gave like gentlemen such a poor reputation that she was duty-bound to disprove it – which was how she'd set upon Monsieur Dupres, their unfortunate pianoforte tutor.

In her defence, she absolutely did not set out to *encourage* him to fall in love with her – she'd just wanted to prove to Sophie that, *even if* a gentleman was impoverished and hopelessly romantic, he didn't always propose elopement.

And if she'd underestimated Monsieur Dupres on this occasion, she was wholly convinced he was the exception, rather than the rule.

Thomas chose not to understand the matter at all, of course, calling her an ignorant, foolhardy girl he'd gladly pack off to a convent were it not for his unwavering belief she'd get herself expelled, before the sennight was up. Instead, he'd talked of Papa's will and bringing forward the dreaded wedding, which had only hastened her own plan, safe in the knowledge that once everything was taken into consideration, Thomas would have to concede he was wholly and utterly to blame.

It was while she was enjoying the comfort of this certain victory, and her brother's well-deserved guilt, that Phoebe spied her new travelling companions gathering in the frosty grass beside the public road, and felt a first rise of doubt.

If only Thomas had let her have a season... If only he hadn't found the elopement proposal from Monsieur Dupres... If only she'd been able to bring some Fairfax Theatrical Company costumes with her... She could have put them to excellent use where she was going.

The thought gave her a surge of strength.

Where she was going was a secret of the utmost gravity that she hadn't even shared with Sophie, her most suspicious sister. Not only was Sophie unable to keep any kind of secret, let alone under pressure, she would also feel duty-bound to read her one of her sisterly lectures which were beginning to sound, uncannily, like dear Mama's. And the truth was, Phoebe's destination wasn't in the least bit de rigueur for a young lady of her social standing, at all.

A rueful smile crept across her face, one that mirrored the gleam in her moorland eyes. Of all her schemes over the past eighteen years, this one had to be the most daring, and she could only imagine Thomas's rage if he could see her now: clad in their brother's hand-me-downs, unaccompanied, and about to board the common stage. If it were divulged in polite company, it could ruin her and yet Phoebe knew her brother far too well for that. The moment Sophie reported her absence, Thomas would concoct some plausible tale of an indisposed distant cousin, while using every means possible to find her – and all to protect his Monstrous Marriage Masterplan.

Let him search. She'd been dreaming of this adventure her whole life long, and even if it was only for three precious months, it would be enough to sustain her for a lifetime.

It had to.

Want to find out what happens next?
Keep reading today!

THE MISMATCH OF THE SEASON
Available in Paperback, Ebook and Audio!

DON'T MISS *THE SCANDAL OF THE SEASON*

'EASIEST FIVE STARS EVER ... A MUST-READ FOR ANYONE WHO LOVES JULIA QUINN, JANE AUSTEN AND LOUISA MAY ALCOTT'

'I wager you this, Miss Fairfax – you'll choose to marry for every reason other than love by the end of the season!'

Miss Sophie Fairfax has every intention of marrying for love, refusing to go along with her brother's plans for a marriage of convenience or title. Throwing caution to the wind at her very first ball, Sophie finds herself in the path of the most notorious rake in the ton.

Agreeing a wager with him may be wicked, but finding herself alone with the dangerously attractive Lord Rotherby might be one scandal too far...

AVAILABLE IN PAPERBACK, EBOOK AND AUDIO!

The author and One More Chapter would like to thank everyone who contributed to the publication of this story…

Analytics
Imogen Wolstencroft

Audio
Fionnuala Barrett
Ciara Briggs

Design
Lucy Bennett
Fiona Greenway
Liane Payne
Dean Russell

Digital Sales
Laura Daley
Lydia Grainge
Hannah Lismore

eCommerce
Laura Carpenter
Madeline ODonovan
Charlotte Stevens
Christina Storey
Rachel Ward

Editorial
Janet Marie Adkins
Rosie Best
Kara Daniel
CJ Harter
Charlotte Ledger
Jennie Rothwell
Sofia Salazar Studer
Helen Williams

Harper360
Emily Gerbner
Ariana Juarez
Jean Marie Kelly
emma sullivan
Sophia Wilhelm

International Sales
Ruth Burrow
Bethan Moore
Colleen Simpson

Inventory
Sarah Callaghan
Kirsty Norman

Marketing & Publicity
Chloe Cummings
Grace Edwards
Katie Sadler

Operations
Melissa Okusanya

Production
Denis Manson
Simon Moore
Francesca Tuzzeo

Rights
Ashton Mucha
Alisah Saghir
Zoe Shine
Aisling Smyth

Trade Marketing
Ben Hurd
Eleanor Slater

The HarperCollins Contracts Team

The HarperCollins Distribution Team

The HarperCollins Finance & Royalties Team

The HarperCollins Legal Team

The HarperCollins Technology Team

UK Sales
Isabel Coburn
Jay Cochrane
Leah Woods

And every other essential link in the chain from delivery drivers to booksellers to librarians and beyond!

One More Chapter is an
award-winning global
division of HarperCollins.

Subscribe to our newsletter to get our
latest eBook deals and stay up to date
with all our new releases!

signup.harpercollins.co.uk/
join/signup-omc

Meet the team at
www.onemorechapter.com

Follow us!

@onemorechapterhc

Do you write unputdownable fiction?
We love to hear from new voices.
Find out how to submit your novel at
www.onemorechapter.com/submissions